# Minding Jackson

Michele Deppe

CRIMSON
ROMANCE
Avon, Massachusetts

Published by
Crimson Romance
an imprint of F+W Media, Inc.
10151 Carver Road, Suite 200
Blue Ash, Ohio 45242


*www.crimsonromance.com*




POD ISBN 10: 1-4405-5043-3
POD ISBN 13: 978-1-4405-5043-0
eISBN 10: 1-4405-5042-5
eISBN 13: 978-1-4405-5042-3

# Dedication

FOR TIFFANY TAYLOR WILLIAMS AND ROBERT REDFORD;
MY FIRST READERS, AND FOREVER DEAR TO MY HEART.

# Chapter 1

Winter had come to England, cruelly freezing the late autumn flowers, and scattering angry showers across the country. Jane gazed from the window, watching as Lydia pattered across rivulets of rain streaming down the high street. Something was wrong. Jane couldn't have said how she knew, but those imperceptable signs, perhaps only obvious to a close friend, conveyed Lydia's distress. Lydia stepped into the Chinese restaurant, and stood for a moment, dripping on the sodden rug, until she spotted Jane in the corner. The restaurant was quite empty; it was well past the lunch hour. Lydia struggled out of her raincoat and hung it on the nearby peg.

"Isn't it relentless," Jane said.

"Yes, and now the wind is getting up, too," Lydia replied, sliding into the banquette. She lifted her fingers through her damp thick hair, gave it a shake, and let it tumble down her back.

Jane and Lydia spoke daily. Now they were companionably silent, longing for the waitress, the owner's daughter, Imogen, to finish chatting on her mobile and bring hot tea. By description, the friends were much alike; both of middle height, slender, and brunette. But where Jane was rather average, Lydia was both striking and delicate. Jane recalled a boy in sixth form, saying, "Lydia's a stunner, possibly the most beautiful girl in Britain." Jane had smiled at him in agreement, not being one to nuture sour grapes.

Lydia leaned towards the table, dropping her chin in her hand, and shot Imogen a cautionary glance. The Chinese Palace was one of only two restaurants found in the village of Hartsbury. The other was the Rapunzel Inn, so named for the native flowering rampion plant, which christened the maiden in the story by the Brothers Grimm. Ale and sustenance had been served on those fine premesis since Shakespeare trod the earth. The Rapunzel stood on the outer edge of the village by an ancient, crumbling stone wall, still marking the last spot of civilization by the abrupt edge of a dense forest. Although the pub was known for serving a decent ploughman's lunch, any private conversation at the long tables in the snug, low-ceilinged, dining room was nigh impossible.

Imogen finally came round with a steaming pot of tea, and a pair of smooth-sided Asian cups. They gave her their lunch order, then took long satisfying sips which inspired chat.

"You look a little worse for wear. I can pick up Jackson if you'd like," Jane assured Lydia. "It'd be no trouble, really."

"No, that's all settled with Clarice. She says that she rather likes going to the school for him, and she feels guilty taking her wage, with Mum doing up the windows and beating rugs. Mum's gone mad on spring cleaning." They talked about Jackson's latest riding lesson. He'd cantered his pony for the first time and was thrilled that he hadn't fallen off. Lydia's smile was replaced with a slightly furrowed brow.

"Lydia, what is it?"

"I am fine, Jane, despite how dreadful you think I look today," Lydia snapped.

Imogen sailed to the table with their meals, set them down and was gone without a word. Her appetite having vanished, Lydia pushed away her cashew chicken and poured more green tea from the lantern-shaped pot.

Jane chastised her friend. "Why you even try to dodge me, I'd like to know," Jane's voice was firm, but tinged with compassion. She knew that Lydia ought to talk about whatever it was bothering her, though it was more in keeping with Lydia's nature to dismiss things, forgoing any decisions, only to have her concerns come creeping back.

These doldrums were occasionally brought on their non-existent love lives. Lydia could easily get a man if she wanted, Jane thought. A weekend in London would conjure a dozen successful bachelors prostrate at her feet, particularly given Lydia's impressive family lines, angelic face, and the posh, teasing airs Lydia could affect when suited her. However, it sometimes seemed as if Lydia was permanently done in after the affair with Jackson's father. Lydia had scarcely left the village since that night, six years ago, when she had spent the wee hours of the morning with the American celebrity. They'd only been too lucky that Lydia escaped the party, at the urging of her friends, before the musician collapsed and the press came pouring into the hotel.

Lydia finally gave up the silent routine. "I've been so tired lately. And I find myself wondering where *he* is. Wondering if I shouldn't be in touch," Lydia's voice became a conspiratorial whisper. "Wondering if Jackson will come to hate me. Because I didn't try harder to inform his father."

"Oh, darling, Jackson could never hate you!" Jane cried, with a gentle, brief squeeze of Lydia's arm. "You're the most wonderful mum in the world. Look. If *he* wanted a relationship with you, then he ought to have contacted you himself, wouldn't you say? Surely, he could have hired a private detective or other to run you to ground. I mean, you've been right here in Hartsbury, not slinking around the world under an alias at luxury hotels. And if he hasn't contacted *you*, why should he be interested in Jackson? You sent a dozen or so letters to the record company address. What more could you do? Or, more to the point, what can you possibly do now, six years later? We've been over it a thousand times, Lydia."

"I suppose. But Jackson keeps asking. Whingeing on about meeting his father. It's doing my head in." Imogen appeared, and replaced the half-full teapot with a new one. A good girl, our Imogen, Jane thought, but rather a nosy one.

Jane leaned back and crossed her arms. She tried again. "What else can be done, Lydia? American rock stars practically expect to go about creating children with strangers. If you got legal help to contact him, the assumption on their side would be that you're wanting money."

"Naturally, I don't want to start some legal quarrel. But, Jane, try to understand, from my view," Lydia said slowly. "If there's a respectable sort of way for Jackson to have a father, whatever the distance, it would fill a void for him." Anger flashed across Lydia's face. "Everyone is willing to pardon me, but it wasn't all you lot who's had a baby from a one-nighter, is it? And it's Jacks that I can't make understand!"

"Oh, Lydia," Jane said tenderly. "You mustn't go on feeling guilty. I do understand the important bits. I understand that you're a good mum. And Jackson is lovely. Children are able to cope with these things. Few families are perfect. Perhaps it's because you get so upset that Jackson feels he must keep asking about his father. Mightn't it be better if you took a positive stance?"

"Yes, perhaps you're right," Lydia agreed.

"And you're exhausted. Maybe you ought to just go home now. Rest."

Lydia could hardly argue. It was obvious to Jane that her friend was a bit run down, what with working, and trying to complete her nursing studies. Jane knew Lydia was grateful that she and Jackson lived at her mother's lovely manor house at Brambleberry Lane. But Lydia drew the line at allowing her mother, or her well-to-do brother, Nigel, to pay the way entirely for her and her son. Lydia's small paychecks from her job as a clerk at the hospital were swiftly gobbled up with tuition and helping with Jackson's expenses. Jane knew that Lydia didn't give much thought to money, having had it all of her life, so it was easy for her to release it to pay bills. Instead, Jane's concern was that Lydia wasn't a particularly energetic person to be doing so much. Lydia seemed a bit overwhelmed.

Honestly, Jane pondered, why does she bother with the nursing bit at all? Lydia enjoyed her job as a clerk, and being friendly to hospital visitors. She'd laughed, telling Jane that people seemed glad to have her give them rather useless information and send them on their way. It wasn't exciting, but it was pleasant, and that suited Lydia. She was happier when things were straightforward and low pressure.

After Jackson was born, Lydia exhausted every means, attempting to get word of their child to Billy Killian, a blues guitarist. Later, Lydia learned that Billy had a serious drugs problem. In recent years, news reports indicated that Billy Killian had long been sober and successful. Thus, Lydia was more confused than ever.

Imogen brought the bill and both women fell silent until she walked away. "Lydia, you know you did well, truthfully recording Billy Killian as Jackson's father, and naming him after some person that he admired. Really, darling, that's quite enough. Jackson will grow past pestering."

"I am sure you're right. And I am ready to go home. Let's leave it," Lydia replied quietly. She shivered again, and rubbed her upper arms with her hands, chasing away the chill of the past.

# Chapter 2

As with every year-end holiday season the world over, the days flew by. Apart from tucking Jackson beneath his duvet for the night, Lydia felt she seldom saw her son. He was growing up too fast, always asking questions in rapid-fire succession. And begging to be given a pony for Christmas. Lydia suspected that his Uncle Nigel had a plan in that direction.

Jane and Lydia enjoyed a holiday shopping trip to London one afternoon, stopping off to see Jane's Aunt Winifred for tea. A beautiful, fluffy snow fell as Jane and Lydia padded along the quiet street. Winifred's house was draped with evergreens, and a wreath hung on the tall front door. White fairy lights twinkled through the window, and the weary shoppers could almost feel the warmth of the Victorian house enfolding them as they rang the bell.

"Oh, you've done a lovely bit of shopping, have you?" Aunt Winifred said as she spied their packages. "Come in, girls. Bloom! Get down! Don't mind her, she'll settle down." Bloom, Aunt Winifred's cottony Westie, jumped about while being generally ignored.

Dropping packages and damp coats in the wide hall, the visitors were ushered into a cosy, paneled sitting room that was golden with the light of a cheerful fire and ornately decorated tree. Lydia sunk down into a large, leathery nest of a chair, while Jane hugged her aunt before they made their way together to the velvet sofa.

"You're looking well, Aunt Winnie," Jane cooed. Lydia knew that Jane adored her Aunt Winifred, her father's only sibling, and wished they lived closer. Jane produced a box of chocolates for her from Fortnum & Mason's.

"Oh, Jane! You never forget my orange crèmes. Bless you. How's the shop? Are you busy with festive arrangements for holiday tables and the like?"

"It's madness. I've got paper whites and amaryllis filling up the entire back room." Jane yawned as though just thinking about all of the orders she must fill from her small flower shop overcame her, and Lydia felt drowsy watching her. Jane had gotten Agnes to mind the store for her. Agnes was the height of dependability, and had retired from the position as head cashier at the supermarket. The grandmother of four relished the fair pay and flowers that Jane gave her, and working occasionally, Agnes was fond of saying, "kept her feet going and her brain firing."

Aunt Winifred poured Lydia's tea, a pungent-scented cup of Lady Grey. "And you, Lydia. I haven't seen you in an age. Jane said you'd been back at school. How's the nursing progressing?"

"Quite well. It's a lot of work, naturally, but the training shall be over next spring, so not too terribly much longer. You're meant to specialize, so I chose the pediatric branch, probably because being a mum makes me feel more qualified."

"And Jackson?"

Lydia snatched her handbag from the floor and proudly produced a snap of her son, taken at a hunt breakfast. The photograph showed a handsome little boy dressed in warm earth-colored tweeds, kneeling by a terrier, and a plump brown pony standing behind. "The children had been allowed to ride around the stable yard amongst the club before the adults left for the hunt," Lydia explained.

"Oh, he is darling, Lydia! And Jane says he is as bright as he is gorgeous."

"Yes, I think so, too. He's begun school and is getting on well."

They stayed and chatted with Aunt Winifred until the dim afternoon sun began to sink, casting long tree-shaped shadows across Winnie's Prussian blue rug. Reluctantly, they packed up their shopping. The temperatures grew more brisk, and the pair were caught out in a wet snow on the way to the train station. Jane enthusiastically predicted a white Christmas, while Lydia longed for a nap on the train.

The following morning, Lydia woke before dawn. She thought she had to go to the loo, but as she rolled out of bed, she stumbled. She was weak. Enormously so. *Perhaps I've got a virus of some sort.*

She turned back into bed, not ambitious enough to make another attempt at getting up. Sleep claimed her immediately.

"Lydia, darling, don't you realize what time it is?" Her mum sat on the edge of the bed.

"I was just awake, but was dreadfully tired, so I went back to sleep," Lydia mumbled.

"I've been over at the church, helping Rose get up the holiday mess. Clarice got Jackson off to school, and you've been lying in for hours. It's quarter of ten!"

"No!" Lydia sat up, intending to bound out of bed. She passed out cold.

"Oh, dear! Lydia! Lydia, darling, wake up!" Her mother chaffed her wrists, and patted her cheeks.

Lydia came to, but the room was moving to and fro, as though her bed was in a ship's cabin on a rough sea. She closed her eyes and encircled her head with her arms in an effort to stop the rocking.

"Lydia?"

"Mum . . . Oh, I feel simply horrid . . . I need a doctor's visit."

*

Lydia saw Dr. Foster late that afternoon. She hadn't been able to hold down her breakfast, and was trying to nap when her mother came to check on her.

"Darling, you really ought to eat something before you take the antibiotics again. It's no wonder your stomach's ill, what with nothin' a 'tall in your system. Here, darling, why don't you take some Scotch broth? It'll do you good."

"Mum, I am afraid I'll bring it right back up. I am sorry." Lydia's damp, pale face gleamed like a pearl. "I am sure I just need to sleep. If I can just get sorted, I am sure I'll rest and be quite well. . . . " Her voice drifted off to a whisper.

*

With Jane's resourceful help, arrangements were made with Lydia's instructors. She would be permitted to make up the days she missed of her clinical training when the nursing students returned from holiday.

Two days before Christmas, Lydia's brother, Nigel Membry, returned to the family home in Brambleberry Lane. Large packages were delivered to the door, full of wrapped presents. Jackson trailed his uncle wherever he went, with Jackson's spaniel, Ausfrid, bringing up the rear. Both boy and dog were eager for play the moment Nigel was free.

The evening following Nigel's arrival, Jane popped round to see Lydia and the family. Her heart gave a lurch when Nigel opened the door to her, speaking as though he'd seen her just recently.

"Good evening, Jane, please step in," Nigel said with his usual dignified tone. Jane surmised in a moment that he was still dreadfully good-looking. He was dressed in charcoal-coloured wool slacks, topped by a black cashmere pull-over. His loafers looked, and most likely were, soft Italian leather, rendering him expensive-looking from head to foot. His eyes fell on her boots, and Jane scrunched her toes within them. He probably thinks these rubber boots are hideous, she thought, but it's filthy and snowing.

Aloud, Jane said, "It's filthy and snowing."

"Yes. Yes, it is," he said quietly, then clearing his throat. The silence hung between them.

Jane took a breath for courage and then greeted him as she would a customer to her shop. "Nigel, it is so good to see you. Its been quite a few months, hasn't it?" She smiled cheerfully and handed off her coat. He gracefully hung her coat on the rack and stood, poised, and gazing at her. She hadn't thought a word like that should suit a man, but it did. Poised. And reserved. Jane couldn't ever be sure what he was thinking. Fortunately, Lydia and her mother were open books, once you knew them. Jane contemplated how much easier life was, when one was honest and uncomplicated.

"Yes," Nigel replied flatly. Had she bodged it again, somehow? Nigel seemed to be at ease with everyone, socially speaking, but with Jane his remarks seemed hollow. She imagined he'd rather his sister's best friend was smart, sophisticated, and attractive. No doubt he was often surrounded with those types of women in his posh job, working for some Middle Eastern royal family or other.

Perhaps he was already bored with her since she'd come in the house, only seconds ago?

"Shall I help you?" Nigel, said, offering his hand and looking at her wellies.

"Certainly, thank you." She placed her left hand in his. His hand was warm, large, and somehow luxurious. Jane balanced against his gentle grip, brought up a knee and dragged off a boot with her other hand. She felt like an odd sort of Cinderella, having a divine moment with her prince, but with rather sad footwear. Wriggling out of the damp boots caused Nigel's fingertips to inadvertently caress her wrist, sending icy little shivers up her arm. *Happy Christmas to me*, Jane thought, and an involuntary smile curled her lips. Kicking the boots aside, she glanced up at him, and saw him staring down at her intently. It seemed as though he might say something.

Yet in the seconds that followed, he didn't utter a word.

Perhaps, it dawned on Jane, he simply wanted his hand back. Flushing with embarrassment, Jane slipped her palm from his and smoothed it over her midriff, a ladylike gesture that seemed to imply his hand had offended her in some way.

"Well, ah, Lydia's with Clarice in the kitchen, if you'd like to step through."

"Oh, right," Jane said, seeking to restore a little of her lost dignity with a nervous chuckle. Holding his hand had been a thrill, however it was also quite pleasing to be dismissed, since Jane felt rather like a housemaid who was eager to join her contemporaries below stairs. Without another glance at 007 — the moniker the villagers had hung on Nigel — Jane deftly slipped away.

"Jane! You're on time to help me wrap presents," Lydia said, looking quite unequal to the task. She sat hunched over a steaming cup of tea at the broad oak table. Her dressing gown hung on her thin shoulders, and it seemed to Jane that she moved her mouth sparingly as she spoke. If only one didn't have to move through one's entire gambit of emotions within two seconds together, thought Jane. Whereas Lydia's brother Nigel had enveloped her in a dreamy cloud of bliss in the entry hall, now Jane was pained through at the poorly appearance of her dear friend.

Time to put on her shop face again. "I shall willingly help for a cuppa and a chocolate biscuit. Hello, Clarice." Jane comfortably poured herself a cup of tea from a large Brown Betty set upon the table, and nicked a biscuit from the blue tin on the counter, where there was always a generous supply of tempting nibbles.

"Did you walk from the high street, Jane? You must be frozen," Clarice said. She was standing in front of a large casserole, capably filling it with aromatic chopped vegetables. It was a short distance, but Clarice wasn't much of a walker.

"Actually, it didn't seem that cold, really. I think I was so ready to quit the shop that the fresh air revived my spirits. So, what are you going to wrap, Lydia, our spoil from London?"

"Yes. Just haven't been up to taking it on since we got home last week. I'll have to hurry with Jackson's presents, he'll be through the door in a tick. He's been next door playing with Toby."

"He's going to be mad for that book on horses that you got him, don't you think?" Jane said, wiping crumbs from the side of her mouth.

"Oh, I don't know. I spoke with Nigel this morning. He's got it all arranged, just as we suspected!"

"You're quite serious? A pony?" Not sure where Nigel was in the house, Jane lowered her voice and added, "He won't stick you with the feed and farrier will he?"

"No, of course not. You know Nigel. It's planned to the least detail. Payment in advance for the box and board, and the equipment has all been purchased."

"A saddle and such, you mean?"

"Yes. The whole lot. So, the book will be a bit shoddy in comparison, wouldn't you say?" Lydia smiled. "I can't wait to see the look on Jackson's face, Jane! I am sure it will be a complete surprise. You'll pop down to the stables with us to have a look on Sunday, won't you?"

"I will. And I'll bring my camera. Well, I am ready to wrap. Shall we?"

# Chapter 3

Jane's prediction about a white Christmas proved true. A downy snow covered Hartsbury during the Christmas Eve midnight service. All were delighted to see the enchanting, frosty landscape when they stepped out of the old stone church, still humming favorite Christmas hymns. Peacefulness and good cheer was abundant in every heart.

The air was still, without the slightest tease of wind. The platinum stars shown hard and white in the black night sky, the dazzling moonlight shimmered on the powdered-sugar rooftops.

Jackson, his chum Toby, and the other children grabbed handfuls of snow and pelted one another, their laughter sounding sharp in the frigid air.

"Isn't it lovely?" Lydia said, gazing at the stars and catching snowflakes on her eyelashes. She stood still for a moment, breathing deeply in the chilly air. She coughed, making the children's shrill voices seem very distant.

"Yes, it is a beautiful sight," her mother agreed. "And it's cold. Let's get moving." She took Nigel's arm and they made their way home, saying good-byes to other villagers and wishing all a Happy Christmas. The Membry family, including Jane, crunched together in the majesty of the snowfall, and, two streets beyond, turned the corner to the manor house at Brambleberry Lane.

*

Christmas morning, Lydia phoned Jane to come join them before waking up Jackson. The day was radiant with sunshine. The air remained chilled and motionless. Clear winter light blazed across the petals of the scarlet Amaryllis placed randomly throughout Brambleberry House.

Jane joined in as stockings were pilfered through, and then Jackson followed his uncle's hints, discovering a halter, bridle, rug, and saddle in various hiding places about the large house. All other presents were put off and a proper breakfast was thrown over in order to get Jackson to the barn before he completely burst with excitement, everyone being reduced to a few slices of buttered bread, taken in hand on the way to the car.

Clarice chose to stay behind. She would not be deterred from her culinary mission, and was in her element with a large meal to prepare, flying about the kitchen with the controlled, merry demeanor of the late Julia Child. Jackson sat in the front seat of Nigel's Mercedes, engulfed by his new equestrian kit, with Eleanor, Lydia, and Jane tucked in the backseat, exchanging grins. The child's joy was boundless, and the Christmas spirit lifted them all.

"Uncle Nigel, you are the best," Jackson said, beaming at his uncle. "My own pony! I can't believe it. It's too fab. Did you know about this Mum?"

"I did, and I am very good at keeping secrets."

Nigel drove the silver sedan into the stable yard's car park and Jackson barely waited for the car to halt before opening the door.

"Hurry, won't you?"

"Just a minute, Jackson. Or shall I say 'hold your horses'?" his grandmother joked, heaving her round form from the backseat. Jane reached inside her handbag and pulled out her rather professional-looking camera.

"You're taking snaps of me and my new pony, Aunt Jane?"

"Yes, darling. I am so happy for you," Jane replied. She hugged Lydia's shoulders, and they agreed that it certainly was a happy Christmas.

Nigel kept pace alongside his nephew into the barn, with the women following.

The barn was dark after the bright winter sun, and smelled sweetly of hay. Nigel and Jackson proceeded down the aisle, between spacious box stalls. As Jane walked by, horses poked out their heads in greeting. The dust danced in the golden light coming in through the barn windows. Jane paused, letting her fingers linger against a heavy horse blanket of black watch plaid hanging on a metal rack. Further in, Nigel and Jackson stopped at a stall, and Jackson's laughter rang through the rafters as he saw his pony for the first time. Jane smiled at hearing Jackson's bubbling voice, and glancing over at Lydia, saw her beaming with joy for her son's happiness.

"Has he got a name, Uncle Nige?" Jackson asked, as he offered the chocolate brown pony a carrot.

"He's called Dudley, but I am sure you could change it."

"Oh, no, that's brilliant. He looks like a Dudley. Sir Dudley the Shetland Pony."

Dudley had a thick, swirly coat and a copious mane and tail. His bangs stuck out like a pom-pom between his small, fluffy ears, and he stamped his hooves, which were smaller than a Great Dane's paws. Dudley's large, liquid eyes blinked kindly, and his little nose crinkled when he took a carrot, and then a small apple from Jackson's palm.

"He likes the apple better than the carrot, I'd say," Jackson informed the group. He was very proud of his new pet, proving his authority in knowing what his pony liked best.

"He's simply adorable, Nigel, thank you so much," Lydia said, grasping her brother's arm and standing on tip-toes to smudge his cheek with a kiss.

"And what do you think, Jane?" Nigel said, turning around to face her.

She smiled, locking eyes with Nigel, and replied softly, "He's lovely."

Nigel softened into a smile in return. "I am glad you approve."

Jackson expertly brought his new pony out of the box and crosstied him in the barn aisle. He chattered incessantly to whomever was listening, while grooming his pony and tacking up. Lydia stepped in to help him slip the bridle over Dudley's ears, and his uncle made sure the girth was properly tightened.

"Can we take him outdoors for a few snaps?" Jane suggested.

"The outdoor arena is this way," Jackson said, giving Dudley's reins a pull to turn him around, leading him out of the double doors at the end of the barn. Having taken lessons at the facility, he knew there was a riding arena surrounded by a copse of tall trees between the barn and the pasture. The group followed the little equestrian. Jane got carried away, taking dozens of photographs. Ever so casually, she captured the child's handsome uncle in a good many of them.

After the little boy put the pony through his paces, Lydia called out, "I think it's best we go, Jackson."

"Right, Mum, just give me a couple of minutes to cool him out." Jackson handled his pony competently and rode well, and the adults remarked that his riding lessons had certainly paid off.

Nigel came to stand by Jane, who was leaning against the fence surrounding the riding arena. "He does quite well," he said, as they watched Nigel's nephew slow his pony to a walk.

"Yes," Jane agreed. "I think he's a natural. Riding has certainly been his strongest interest to date. And he couldn't be more pleased with his pony."

"I hope I've something here that will please you."

She turned to look at Nigel, who was holding out a little present wrapped in glossy red paper with a white velvet bow.

"Oh, dear!" Jane said. "For me?"

They held each other's eyes and for once Jane knew what Nigel was thinking. He was delighted to have her caught off guard. She carefully removed the heavy paper and velvet bow, stuck them in her deep coat pocket, and took a moment to read the inscription on the jeweler's box. *Van Cleef & Arpels, Paris.*

Reverently, Jane lifted the lid to find a dazzling necklace. From it, hung a not-too-large pendant, shaped in white gold to resemble a smooth calla lilly. A row of small diamonds graced the stamen at the center of the bloom. Jane's hand flew to her mouth. Nigel took the box from her hand, removed the necklace, stepped close behind her, and drew it around her neck. She felt his fingers lightly brush her hair aside and the necklace was fastened and it's cool weight fell inside the collar of her festive, holly colored sweater. Her fingers rested on the necklace's smooth, beautiful shape, while Nigel put the jeweler's box into her other hand. She slipped the gift box, along with her camera, into her handbag.

"Thank you . . . ." she managed.

"My pleasure."

Jackson was coming through the paddock gate and Lydia was asking Jane a question, and no doubt wondering why her friend looked so completely carried away.

*

An hour later, the group returned to the house chilled, smiling, and ready to eat Christmas lunch. Clarice retrieved a golden turkey out of the Aga, as "Come All Ye Faithful" rang out from the radio. The feast sent warm, comforting smells of chestnut stuffing, buttered Brussels sprouts, and mincemeat pies throughout the house. Lydia busied herself by carrying clinking crystal glasses full of water to the dining room table, while Eleanor dished up steaming red cabbage into a large amethyst-colored glass serving dish.

They sat down to the meal. Nigel ceremoniously offered a blessing, thanking God for his family and guests, and then he expressed appreciation for Clarice and her hard work. Jane's thoughts left Nigel's gift long enough for her to think of her mother, in Scotland with her second husband, and felt a pang of homesickness for her. She remembered her childhood home, in a village not five miles distant, and wondered what sort of strangers was gathered inside its walls. Her secure childhood seemed a lifetime ago, as though she'd never had a true home. But she was glad for this family, and thankful they saw her as one of their own. And she felt quite at home being with them at Brambleberry House, with its grand old rooms, warm fires, and unchanging furnishings.

Clarice was deeply touched by Nigel's praise during the Christmas prayer, and Jane saw the housekeeper brush a sentimental tear away from her pink cheek. After Nigel concluded with a firm "Amen," Clarice described all of the foods available, though each dish was obvious to all, as a sort of enticing advert of all they were about to consume.

Afterwards, it was time for coffee and crackers.

"Gram! Read yours!" Jackson squealed. He had managed to forget about his new pony for several minutes while the family pulled apart their Christmas crackers, spilling gifts and paper amongst the table napkins and gravy-streaked dinner plates.

"All right," Eleanor Membry slipped her glasses over her nose and unfurled the paper. "It says, 'Doctor, doctor . . . I keep thinking I'm a pair of curtains!'" Gram chuckled as she read the reply. "'Well, stop moaning and pull yourself together!'" Even Nigel laughed at the corny joke, caught up in the gaiety of the moment.

The meal had been substantial, and Clarice received further congratulations for having outdone herself. She fobbed these off, saying that she had enormous amounts of help from Gram, and had even put a few things in the deep-freeze earlier in the week. Clarice cared for the Membrys like her own family, for in fact, like Jane, they were the closest to family that she had anywhere near the village.

Jane was pleased to see that Lydia made a change by eating a full plate, and appeared to feel the anesthetizing affects of the heavy holiday meal. With last night's excitement, the trip to the stables early this morning, and all the preparations in the kitchen, Lydia declared that she was quite put under. "I think I'll pop upstairs for a lie down, if you don't mind, Mum. I am sorry to be a bore, Jane, and I wish I could help more, Clair."

"No, you mustn't, Mummy, we need to go back to the stables to visit Dudley! He's been alone now for hours, and on Christmas Day!" Jackson was appalled by his mother's lack of dedication to his new pony. His face was pulled into the most hurtful frown he could muster. Lydia said she might go face down into the turkey remains if she was kept from bed a moment longer. As always, Nigel came to the rescue.

"Well, it looks like it will be just us men folk then — you, me and Dudley."

"Yes!" Jackson emphatically shot both fists in the air. He jumped up from the table, nearly dragging the cloth with him, his napkin lost on the floor. He'd insisted upon wearing his breeches and boots to the table, and so only needed a jersey, hat, and gloves to be barn-ready.

*

Lydia smiled in appreciation at her brother, and was glad that Nigel could spend some time on his own with Jackson. Now that she was free to go to bed, it seemed too far off when she was so comfortable on the dining room chair.

"C'mon, love," her mother coaxed and helped to hoist her up by a hand under her elbow. "You seem done in, but you'll be right as rain after a bit of a lie down."

Lydia pushed her head deep into the down pillow, and studied the golden pink rays of light that glazed her dressing table. Her silver hairbrush shimmered in the late afternoon sun. Her nursing text book looked out of place among the delicate flacons of perfume, container of lilac hand cream, and china bowl holding a white jasmine brought by Jane, its mysterious fragrance softly scenting the air. Time to think of studies after the holidays. As for now, she felt as though she could sleep through the New Year.

# Chapter 4

January was bleak in southeast England. The wet skies looked as though they'd been smeared, a dirty wash left behind by a painter's brush full of ebony and rain.

Lydia's first day back at school was dismal. By mid-morning she was completely knackered. The other nursing students exchanged stories about Christmas parties, as they floated from one hospital room to another, bathing patients and checking vital signs.

The gleaming white walls and hospital floors seemed to dazzle Lydia's eyes, and the antiseptic smells nearly took her breath. Having finished with her first patient, Lydia wondered how she'd get through the rest of the day. A kind fellow student, Joanna, graciously insisted upon taking her other patients, telling Lydia she ought to have a lighter load her first day back.

Lydia was too grateful to be embarrassed. She scanned the nurse's station for an available chair. A moment off her feet, to rest and do her paperwork, would be just the thing. She saw her preceptor approaching her, and presented a brave face.

"Miss Membry, you aren't quite yourself, dear," Mrs. Fowler said, as she laid her hand on Lydia's shoulder. "I really think you ought to finish up your recording and go back to your doctor."

"I am sorry, Mrs. Fowler, really. I didn't mean to fall behind."

"No, dear, not at all. I simply think for your benefit, you ought to be examined again. I know you said doctor's given you antibiotics, but they don't seem to be helping much, do they? Perhaps there is something else we can try. And, of course, Lydia, whatever it is, our patients already have their own troubles, don't they? We wouldn't want to bring anything else. You'll call my office later this afternoon, then?"

"Yes, of course. Thank you, Mrs. Fowler."

Lydia took an unacceptably long time to write a single progress report. She had missed lunch. She didn't really mind. Food didn't appeal. She ought to just phone her doctor from here, to save driving home, and then have to go back out.

*It's dreadfully hot in here*, she thought, slipping off her sweater. Patients liked the stifling heat, as they were nearly naked. Lydia pushed her damp hair from her face. She tried to remember where she might find her doctor's phone number.

Joanna was just coming from a patient's room, and Lydia felt the oddest sensation sweep over her. She was unable to keep upright, saw the ceiling dash by, and then felt her body begin to slip to the floor.

*

Jane longed for spring. She'd removed the holiday decorations, and now the florist shop was done in a winter-white motif. Pristine paper whites, with starry bunches of tiny flowers on their spear-like stems filled the air with a heady fragrance. Jane thought she liked the smell of paper whites, but today she thought they smelled of ammonia. She was tempted to throw open the shop's door.

Soon, she would put up St. Valentine's Day, and decorate in jovial reds. That would do nicely to buoy her spirits, until spring's first hyacinth arrived.

Her thoughts were interrupted by the shrill ring of the telephone.

"Petal Pushers. This is Jane, how can I help?"

"Jane! Dear, you must come quickly!" Eleanor Membry sounded awful. "Jane, are you there?"

"Yes. Eleanor, is it Jackson? Do you want me to go to his school —"

"No, love. I've just gotten a call from a Mrs. Fowler, who is something at the hospital. Lydia's collapsed, and they've admitted her. I am just beside myself."

"Oh, Lord! Well, listen, it will take me a moment to close up shop, but I'll be there straightaway. Jackson?"

"Clarice will be here when he comes from school. I don't mean to drag him to hospital to see his Mum. Do hurry, dear."

"Try not to worry."

Jane laid the phone down, feeling the knife edge of fear pierce her chest. Drawing in a deep breath, and brought up sharp by the pungent smell of the paper whites, she forced herself into action.

She flipped the shop's sign to "Closed." She locked herself out of the shop, then let herself back in with the keys in her hand to get her bag. Now to the van.

Jane used her bare hands to push the snow from the delivery van windscreen. She climbed in and started off towards the Membry's house on Brambleberry Lane. The weather report predicted continued snow and freezing rain. Jane furiously clicked off the radio. One crisis at a time.

Turning in the drive, she saw Eleanor dressed in a navy wool coat, her face pinched with worry. Before Jane could make a complete stop, Eleanor's plump hand pulled the van door open.

"Oh thank you, dear, for coming so quickly."

"You know I am happy to help. Sorry it isn't warmed up. The old thing takes a bit to put out heat."

"And we're due for more snow," Eleanor replied, both of the women eager to control the rising panic they felt.

"Yes, that's what I've just heard. So, what is it, exactly, they've said about Lydia?"

"Well, very little, really. They mentioned that she was very feverish, and that she fainted. Her friend, Joanna, rang me, but of course I hope the doctor will have more details. I've told Lydia she must eat something. Silly girl. Oh, Jane, I am so worried."

"So am I."

They said little else on the drive to the hospital. Jane swung the groaning old van into the car park and came to an abrupt stop in the space closest to the door.

Without a word, Eleanor opened the door and slowly sank her feet onto the slushy tarmac. Jane ran around the back of the van, to offer her a steady arm.

"Thanks, love."

"Did Joanna say what room?"

"Yes. 410. Isn't that odd?"

Lydia's birthday. "Let's see it as good luck, shall we?" She smiled but Eleanor didn't see. Her thoughts made her unseeing, and Jane's voice only seemed to be reaching Eleanor at random intervals.

They walked through the automatic doors, passing the desk where Lydia worked as a clerk, across the broad hospital hall, and straight to the lift. Jane pressed the button, and the doors swung open immediately, revealing a somber elderly gentleman inside. He shuffled slowly out of the lift, while Jane kept her hand against the door. His neck bowed like a cane, his eyes cast down. The elevator's mechanism began to beep loudly, in objection to having the doors open for too long.

"The poor dear," Eleanor said absently as they stepped into the lift. "I don't know how he'll get on in this weather." Jane selected the button labeled "4th Floor."

The doors drew together in a shush and the air became still. Their eyes moved with the small round lights as they passed each floor. Jane didn't cope well with medical situations, hospitals, doctors, and the like. She took deep breathes, determined that she would be cheerful when she saw Lydia, and not chide her for eating poorly.

"How is it that you want to be a nurse, and work in one of those horrid places?" Jane had asked Lydia, months ago. She remembered Lydia's sour expression, her breath escaping with a little hum. That was how she bought time, when she was thinking of what to say.

"Jane, you know I'll never lack for job security. I could work most anywhere, in all sorts of different situations. With the aged, or with young mothers, or anyone. Never surgery, but I should want to do something helpful. I've always just sort of watched everyone, and, I don't know, I've always would rather be at home. But surely I need to stop wasting my life."

Jane tried to feel supportive. "It is an important career, I'll grant you that. Are you sure you'll be happy though?"

Lydia's eyes betrayed her bewilderment. "I don't know how I shall get on. I'd rather just take up with you at the shop. Get a string of greenhouses, and supply you flowers. But that doesn't seem to be doing much, or something."

"Oh, thanks a lot!" Jane was angry. "I suppose that means that I contribute nothing to society? Gardenias for Mother's Day, bouquets for lovers, flowers for caskets . . . who needs them?"

"Jane, you know that wasn't what I meant."

It was a terrible row. One of the worst they'd ever had. It wasn't that Jane really thought Lydia was running down the floral industry. Well, maybe that was part of it. But Jane was angry because Lydia never really followed her heart. She wanted her friend to feel passionate about her work, like Jane felt about the shop. Lydia shouldn't be a nurse, any more than Jane ought to be Prime Minister.

Eleanor and Jane quietly peeked into room 410. It was empty. Eleanor was undone. "Where could she be?"

"Don't worry. She could be at a test. Let me check with the nurse. I'll be right back."

*

Waiting, Eleanor leaned against the wall for support. A tear slipped down one cheek, but she didn't notice. It was at this hospital that her sweet Georgie died. She missed him with a pang in her heart, as though he passed away just a moment ago. Time was meant to heal, but Eleanor thought that was rubbish, because the past caught you up in a moment.

Jane returned, and Eleanor's full attention was upon her troubled face.

"They've moved her, Eleanor. That's all."

"Where?"

"Down to the second floor."

"Oh, my God, not the High Dependency Unit?"

Jane was silent. Now it was she who felt as though she'd left reality to act out some strange drama. They studied each other, looking for courage, and finding none.

Both turned back towards the lift, not feeling the floor beneath their feet.

Lydia was in 203. Jane followed Lydia's mother into the room, passing a glass observation window that faced the south side of the nurse's station.

And there she was, looking too pale, too lifeless, and dressed in a blue and white patterned hospital gown. Eleanor looked at her baby girl, now a mother herself. Where had the years gone? She walked to Lydia, and took her hand, expecting her daughter to open her eyes. But she didn't.

*

Jane had learned from the nurse that Lydia was in an unconscious state, but when Jane asked for more information, the nurse asked Jane if she was a family member. Jane almost said, "Yes, of course." But, of course, she was not. It seemed strange that she had no right to Lydia's medical information. She knew Lydia better than anyone else in the world.

And her best friend looked simply dreadful. Lydia's eyes were ever so slightly parted. Despite the oxygen-rich cannula that rested in her nostrils, Lydia's lips had a slightly blue cast. Jane felt her stomach start to squirm about, causing a wringing sensation to move through her bowels.

With a voice she didn't quite recognize, Jane said, "Eleanor, perhaps we ought to let the doctor know you're here? Maybe he could tell us what he plans to do for Lydia next?"

Eleanor never took her eyes from Lydia's beautiful, pallid face. She ignored Jane's suggestion with a slight shake of her chin.

A few minutes later, Eleanor turned and murmured to Jane. "Ring Nigel."

Jane had known that it would be up to her to do so, somehow. She began to hurry from the room, and plowed into the doctor. The doctor hesitated for a moment.

"She's very badly off, isn't she?" Jane croaked.

"Yes, quite," the doctor began. Eleanor greeted him, but her eyes never left Lydia's face. The doctor's voice picked up strength and speed. "Miss Membry has contracted influenza, complicated by viral pneumonia; a very bad case of it. She also has infection of the blood. Do you understand?"

Jane nodded her head in the affirmative. She smiled, as though being compliant would somehow relieve Lydia's suffering. Jane was grasping for hope, but didn't want the doctor to say anything further that she would be doomed to remember for the rest of her life.

"Um, she's been on a lot of antibiotics, you see," Jane began.

"Yes, right. Well, they'll do little good in this case," the doctor said. He laid a hand on Jane's arm. "The pair of you will be all right, then?"

"I, yes, I suppose . . ." the doctor was already gone as the words sputtered from her lips.

She stepped into the corridor, fumbled with her mobile, and pressed the auto-dial for Brambleberry Lane.

"Hullo?" Clarice's voice was as tight as piano wire.

"Clarice, Jane here. We've seen Lydia. She's resting. Could you be a love and give me Nigel's telephone number?" A nurse hastily walked by, into Lydia's room, followed by a different doctor, who was blocking Jane's view.

"Jane, what's happened? . . . .Are you there?"

"Yes, sorry, Clair. Lots happening here. Medical people going into Lydia's room it seems. Uh, well. I wouldn't say I've any good news at the moment. I, I certainly don't know. . ."

"Listen, duck," Clarice said quietly. "Let me ring Nigel for you, will that do?"

Jane emitted a watery sob in reply, and then an involuntary high-pitched whine. Clarice waited until Jane could speak. "I . . . think . . . Oh, Clarice!"

"Jane, darling, listen to me," she said. "I am going to ring Nigel, drop Jackson at Toby's, and then I shall be there in a tick. You just try to put on a brave face, love. Eleanor needs you." She rang off.

Jane slid down the wall, and was sitting with her knees to her chest. Her head pounded the way one's always does after crying. With another deep breath for courage, she made her return to Lydia's room.

She rounded the corner, listening to Lydia's voice in her head. A remembered conversation about hair products. One mousse left too much build-up, and Lydia wasn't pleased with it. "It feels as though I've put floor wax on my head." Jane had laughed at Lydia. The two bent over in giggles, and the hair product slipped from Lydia's fingers and crashed to the floor.

When Jane entered the hospital room, it smelled of something odd. Sort of like the paper whites. Her eyes skipped to Lydia. Her friend looked incapable of laughter, and her usually thick, lustrous hair was stringy. It never looked that way, and it was terribly upsetting. Lydia could've done hair commercials, she had that sort of hair, full of body. Full of life. The nurse and doctor were staring at her, as she stared at Lydia.

Jane wanted to speak to Eleanor, whose fingers were pressed hard to her lips, but Jane could not. There wasn't anything to say. Lydia was dead.

# Chapter 5

Jane looked at her accounts with dismay. It was rather sickening that her shop profitted from Lydia's death. She had nearly wiped out her whole inventory at the flower shop last month, with everyone sending large bouquets to the Membry's. She needed to restock ribbons, cards, baskets, and arrangement stands. The whole village had turned out for Lydia's memorial service, and Eleanor's house had been full of visitors bringing dishes of food that the other visitors would eat.

Jane shed fresh tears daily. The rather stupid thing was, she had the urge to ring up Lydia and to tell her how depressed she was feeling. It didn't seem right that she should have to go through something so hard as losing her best friend, without Lydia's support. How perfectly ludicrous. But Lydia had been there almost her entire life, helping her through the rough spots, and so this coping on her own was new business. It didn't seem quite real that she was gone, yet Jane couldn't stop crying for missing her. Lydia had passed on, and Jane wondered when she would pass through; to get to that part of the grieving process when she was no longer in a miserable flux, but seeing an end to it all.

Jane's heart broke all over again when she looked at Jackson, Lydia's dear child. Little boys cry like banshees and then they stop and want to do something else. His resiliency was somehow sadder than if he'd lapsed into depression. Sort of like a cheerful dog who doesn't know he's going to the vet for the last time, but you can't possibly tell him what it means. Jane couldn't have possibly told him what a future without his mother would be like, because she was beyond imagining it herself.

Eleanor had been doing poorly since Lydia's passing. She managed getting through the first seven days, then had a stroke. She was home from hospital now, and Jane popped in every evening to check on Eleanor and to relieve Clarice, who was really struggling too much herself to be Eleanor's nursemaid and run the house. Jackson was often to be found with Jane or at a mate's house.

Clarice, usually one to go into an energetic overdrive during a crisis, was completely put under by Lydia's death. In many ways, she mourned as deeply as Lydia's own mother, and with every reason, given her long, intimate acquaintance with the family. Several times, Jane arrived at the house to find Clarice weeping at the kitchen table. The only thing to be done was to feed her, dose her with a sleeping pill, and put her to bed, with hope that tomorrow would be better.

Nigel was a different kettle of fish altogether. Surprisingly, he *stayed* after Lydia's funeral. To help. Jane was shocked to discover his handiness in the kitchen, and marveled at his nurturing way with Jackson. He discreetly carried on his business dealings in his father's old study, but was very accessible. He was the height of compassion to Jane, holding her when she broke down at the hospital, as it was she who discovered Eleanor after her stroke, lying on the bathroom floor. Efficiently, he handled bills, phone calls from the university bursar, issues with various hospital staff, and necessary documents regarding Eleanor's medical care.

The Membry family seemed an odd one now, Jane thought: Eleanor, an elderly half-paralyzed woman; Nigel, her son and an international business tycoon; and Jackson, a little boy of five. And then there was she and Clarice, constantly in and out, their roles changing as needed.

Jane finished her accounts and put her ledger aside. She drew her cold hands across her forehead, felt comforted by stretching the skin up to her scalp, and dreaded the tears that were making their way from her grieving soul to her saltworn eyes. Lydia's laugh echoed in her mind as a few large tears puddled on the green ledger cover, smearing a bit of potting soil and making mud on the worn surface. Jane was so weary of these quiet moments, when everything about her memories of Lydia seemed loud and overwhelming, turning Jane's reality into a pale, seemingly unreal state.

The phone rang, and Jane sniffed violently. "Petal Pushers. This is Jane, how can I help?"

"Jane, you're still there."

"Hullo, Nigel. Is everything all right?"

"Yes. We're doing well here. I would like to meet you for dinner if you're able. Away from the house."

"Certainly, Nigel, I can meet you."

"Chinese Palace?"

"I'll see you there."

They rang off. Jane was puzzled as to what Nigel needed to speak with her about. Surely she could've just nipped into his father's old study when she came round in the evening? Perhaps he was getting ready to make one of his abrupt escapes and wanted to forewarn her. He'd been wonderful. How would she manage helping Eleanor, Clarice, and Jackson on her own?

Whatever Nigel's conundrum, she was thankful for the distraction that had spared her from weeping again.

The evening was unseasonably warm. The shop was busy, and Jane had nearly sold out of forced blooms of sweet-smelling hyacinth, lipstick-red tulips and a new variety of purple bleeding heart. The cold would return and remind them it was a false spring, but that would be tomorrow, and no one could bear thinking of it.

Jane's spirits lifted as she walked the village streets to the restaurant. Quite suddenly, it was the best she'd felt since Lydia passed away, and she selfishly hoped that Nigel wouldn't say anything too upsetting. She liked feeling normal for two seconds put together.

A bell tinkled as she pulled open the door to the Chinese Palace, and she spied Nigel at a booth in the corner, reading a newspaper. She knew that he would be more than punctual, and that he would be making use of his valuable time by having some occupation while he waited on her to change her clothes and walk to the restaurant.

"The weather is glorious, isn't it?" she said, hanging her light coat on the peg before sliding in.

"Indeed it is. And you're always a bit of sunshine, Jane," Nigel said, with a smile.

Jane felt a flutter across her tummy at his compliment. She suddenly felt like a woman meeting her lover. She had grown accustomed to seeing Nigel as the other nursemaid of the Membry household. Here in a public place, he was the dashing 007. She quickly glanced around, but no one was looking at them. She drifted back to earth by pretending to study the menu. She felt a pang when she saw Lydia's favorite dish offered as the special.

"Jane, you've gone black," Nigel said gently. "You came here often with my sister, didn't you?"

"Why, yes, as a matter of fact I did," Jane replied, ignoring his attempt to care for her feelings. She fought to keep the good feeling she'd had walking through the village.

The waitress, Imogen, came by and took their orders, and Jane busied herself with arranging the dragon-red cloth and utensils. She knew Nigel was staring at her. Instead of feeling thrilled to be sharing a meal with a gorgeous man, she suddenly felt as though she were about to be put through an inquest. She felt a flash of inexplicable anger.

"I'll come straight to the point, Jane," Nigel said. Jane repented, realizing that she would have done better to respond to his gentleness. She had never been comfortable when Nigel assumed his business airs, and she listened to him intently, so that if he said something complicated she wouldn't be caught out with nothing intelligent to say. And yet, he wore a slightly pained expression, not at all like corporate indifference. Whatever could be the matter, now?

But he didn't come to the point, and began fussing with folding the newspaper. He laid it aside and gazed at her. She looked into his eyes, and tried to think of herself as being a glamorous person who would be his equal.

"You realize that we can't carry on this way."

Jane started giggling. She couldn't help it, what with the things that had just been playing in her mind. The clandestine meeting between lovers, as it were. Carried away on the novel feeling of mirth, she gave way to hearty laughter.

"Jane! Whatever are you laughing about?" Nigel was stern. Jane's frivolity deflated like a balloon.

"Sorry, Nigel. Do go on, please. I shan't let it happen again."

"As I was saying, you and I have our lives, don't we? I don't think either of us are prepared to continue on with our current responsibilities."

Oh. No wonder he wanted to speak with her away from Brambleberry Lane. It was time for a family counsel, and, well, she was more or less family.

"You're quite right, Nigel. Only I haven't figured out what should happen. I didn't realize that Lydia was the glue holding us all together."

She swallowed hard, considering this revelation. Lydia had given everyone their place in the world. Eleanor had been ill before, when Lydia was alive, and Lydia managed to tend to her, be a mother to Jackson, assure Nigel that all was well at home, and keep Clarice from worrying herself ill. And she always knew when to call in Jane for extra support.

Clearing his throat, Nigel continued. "I've sought legal advice, not knowing whom else to speak with. You'll remember Mr. Beacon, father's old chum in Dorchester?"

Jane nodded. Meals were set before them. Her sweet-and-sour chicken smelled noxious and looked ridiculous. Who could be expected to eat food with thick orange gel on top?

Nigel continued on, "Mr. Beacon knows, of course, that Clarice is more than an employee. More like a sister to my mother, than housekeeper. So, we've considered her in all of this. When you and I get on, there'll be a visiting nurse to check in." Nigel systematically cut a piece from the strips of beef and pepper, and stuck the fork in his mouth. Jane wasn't having a bit of problem keeping up, he was speaking rather plainly. But it was terribly impersonal. And somehow still difficult to grasp. She was huddled over her plate, her arms folded and resting on her hip bones. She wanted to disappear from this conversation. Clarice and Eleanor were the most caring and loving of women, and apparently they were being assigned some cold-hearted, visiting medical worker.

"Now, Jane, this doesn't have to be horrible. We will be careful to hire on someone who'll function in the role with all of the convictions that we've had, you see? Someone who is kind, has a sense of caring, not just a pop-in nurse."

"Oh, yes, of course." Jane was immediately encouraged by his description of a helpful person. "Perhaps even one of the nurses from Lydia's training course. They're to graduate soon." She took a deep breath. The bell tinkled and her gaze went to the door. Seeing the sunshine, she was revived again. She became aware of her defeated posture, sat up, and began eating. Orange gelatinous food was quite good, really.

"Yes. We'll carefully screen this person. Pay them well. Make sure they've a heart for the job. It's more than medication dosing, providing transporation to stroke therapy, and checking blood pressures. We shall only take on someone that doesn't mind doing things that we do. Light housework. Doing the shops. Reading to Jackson. There is such a person, Jane, and you'll help me to find her, won't you?"

"I can't think of anyone suitable in the village, so I'll make some calls to Lydia's former teacher, for a start."

"Excellent. Now, for our larger problem," Nigel said, giving Jane a knowing glance.

She froze. This would be the part to make her feel an imbecile. What larger problem?

"Obviously, Jackson won't benefit from living in a home with two elderly and ailing women."

"Why ever not?" Jane shrieked. Several diners turned round. Her heart thumped wildly. Nigel leveled his gaze at her in a way that intimidated her into silence.

"Jane. I know that Jackson is dearly loved. But little boys need a bit more direction than can be given by a stroke-recovering grandmother and her housekeeper who appears to be going crackers over the death of his own mother. Be fair, Jane. It isn't sentimental, raising children. It's work. And speaking of which, I've got work to do, and you've got your shop."

Nigel took a long sip of coffee, and pushed away his half-eaten lunch. Jane remained suspended over her plate, not trusting herself to utter a word. How long would this go on? What devious plan would Nigel deliver up, next? She didn't think he was fit to be compared to James Bond anymore, and she certainly felt as though she'd never known him as he truly was. At least she wasn't going to cry, she was too numbed with shock for that.

"When I raised the dilemma to Mr. Beacon, he brought up a point I had rather forgotten, Jane. Jackson is under custody of his parents. With his mother deceased, we have a lawful obligation to notify his father."

At this intelligence, Jane dropped her fork.

"Nigel, you can't be serious," she said in an anxious whisper. "Do you know who he is?"

"Yes, Jane, I do. And Beacon is already in the process of contacting him."

Jane struggled with her composure, wanting her voice to sound steady and sure. "I could take Jackson, Nigel. I am sure that's what

Lydia would want. I could adopt him." The moment the words flew from her mouth, she knew them to be a lie. Her flat only had one bedroom. And how could she continue her present schedule, working ten to twelve hour days at the shop, then making her way three or four evenings a week to Brambleberry House, to help for two or three more hours? Plus, she'd worked so hard, for so long, that the shop was finally supporting her well, without any financial help from her mother. On the other hand, many single parents made all sorts of sacrifices. It's not like she was incapable; in so many ways she'd always been more responsible than Lydia.

Nigel regarded her for a moment, and then said quietly, "Jane. You're a dear. But the child's own father must be the first legal route to pursue, you understand that. And — "

"Don't you care about your own nephew? Don't you know that his father was some drug fiend, some American rock-and-roll star? Nigel, how could *he* be better than Jackson staying at home? How could Jackson do well, living all the way in America?"

Jane sobbed into her scarlet napkin, the threads of the rough, gold dragon scratching her nose. She no longer cared if she was making a scene. Without the benefit of having received a bill, Nigel laid a large sum of money on the table. Calmly and with all of his usual grace and dignity, he stood and brought Jane to her feet, reaching behind her to retrieve her coat. With his arm around her shoulders, they made their way from the restaurant.

The fading sunshine revived Jane a little. She couldn't believe she wasn't embarrassed, but her emotions were too strong to feel the sting of public scrutiny. She wondered if she would care about throwing a fit in the Chinese Palace later on. Nigel was looking at her intently.

"I am sorry, Nigel. Help me to understand."

"I've done a bit of checking. It seems the old chap has cleaned his life up. And to be fair, he never has known Jackson exists, so we mustn't make judgments on how he'd react to his son."

"I wanted you to help me understand, Nigel . . . not from a barrister's point of view. *From yours*. Is it always business first?"

"That's not fair, Jane."

"Why not? What do you think Lydia would have you do?"

Nigel drew in a long ragged breath, put his hands on his hips, as he studied the cobblestones edging the street. It seemed a full minute before he spoke.

"You must understand that I am not ready to act as Jackson's father, Jane. There are short-term legal commitments attached to my job, so it's impossible, at the moment, that I step in where Jackson is concerned any longer. We haven't any family members that are coming forth to give a hand in this. We have a cousin in Oxford, but she has two children of her own, and going through a divorce, as well. And this isn't totally up to me."

"What do you mean? Because of some legal technicality? Nigel, with your mind and money you could win against sending Jackson away to a man he's never met. I know that you could! It is up to you, because surely you are more a guardian to Jackson than his natural father! Don't you see?"

Nigel avoided her eyes. "Jane, it isn't my decision. Believe me or not, here's the truth: going to his father is what *Jackson* said that *he* wanted."

# Chapter 6

Eleanor Membry was sitting at the highly polished, cherry desk in her comfortable sitting room, looking through the mullioned windows at the large oak that dominated the front garden. The oak had long been the largest tree in the quiet village of Hartsbury. It created a canopy over the shade-loving English primroses dotting the brick walkway leading to the front door, plucky bright yellow, deep scarlet and crisp white bouquets. She would tell her friends later, over a cup of tea, that she would always remember that poignant conversation with Jackson. And the way he looked so tiny that morning.

Eleanor's soft, matronly body was sheathed in a dress covered with tiny pink flowers on a white ground, one hand held the telephone to her ear while the other listlessly smoothed her thick gray hair.

She had her friend, Rose, on the line. "Our Lydia never seems to leave my thoughts, Rosie." Eleanor had to put the phone down a moment, and blow her nose. She and Georgie'd had Nigel as a young married couple, and were told there wouldn't be any more children. But along came Lydia as a lovely surprise when Eleanor was in her mid-forties. She'd been delighting her mother ever since. Eleanor's life was so empty without her girl.

"Rose, there's nothing worse in the whole world than losing a child. Except having to share your loss with a grandchild," Eleanor said. "Oh, my lands, I am sure I don't know what to tell that precious lamb. It's all a body can do, to stop grieving when he walks in the room." She poured out her heart to Rose, who'd been her friend since their school days.

*

Unbeknownst to his grandmother, Jackson stood in the hallway listening to her talk on the phone. Gram had made him stay away from his mother's funeral. He was sent to Toby's for a few days.

But Jackson knew the truth, as would any five-year-old would who is shuttled about from one well-meaning adult to another. He figured that his mum wouldn't be coming home from hospital, and he wasn't sure of what his grandmother meant to do with him. Gram was in ill health. His uncle, Nigel, was often traveling all over the world on business.

He saw that Eleanor had caught sight of him, standing in the hallway. He couldn't help clinging to the wall like a pensive twist of ivy.

"I'll ring you back later, Rosie, after tea."

She put down the receiver, never shifting her eyes from his. "Come here, pet . . . Gram's got a bit of bad news to tell you, and you must be a brave soldier now, mustn't you?"

Jackson climbed into her lap and leaned his head against her breast. She cleared her throat, and Jackson felt very sorry for her, having to be a grown-up and give him the news he already instinctively knew. He wanted to tell her she didn't have to say it, but his voice seemed inoperable, his lips pressed firmly together. Being quiet would always be his comfort. She began to rock back and forth with the telling of Mummy's dying, and his mind drifted. He studied her sturdy brown shoes, and heard Clarice in the kitchen, putting the kettle on for tea.

After Gram talked for a while, she started to cry. He wriggled out of her lap, and said he should like to take Ausfrid outside. She lifted her glasses, wiped her eyes, and said, "Okay, Pet."

He called his spaniel and opened the door for them to the back garden. Jackson couldn't shake the feeling that his mum would show up, just when he least expected it, and ask him if he had missed her. She had spent many hours away, leaving him in Gram's care while she went to university and worked at her job. It still sort of seemed like she was super busy, and all of this was a terrible mistake. That was as far as he could get with it, and so, he wasn't really sad to go to America to meet his dad, except that he would miss Gram and not be here if there was a mistake and Mummy came home. Dudley could fly, like a show horse, so that wasn't a worry.

He had a picture of Mummy along with other treasures in his special box, that he planned to tuck into his case.

*

Jane was more than ready for a cup of tea when Charlotte Lloyd breezed into the shop.

"Oh, putting the kettle on? No, none for me," Charlotte said, fanning her long artificial nails. "I gave it up. One needs to make sacrifices to keep a dazzling smile, don't we, darling?"

She knew perfectly well that Jane didn't pay to have her teeth brightened, and in fact, was rarely even bothered to apply lipstick. Charlotte was committed to a beauty regimen that smacked of status, to the point of going on holiday to Switzerland and checking into a posh spa. Today's outfit was stunning, too; Charlotte's womanly figure was tailored to perfection in a light wool teal-colored suit, complemented by a stunning necklace wrought of gold and twisted with a strand of pearls.

On occasion, Jane secretly coveted the beautiful clothes in Charlotte's shop, but lacked the nerve to try them on. Her business was going well; she may be able to afford them. Still, it seemed too daunting to try something besides the khaki trousers and polo-necked jerseys she wore daily to work. Not to mention Jane was on her feet a lot, and she supposed that smarter clothes demanded higher heels.

"How are things going?" Jane said, ignoring Charlotte's inspection of her humble attire.

"Absolutely soaring, darling. I've picked up a few lovely things in France, casual seperates for spring, and I am going to put them in the window this evening. You'll have to match up the floral displays in your window to my clothing ranges, wouldn't that be dishy?"

Charlotte swept grandly towards the refrigerator under the pretense of looking at the bouquets. Jane knew that she had no interest in the floral arrangements, but was spying on the delivery cards, in an effort to see who was sending flowers to whom.

"Actually," Jane responded, coming to stand quite close to Charlotte to interrupt her snooping, "perhaps you'd like me to provide arrangements to stand by the till? Ladies always love to be surrounded by flowers, and the fragrance is lovely, too."

"Hmm, I'll think about it, dear," Charlotte said, dismissing her suggestion. "I've got that potpourri from Provence for fragrance, of course, and I don't want things dying and dropping off like flowers do. Anyway, I came over to let you know that you can give me your insurance payment directly."

"Oh? You don't want me to pay the solicitor anymore?"

"No, dear, I am handling all of that, now. Becoming a full-fledged landlord, you know. Why pay someone else to do it? All the renovation I've done at Panache has made me feel quite capable. Roland never let me raise a finger, but I think I am doing rather well, don't you? Now, I won't keep you from your potting, or whatever you call it. I've got to speak with my other two tenants. Ciao!"

Jane watched as Charlotte click-clacked out of the shop, turning to flash her fingers in a saucy wave as she stepped over the threshold. Jane pushed her cheeks into a goodbye grin. No doubt Mr. Collins, Charlotte's next victim, would be annoyed to see her come into his violin shop. Perhaps she ought to nip next door and take him a piece of candy after Charlotte left him, to help him recover. Mr. Collins is such a dear old soul, Jane thought. So gentle, and always smiling.

Jane heard the kettle click off, and released a long sigh. Everything about Charlotte Lloyd annoyed her. Jane missed the days when she used to rent her shop and flat from kind old Mr. Hoffmann. Ever since the newly divorced and on the pull Charlotte had been in charge, one never knew if she might try to break their contract and toss her out to expand her ladies' clothing and accessories store. Jane had to admit, Panache did bring in a lot of clientele, and many tourists who saw Charlotte's glossy ads stopped by Jane's shop. Business had improved.

But that wasn't only due to Charlotte Lloyd's customers' stopping. Jane smiled as she remembered those hours she spent brainstorming and doing research. Lydia had tried to discourage Jane from adding a range of gift items. She said people wanted flowers from the florist's shop, didn't they? And where was there any room for anything else?

Lydia's brother Nigel had understood. He'd been home for a long weekend, and listened to Jane's ideas over dinner with the family. He didn't say anything at the time, but Jane felt certain he admired her entrepreneurial spirit, as he'd given her a warm smile and a slight nod. Figuring how to begin had been frustrating, though. Especially since she couldn't afford to renovate the shop, and move the oversized counter for something less monstrous.

One afternoon, Jane was about to bin her new marketing plan, when a curious, large shipping box arrived. Inside were circular display racks, perfect to occupy the unused corner by the cold storage unit. Jane was elated. There'd been no doubt as to who had sent them; she guessed Nigel knew all sorts of people, and probably made a phone call to a manufacturer on her behalf. Besides, he was the only person, aside from his sister, Lydia, his mother, and Eleanor's housekeeper, Clarice, who knew about her aspirations, and certainly the only person who had cash enough to realize them. She noticed his careful surveyance of the new retail display when he last visited the shop. He said he was just popping in to buy a bouquet for Clarice's birthday, but obviously it would have been easier to ring her up and have her bring the bouquet with her for Clarice's birthday dinner.

After assembling the new racks, Jane purchased hand-crafted English garden tools, floral note cards and books by popular television gardeners. A month later, Jane had the decorators in. They painted the wall in a soft yellow, over a plastered texture that complimented the age of the building. It made such a welcome change to the previously dreary gray-white walls, and Jane's fresh flower offerings seem to sing in harmony with the new backdrop. Jane found some lovely, rough hewn timber, and installed new shelving below her front display window, to accommodate even more gift items. The shop had a natural, welcoming warmth, and even the villagers came flocking in more regularly.

Jane had been surprised how well the gift items sold, and had made a good deal extra money by offering them. She wrote a heartfelt letter of appreciation to Nigel, and sent it off to his current office, in Cairo. She decided what was good for the shop was good for her, and took her new decorating savvy upstairs, to her flat above the shop.

The decorators returned, this time painting the entire, tiny flat in robin's-egg-blue. Jane changed out the curtains at every window, and bought beautiful new linens and a soft, generous rug for her bedroom. A new, small sofa upgraded the little sitting room, and Jane stood an iron-and-glass table in front of it. A new mirror was hung in the bath, and fresh white tiles made it sparkle. The flat was lovely, and Jane even contemplated throwing a dinner party to show it all off, but it was a challenge to have more than two guests at a time. Jane thought there was no place lovlier than Lydia's family home on Brambleberry Lane, but she was full of new pride and affection for the flat, now that it was given a make-over. She truly had a charming little home of her own, and a thriving business below. She longed for a special man to share it with, but in all other respects her heart was content.

Jane drained the last of her tea. She was looking forward to this evening. On Friday nights, she often had Jackson come to stay. They usually played games, took a walk, shared pizza, and then he slept over on her sofa. It had been their long-standing Friday evening tradition, giving Lydia a chance to get some extra time in with her studies, and Jane thought it best to keep Jackson's schedule as unchanged as possible. Especially since it was often the highlight of her week.

# Chapter 7

Billy Killian looked out of the 50th floor window, from the conference room at the elegant Four Seasons Hotel on Fourteenth Street. The city of Atlanta was engulfed in spring blossoms, and the day had been hot. He could see small figures far below, their tiny legs reaching out, forwards and backwards, as they hurried along the pavement. We must all look pretty funny down here to God, he thought. Smiling, he turned towards the room of elegantly dressed people who were networking and making urgent requests of one another for the upcoming year.

He found a place to sit and settled onto the tapestry banquet chair. Opening the burgundy presentation folder, he was greeted with a photograph of himself receiving an award from a beautiful actress. The shot was over two years old, right after his fifth album went platinum. And to think he almost lost his life, not so long ago.

Instead of dying as a junkie, he was here for a meeting with the most elite musicians and members of America's blues music community. A number of them were sobered up, so they had more in common with Billy than music. They were glad to be alive. Sometimes his strong emotions, unhindered by chemicals, surfaced without warning. Billy just figured it was part of cheating death. It made you grateful, maybe more than most people.

"Hey, I was just talking to Webster Street, and he thinks you ought to do a greatest hits instead of new material," Billy's brother, Yancy, remarked as he mechanically straightened his already perfect tie and took a seat beside Billy.

Yancy had always been particular about his dress, whereas Billy's tastes were more assorted, occasionally bordering on the flamboyant. He cleaned up a lot better than he used to during his drug days, but he didn't mind suiting up in daring colors and heavy jewelry. Besides, Billy knew he was a rock star, so he might as well dress any which way that tickled his fancy. When you're a celebrity, people think it's cool. At least, he hoped so.

"Webster is all about making the most money for the least investment, Yance, you know that. Besides," Billy added with a mischievous grin, "this new stuff we got is too hot to keep under wraps, Bro!" He laughed and rubbed his hands together. "We've got to start laying down tracks 'cause I can't keep it to myself."

Yancy nodded, but he wasn't as quick to ignore Webster Street's advice. Yancy Killian could be swayed by the financial aspects of the music business, and he also knew his brother needed to produce quality albums to keep his fan base interested. He contemplated the opposing views, his face giving away nothing. Then a thoughtful smile spread across his face. His brother always produced the best music he'd ever heard.

He slapped Billy on the back. "Well, if it's all as good as what you played me last week, I am gonna have to side with you. You know you've got first dibs on the penthouse studio," Yancy assured his brother. He was proud of the fact that Billy always came to his place to record. He was handling so many new artists now that he'd added ten more recording studios.

Industry executives, artists, managers, marketing personnel, and board members found their seats as the meeting came to order. Howard Sultz introduced himself, and welcomed them all to the annual meeting.

"I appreciate you all being here, and taking precious time out of your busy schedule to join us today. The Preserving the Blues Music Hall of Fame Museum is an organization that exists only because of your generous support." As Howard Sultz spoke, the lights dimmed and images of a modern facility materialized on a screen.

The roof line was in the shape of a guitar, with the front entrance leading into the circular hole, representing the front of guitar, and a long Hall of Fame was fashioned on the outside to look like the neck of a five-string. The immense building was skirted by a huge parking lot, laid-out among colorful plots of southern landscaping.

"Here we have our new Preserving the Blues Music Hall of Fame Museum that was finished in February. If any of you haven't marked your calendars yet, please note that we'd love to see you all at the Grand Opening in May. We've reserved suites at the new hotel accommodations in Tupelo, where the security is excellent. Simply advise us of your needs."

As the multimedia screen silently withdrew into the ceiling, their attention shifted to a striking young lady who was gracefully pushing a large cart that displayed T-shirts, program books, key chains, and caps.

"Here is an example of some of the fine quality merchandise that we'll be offering at the gift shop." The young lady waved her arm decoratively in front of the merchandise, reminiscent of a television game show hostess who functions as a human accessory. Enjoying her moment in the limelight, she took a stiff navy cap from the cart and placed it on her head, then struck a pose with her hands on her hips.

"Our marketing team is using only licensed images, preapproved by each artist's management. I can assure you that these items will be treasured by visitors to the center. You each will have an opportunity to donate a percentage of the sale of your items to the Preserving the Blues Music Hall of Fame Museum. Your gifts, as always, will be greatly appreciated. Thank you, Becca."

Becca discreetly removed herself from the front of the room, her smile unaltered as she went.

Howard Sultz paused for a drink of water. "Now I'd like to introduce a local resident from here in Atlanta. Serena Berquist serves on our national directors' board and has been instrumental in procuring items for the museum. She is the granddaughter of blues legend Cletus Mains. Please give her a warm welcome."

Billy turned to see a statuesque blonde approaching the podium. Her smile was easy and sincere. She was dressed in a tailored, mint-colored shantung-silk suit. Pearl earrings bobbed attractively from her small ears, and she casually tucked her straight blonde hair behind them, revealing beautifully sculpted cheek bones. Her face was lightly sun-kissed, making all of Atlanta seem more warm and inviting.

Her voice was low and clear, attractively tinged with a southern accent. Billy melted in his chair. She was the classiest woman he had ever seen. She'd told a joke and everyone responded with laughter, but Billy missed it.

"So, that is why I am speaking to you today," her eyes skimmed the room, embracing each listener. Billy's heart skipped a beat as she focused her gaze momentarily in his direction. "Of course, we realize that many of these items have great sentimental value, but that value only doubles when your keepsakes are shared with your most dedicated fans. If you could look through your closets, sift through your mementos, and find something to donate to the museum, we would be so honored to display it for you in this illustrious new facility. The types of items that we are looking for include performance clothing, personal correspondence and photographs not previously shared with the public, private audio and visual footage, retired instruments, or awards that you've been given."

Billy wished he had every award he'd ever won. He would place them at her feet right now.

"Feel free to contact me and I'll arrange to have your donations safely conveyed to the museum. Of course, we will manage each item with tender loving care, and it will be enjoyed by millions of visitors. Thank you in advance for your generous support."

Serena Berquist shook Howard Sultz's hand and said something to him with a charming smile. Billy's eyes were glued to her pleasing form as she returned to her seat.

She appeared to attend today's meeting by herself, and sat at the back of the room with the presentation technician.

Forty minutes later, the meeting finally concluded. Billy stood up from his chair and bolted towards Serena Berquist.

"Billy!"

He pretended for a moment not to hear. He glimpsed the back of Serena's head as a sea of people filled the gap between them. She was talking with his distribution manager, Webster Street. Webster was stylish and smooth, and had a reputation as a ladies' man. Billy quickened his pace, but someone caught him by the arm. It was Rusty, a fellow blues artist from Texas.

"Good Lord, Billy, where's the fire?"

"Hiya Rusty. Didn't know you was going to be here. I was hurrying over there to catch Webster."

"Do you wanna join us for dinner? The guys and me thought we'd go around the corner, on Peachtree. . . . "

"Um . . . could I take a rain check, Rusty? I am not sure I am free tonight."

"Sure, Billy." Rusty studied Billy's distraught face for a moment, and figured there might be a woman on his mind. That girl with the T-shirts made for some yummy eye-candy. Maybe Billy had designs on her.

"I'll let you go. If you change your mind, you'll call me?"

"Yeah, sure. See ya."

The crowd stood in tight little groups and Billy had a difficult time shouldering his way to the back of the room. A few artists stopped him for a quick handshake and congratulations for the success of his last album. Finally he reached the area where Serena had been speaking with Webster. She turned, and his heart dropped into his boots.

He stated his name and blurted out his intention. "I'd like to donate a guitar to you."

She smiled. "That's wonderful!"

"How do we do that?" He couldn't believe how un-smooth he was. Yancy would laugh out loud if he could hear him now.

"Well, why don't we get coffee downstairs, and we can talk about it."

"Sounds good. You're as smart as you are pretty." The compliment came rolling out, but Serena didn't seem to mind. She just smiled again, and walked closely beside him.

The hotel elevator doors opened on the neoclassical tower of marble and rose granite. As they entered the dimly lit lounge, Billy silently led Serena across the plush, ivory carpet. There was a cozy table in the back corner, somewhat hidden from the rest of the room by a large potted palm in a stone planter. They sank into the hug of a pair of cushy cocoa-striped club chairs, and Billy ordered de-caf.

"I called you 'Miss' before. Is that right?"

"For the time being. I am engaged," Serena said. She seemed distracted for a moment, and avoided his gaze.

"Oh, okay." Now what?

Suddenly upbeat again, she said, "I am a big fan of yours. May I call you Billy? I was hoping that you'd be here, and that I would get the opportunity to talk to you. Your *Message* album is my absolute favorite!"

"So, you're Cleatus Mains's granddaughter, huh? That's really somethin'. Do you play?"

"Me?" Serena threw her head back and laughed. "No, I don't play. I wish I could, you know? Give Bonnie Raitt a run for her money. But, no."

"Did you ever want to learn? I mean, how do you know that you don't have the gift?" Billy said.

*

Serena was touched by the thoughtful expression in Billy Killian's eyes. He was concerned that she might be overlooking something special in her life. The magic in music that he'd found. What a nice guy.

She drew in a breath. "Well, I've never tried to play. And to be honest, it scares me. It's one thing to sing in the shower. It's quite another thing to sit down and put an instrument in your hands and be that . . . vulnerable. Do you understand what I mean?"

"Yes, ma'am I certainly do. I've felt, when I am playin', that the whole world was hearing me pour my guts out. It's a powerfully personal thing sometimes. Music doesn't lie, ya know?"

"Mmm, I guess you're right. And, that would be your experience, but it isn't *music* for a long time, is it? I don't relish making awful noises while trying to learn."

Billy laughed and shook his head. "I've had plenty of those days, too, believe you me!"

*

Later that evening, Billy walked Serena to her car. She slid in and he closed the door as she waved and turned over the key. After she pulled away, he stood in the parking garage for some minutes. Replaying her voice was like a sweet melody, a song he wanted to hear all of the time. He walked back to the entrance to the hotel.

He closeted himself in the elevator. The chime signified his accent to the 48th floor, and he fumbled for his keys. As he stepped into the dark hotel suite, a feeling of cold loneliness poured down his chest. He fumbled for the light switch and shut the door behind him.

*Lord, what has come over me? I was fine. I spent the better part of the evenin' with the most gorgeous woman on earth. And now I feel like I've dropped to the bottom of a well.*

And he wanted to drink his way back to the top.

His gaze shifted to the minibar in his room. He knew there would be some comforting alcohol in there. And not too much, either. Just a little to calm his nerves. No one would know, and it wouldn't have to mean anything.

This commitment to being sober would be a battle that he would fight for the rest of his days. But why tonight? Was it Serena? Did she somehow bring out the worst in him? Why should he care? She belonged to another man, and he would never see her again.

Billy heard voices in the hallway, and he recognized his brother's among them. *Thank you, God. The cavalry just rode in.*

He dashed out into the hallway, closing the door on his temptation. He caught up with Yancy and asked him to get a cup of coffee with him. Yancy said that sounded just right. Billy had won this round, and he desperately hoped he'd be in a better frame of mind when it was time to enter his room again.

After talking with Yancy, he was.

The next morning, Billy was boarding his flight back to Texas when his subconscious tickled him with a thought. They hadn't talked about the guitar. A grin creased his face. He was glad to have an excuse to contact Serena again.

# Chapter 8

Serena Berquist parked her convertible in the garage of her brick home on Montgomery Ferry Drive. Coming into the cheerful Prussian-blue-and-yellow kitchen, she was greeted by Taffy dancing with delight, jumping up to her knees. Dropping her purse on the counter and kicking off her high heels, Serena swooped down to pick up the dog, who weighed less than a sack of sugar.

"Taffy! Hello, precious girl! Did you think Mommy was never ever coming home?" She smoothed the dog's silky steel-blue-and-tan silk coat, while they made their way to the sun room and out the back door. She put Taffy out for a quick potty, then let her in again.

She had a message on her phone. Probably Richard. She pressed the button and heard his voice. "Just checking in from New York." There was a pause. She knew he was trying to remember what was on her agenda, so that he could express an interest in how it went. He gave up after a moment and ended with, "Saw on the TV that you had a thunderstorm yesterday. Hope it wasn't too bad. I'll call you this weekend." Click.

"I am going to marry him, Taffy. Richard's a very wonderful, successful, sensible man, you know? Hmm," Serena mumbled softly, "of course you don't agree." She recalled Easter weekend last year. They'd come home from a luncheon with her parents to find Taffy on top of Richard's briefcase, chewing the leather handle. Richard had already called the dog, "Rodent." Found guilty of ruining his property, Taffy was immediately upgraded to "The Destructive Rodent." Taffy had never been a problem before, but she wasn't sure if Richard would allow her to keep Taffy after they were married. He would put it in a way that seemed logical. Richard would insist that of course she would prefer the comfort of her husband over that of a dog, right, honey?

Serena picked up her teacup-sized Yorkshire terrier and whisked her upstairs to bed.

For the most part, Serena had always been malleable, although she did exasperate her parents when she was younger. Despite their officious encouragement, she wanted to dig in the dirt with the family gardener, sleep with dogs in her bed, and take up the sloppiest of hobbies.

Serena's parents garnered a lot of cooperation from her with a single compromise. They allowed her to ride horses. Except for a sporadic reminder not to "break her fool neck" the Dr. and Mrs. allowed Serena to ride in peace. They didn't meddle with affairs at the barn or attend her horse shows, which she considered the greatest blessing of her teen years. Serena walked through the show barns with a variety of friends. She drank pop out of a can, cussed now and then, wore whatever clothes she wanted, and enjoyed her freedom.

Serena dreamt she was falling from Logo, a horse she used to jump until she had a fall from him that broke her arm. Of its own volition, her leg kicked beneath the bedcovers, waking her up. It was only excess electricity from the nervous system, she reminded herself. The clock read one a.m. Taffy sighed and rolled over. Serena felt wide awake and agitated.

They hadn't talked about the guitar. But not because she forgot.

What kind of game was she playing? She needed Richard. When she was with him, her life came together. She was protected, and her parents' expectations were fulfilled. There was a lot of security in that.

She need only to set a date, and pick out her dress. Her mother and the wedding planner would glory in taking care of all the details, while she toiled at the hospital with her huge engagement diamond throwing scatters of light from her computer keyboard. It was time to make a decision.

Impulsively, she threw back the sheets from the bed and went to her office. Everyone got married in April, May, or June. Or messed up other people's schedules by having their ceremony over a holiday weekend. Serena arbitrarily picked the second weekend in . . . October. Yes, that would be it. Her finger pecked the square labeled the 13th. A Saturday, so the date was okay. And it gave ample time for arrangements to be made.

And that's all there was to it. She scampered down the hallway, her feet chilled, and crawled back into bed. She switched off the light, settling down into the darkness, hoping for sleep to claim her.

*

Mrs. Adele Berquist laughed aloud as she modeled a large brimmed, butter-yellow hat that flopped about her shoulders. The ladies all clapped their hands and encouraged her to buy it.

"Oh, I couldn't!" Adele gushed. Then she turned to her daughters, Serena and Caroline, and asked, "What do you think, girls?"

"Mother, please," droned Caroline. "It's simply ridiculous. So buy it!" Another peal of laughter ascended above the bubbling song of the outdoor fountain.

April held a yearly tradition of a garden tea with a trunk show. For the last three years, Pooch Kennedy hosted the event, and invited a hat designer up from Charleston to display her latest creations. The hats were such a smashing success that everyone would've missed them in lieu of something different, so Pooch decided to keep the same theme again this year. The ladies sipped Darjeeling from china cups and tried on dozens of hats, which were prettily perched on golden stands upon a table dressed with a lavender linen cloth. Pooch and her husband, Bob, a real estate broker, owned a beautiful property, with dozens of pink rhododendrons hugging the spacious patio. There were half a dozen round tables set up, with the guests approaching every so often to try on another hat, and admire themselves in a twelve-foot-high Louis XIV-style mirror framed with climbing rosebushes. Servers in white uniforms discreetly refilled teapots and replenished the disappearing cucumber-and-ham on brown bread sandwiches, assorted quiche tartlets, pink frosted petit fours, fresh sliced fruit, shell-shaped orange-flavored madlines and hard-chilled white-chocolate-covered strawberries. They smiled as they passed the fountain and came onto the patio, knowing that Pooch would not tolerate the hired help bringing sour attitudes to her tea party.

Caroline Berquist-Von Berge had already decided on her purchase. She choose a tastefully small hat that looked like a present wrapped in pale golden silk. "I can't wait to wear this . . . you know what it will go with!"

Serena said she didn't have a clue.

Caroline gaped in disbelief. "My new Vera Wang, you know *the one for your wedding*?"

"Oh, of course. I am sorry, Caroline. That will look gorgeous with your dress. It will."

"I know, I can't believe she had one that is so perfect. Which hat are you getting?"

"Oh, I don't know. Sometimes I just feel silly in a hat, even though I love the way they look on other people."

"Serena you should buy something, even if it's that little straw one I saw you try on. Actually, that looks like you. You could wear it to a polo match or a horse show or something."

"Yes, I do like that one." Serena absently sipped her tea. She was thinking about the brief conversation she'd had with Billy Killian, about her coming to Texas to personally pick up the guitar he was donating to the museum. She had been all business and so was he.

"You're preoccupied. What's going on with you?" said Caroline. She was taking another bite of a madline which Serena knew she wouldn't finish. Caroline's dieting approach was very French; eat anything you want, just in minute amounts. She thought Caroline probably liked the idea of wasting food at social events. She was naturally thin like her mother and sister, but she liked to present herself as someone of great personal control who ate only bird-like portions.

"Well, this afternoon I am flying to Texas to collect a guitar for the blues museum."

"Oh, uh-hum," Caroline chewed the sweet Madeline slowly, savoring the second and last bite that she allowed herself. Serena saw her eyes glaze over. Caroline had little interest in any music outside serving on the ladies' auxiliary that raised money for the Atlanta symphony. Her sister always politely expressed an interest in Serena, and tried to have meaningful conversations with her, but they seldom connected.

"So, I was thinking about the musician," Serena added, even though she knew Caroline wasn't really waiting for more of an explanation.

Caroline gingerly rubbed her fingertips together to rid herself of crumbs, and then took up her lavender napkin and began to massage away soiling bits of food from the edges of her mouth.

"What did you think of me in the white wool cloche? For winter, of course," Caroline said. "Maybe for Christmas." Caroline never really wanted opinions, just compliments on her choices.

"It looked nice, too," Serena replied. She felt a sudden hot tickle of pain in her nose, and she concentrated on not allowing tears. Caroline and her mother had been living on a different planet her whole life, so why did it suddenly matter? Maybe she should chalk it up to wedding emotions. Everyone always says it's a stressful time.

"Darling, what are you getting?" Adele had traded the bright yellow hat for a more subdued navy and Kelly green. She removed the hat and smoothed her hair, looking sideways at Serena.

"The straw hat with the black band, probably."

"Oh, yes." Adele wore her auto-smile. It wasn't that Serena had bad taste. Quite the contrary, but she didn't share *exactly* the same preferences as Adele and Caroline.

Serena left the tea, her new hat in hand, a little early. She knew the security line at the airport would take forever, and she didn't want to miss the only flight out tonight. Having gotten to the gate uneventfully, she settled in as best she could on a hard plastic chair and opened her briefcase. She reviewed her paperwork for the acquisition of the guitar, and then moved on to some policy revisions for the physical therapy department. The joint commission was coming to review the hospital this summer. Everything in her department had to be in order, or the hospital could incur some heavy fines. Her flight to Dallas was called. She picked up her briefcase and walked up the slightly sloping tunnel and boarded the plane.

# Chapter 9

Billy hoped he wouldn't be a blundering idiot when he saw her. He knew that she'd look beautiful, but he would have to ignore that.

And this was business. Although he was incredibly attracted to this woman, he respected her. He didn't want to creep her out by getting caught looking her up and down. She was engaged, and she would be here to get a guitar. He didn't want to disgrace either of them by coming on to her.

He flipped on lots of lights and picked up the guitar. He put the instrument back down, then turned on some music, then turned the music down a notch, and decided to put the guitar on the desk. It looked stupid on the floor, sitting there like a trash can beside the chrome table. Satisfied that the room and instrument were presentable, he started back down the hallway towards the front of the building.

He reached the glass double doors just in time to see her limo arrive, issuing out of the sunset. The sprinklers turned off as he opened the door, as if they were on cue. He paused on the pavement, watching her as she turned back to the car to retrieve her things. The driver had gotten out and was placing her single piece of luggage on the pavement.

Billy couldn't help himself, he drank her in for a few seconds while she conducted her business with the driver. She was wearing a sleeveless blouse and fluid pants in a cool turquoise shade. She had high heel sandals on, and her toes were polished in soft coral. She was stunning. Smiling.

He moved forward to get her luggage as the limo driver stepped back into the car.

"This is impressive, Billy," Serena said, studying the sandstone colored building. The sign above the doors announced Killian Studios in dark purple, and the building was situated on four acres of prime Dallas real estate.

"It's my brother's dream come true, that's for sure," Billy replied. He was calm, now that she was actually here. She was the girl he'd talked to so effortlessly for hours in Atlanta.

She followed him up to the door and passed inside as he set her luggage in the reception area, which was a grand, tiled affair with a fish tank that circled the whole foyer.

"Oh, my!" she exclaimed with a laugh, pivoting around to view the aquarium.

"I am just glad it isn't my job to clean it," Billy said. "Follow me, and I'll give you the two-penny tour."

"I can see why artists are wild about this place," Serena remarked as Billy showed her one of the recording suites. The black, red, and silver room boasted a large screen television, bathroom, and full kitchen with a dining room table, seating enough for twelve, and a broad glass wall that separated the recreation area from the studio. A desk was available to the guests, complete with pads of paper embossed with Killian Studios across the top, and a computer and printer. A cabinet opposite housed a sound system. A drape was drawn half-way across a set of French doors that led out onto a second-story balcony. Serena stepped over to the window and looked out. Below was a beautifully manicured garden, lake, and a picnic area, bordered by wide walking trails. The state-of-the-art equipment and generous room dimensions made recording a luxe experience. On the walls there were photos of dozens of entertainers who had been guests of Killian Studios.

"They've got their own e-mail address while they're here, all that sort of stuff. And we've got a little inn on the other side of the property that everybody likes to stay at. But, a lot of 'em come back for Mama's cooking, more than the digs," Billy said.

"Are you serious?"

"Oh, yeah, I am serious. If we've got a band in here who are going to be holed up for a while, doing a start-to-finish project, then Mama will bring them over a couple of home-cooked meals. Texas-style BBQ, mostly. They love it."

"That is so nice," Serena said.

Billy smiled, enjoying himself. He was proud of the family business. "Yancy is really into service, ya know? He has the interns wash our clients' cars and everything."

"But besides all of that, we've got the goods when it comes to the technical stuff. We've got a 65,000 square foot facility here, with all the bells and whistles."

"Do you have a Custom API Legacy Plus in every studio?" Serena asked. Billy was surprised by her question. He saw her checking out the console from where they were standing.

"Yeah, and each has processors, dynamic gear, and monitors that are all top-notch. Every studio has four isolation booths, with good cueing systems, and we've thrown in a baby grand, too."

"All of that with good security, and just fifteen minutes from the airport, huh?"

"Yes, ma'am," Billy said with a grin.

He led her from the studio to see the meeting rooms, and then lastly to Yancy's office.

"Please, have a seat. How 'bout a drink? We've got juice, pop, water, uh, what else. . . ."

"Water, thank you. I've had enough juice and peanuts for a while."

"Yeah, isn't that terrible? They used to serve you *something* to eat on commercial flights. I guess we all complained about the food, then, and now they've taught us it was better than nothin'."

Billy emptied a bottle of Evian, and was proud of himself for remembering to put a lemon slice on the edge of the glass. He'd seen Sandy, Yancy's secretary do that. Sandy was classy like Serena.

Billy picked up the guitar case and took out the instrument.

"Well, it certainly looks like it has a history!" cried Serena. The guitar was scarred from heavy use. "Mind if I record your comments about it? The museum display people will strangle me if I don't get everything they need, so I've learned to record."

"Sure, no problem. Well, first of all, this is a 1982 Strat that my brother gave me way back when. I used this guitar for about half my sets, with an old Vox Wah pedal and an Ibanez Tube Screamer."

Serena smiled. "Have you been using this guitar since you got it? Did it go on your last tour, and have you had it lately in the studio?"

Billy paused. He was holding the dark red guitar lovingly, and deftly touching-out chords on the strings with his left hand.

"It's funny you should ask that, ma'am."

Serena saw emotion pooling in his eyes. She knew he was about to tell her something personal, and she wasn't sure if she should pause the recorder app on her cell phone out of respect.

"The last time I used it was the night I . . . well, I left this life for awhile. This baby here was in my hands, right then. Somebody showed me a picture of myself, all laid out before the ambulance came. Have you ever heard that story?"

Serena looked away when his eyes lifted to hers. She replied tentatively, wondering how much she should let on that *everyone* knew the gory details. "I've heard bits and pieces. The press said that you collapsed, and then shortly afterwards you entered a treatment center. But everything else was hush-hush. That's what I remember about it." For some unfathomable reason, her voice filled with emotion. He was so accessible, a quality that seemed to Serena everyone else in her life was lacking.

"Well, I can't say that I remember it that well, ya know? It seems like a million years ago. I am sure it's been that many miles. Sometimes the pain of it just comes up, and surprises me. That night, I guess I had a heart attack and they lost me for a few minutes. Actually, that happened to me twice, but I don't remember much from that first time at a hotel in London, I was so high."

He grew quiet. Serena was about to turn off the recorder, but then he regained his composure.

"But I am doin' real good now, for the last five years. I eat right, take good care of myself, and I thank God I am alive every single day." He cocked his head to one side, his face folded into a sweet grin, and Serena laughed with him. They were about the same age, but his past made him seem older.

"I used this guitar all the time before that night, though. In the studio on my first two records, and on the road, too. After the whole business in England, I just sort of retired it. I don't wanna say that I thought it was bad luck to play it or anything, but for some reason, well, it was kinda like I needed to let it rest with the past. You kinda get to thinkin' about an instrument as a person, and this one partied with me too much. It sounds stupid, but you understand what I mean, don't you?"

"Yes, I think I do."

"Yance got this guitar in a second-hand shop somewhere. I had just discovered how to use a whammy bar, and I went to town on this ole' thang. It was a different band then, too, because we hadn't picked up Mason yet."

"Oh, and didn't he join up a year later, right before you went in the studio for the second time?"

"Wow, darlin' you sho know your history. I am flattened."

She didn't know if he meant to say that he was flattered, or that he really felt knocked-down by her knowledge of the Vipers. It didn't matter. There was genuine feeling in everything he said, and she liked that about him.

They talked for a while longer, effortlessly jumping from one subject to another, like old friends. Billy finally stood to return the guitar to its case.

Serena said, "Are you due to be somewhere else, or can you have dinner with me?"

Billy felt easy on the subject. They got along so well that it was just like being with his sister-in-law, except for those occasional snaps of fizzy excitement that came and went. Billy knew his behavior was honorable; nothing he'd done or said couldn't have happened right in front of her fiancee. And soon, she'd be gone.

"Let's go over to Slyder's. It's about ten minutes from here, and they've got a little bit of everythin'."

They switched off some of the lights and Billy set the security system. He handed her the guitar and picked up her luggage on the way out. He loaded his trunk, handed Serena into the car, and they drove away.

*

It was late when Serena checked into her room at the Mansion on Turtle Creek. Once owned by a Texan cotton magnate, the beautiful inn felt like staying at a wealthy relative's home. She was also five minutes from fabulous shopping, so Serena thought she might hit a few stores before she left Dallas. She hadn't seen much outside the city on previous visits, and so Billy had agreed to be her tour guide tomorrow.

She went into the bathroom and started a bubble bath in the expansive honey-colored marbled tub. She checked her voicemail while the water ran. Nothing from Richard. Perhaps he'd forgotten that she was out of town and left a message at her house. She'd call him back after her bath.

She slipped into the silky water, reclined with her head on a terry pillow and sighed deeply. The tea party and hat trunk show seemed as though it happened a very long time ago.

Her time with Billy felt cut short, even though he hadn't dropped her off until after midnight. She was content with him. Standing in the crowded restaurant waiting for a table, he moved in close to hear what she was saying, and she had enjoyed his attention.

The bath was cooling, and Serena decided to get out, her thoughts still on Billy. He'd answered her question; no, there wasn't anyone special in his life. She didn't worry about being attracted to him. He was a perfect gentleman. It was okay that he made her feel pretty, feminine, and well taken care of. She knew that he didn't expect anything of her, and she also knew that if she were free she would let herself fall in love with him. It wouldn't take much to make that jump, but he would hold them safely where they were, in friendship. In fact, after she boarded the plane on Sunday, she'd probably never speak with him privately again. She might see him at a distance, during public functions like the opening at the blues museum, but it was doubtful they'd connect this way.

She thought about Richard and grew irritated, knowing how he would misinterpret their friendship. He never understood about her inherent love for music. He couldn't comprehend the intangibles in life; he didn't know how to just "be." She decided she needed to drop that line of thinking. Why analyze everything, anyway? She'd leave that to Richard.

She slathered on lotion, and happy thoughts ensued. Billy told her about his Uncle Eustus. Uncle Eustus was a rodeo clown who once foiled a robbery that was happening in a grocery store. Serena giggled, remembering how proudly Billy related the story.

She grabbed her cell phone and climbed into the large canopy bed beneath a heavy cover of golden and red flowers. She settled deep into the goose-down mattress, and pressed the auto-dial for Richard's condominium in Atlanta.

"Hello?" a sleepy female voice answered.

Serena froze.

"Hello? Is anyone — " There was a click and the phone hummed.

# Chapter 10

Serena's first befuddled thought was to berate herself for calling so late, and waking people up to answer the phone. She'd forgotten it was after one a.m. and that civilized people were sleeping. A split-second later, she remembered that her fiancé ought to be sleeping alone.

She dropped the phone, her emotions heading for a crash. She felt like a test dummy in a vehicle, rapidly heading for a cement wall, powerless to change what was happening.

Maybe she shouldn't jump to conclusions. She remembered that Richard has a sister. *A sister who lives in South America, and never visits.* Maybe she hadn't dialed correctly? *The number has been programmed into my phone for a year.*

Impulsively, she called back. The phone rang, the pattern of the tones were familiar and they afforded Serena a little comfort. He would answer, and explain everything.

But no one picked up. Richard's answering machine switched on, and Serena clapped her phone shut. She was in a mild panic. She imagined Richard arguing with the woman who answered his bedside phone. Was the woman someone Serena knew? Should she have suspected something was going on?

She leapt out of the bed towards her purse. She looked for Billy's card, his cell phone number was scribbled on the back. She dialed it.

"Yeah . . . hello?"

"Billy? Oh, I shouldn't have called you. I am so sorry. I am just . . . a little upset." *And you seem like my closest friend in the whole world.*

"Serena? Serena . . . . What's wrong, baby?" The warmth and kindness in his voice was too much. She began sobbing, quietly. "I . . . I am not sure," she said, clasping her hand over her mouth.

"I'll be right over, okay?"

Serena hung up. Numbness set in as she mentally repeated the woman's voice, over and over. She folded a pillow between her knees and chest, and sat motionless, her thoughts tumbling. Minutes later, there was a knock on the door. Billy. Somehow she'd almost forgotten he was coming.

She scrambled off the bed, running through the suite. She caught her reflection in mirror in the sitting room, and didn't recognize the frenzied woman. She paused before opening the door, wanting to stop, think things through, take stock of the situation; but it was too overwhelming and she couldn't seem to summon any self-control, she was just confused, raw, and feeling as though she were floating in space. Billy would anchor her. She opened the door, stepping aside to let him in.

"No photographers to make a scandal of you at this hour," she joked. Her voice was too strained to convey any humor.

"They don't find me that interesting, unless I win some award, or I am talkin' to some actress or somethin'," he said, as though he was in the habit of making social calls in the wee hours. Billy had stepped into a pair of jeans, a white T-shirt and hadn't done a thing with his hair, which stood up in a goofy cowlick at the crown. Serena thought he looked incredibly appealing. A funny observation, considering her life was probably falling apart. It just didn't seem that serious, as long as he was here. She almost felt guilty for calling him, because his presence had quickly enthused her with courage.

He eased his tall frame onto a low French salon chair in the corner, and smiled at her to give her confidence. He waited for her to begin, but she just sat there, grinning back at him. Billy decided small talk must be in order. But what came out wasn't as trivial as he was aiming for.

"I had a really great time with you today. Well, yesterday," he said. "I almost chickened out of meeting you with the guitar, ya know that?"

Thankful for the diversion, she said, "You did? Why?"

"Oh, because I like you so much. Probably too much, seein' how you are gettin' married soon. I thought maybe I'd put my brother up to it, tell him to meet you instead. But I was worried about having to admit to him that I hadn't stopped thinkin' about you since we met in Atlanta. I am only good at keepin' my secrets if I totally keep my mouth shut. Once I start talkin' I am afraid I tell everything."

*Like now*, Serena thought. "Yes. It's like opening Pandora's Box sometimes."

"I am not gonna pretend I know who that is, but I do know the worse news usually comes in the witchin' hours, and since you were fine when I left you, you must've gotten some bad news. Question is, what was it, and then we'll figure out what to do."

Serena smiled. The woman's voice played in her mind again, and her emotions went reeling.

"Hey, it's okay, honey. Talk to me." Billy leaned forward on the chair, his elbows dropping onto his knees.

"I don't know what to say, exactly."

"Don't think. Just let it come out. You'll feel better, because when things are just in your head they grow like weeds. If you say it out loud, it brings everything down to a managable size. My mama tells me that, and she's pretty smart."

Serena sucked in a deep breath and sat on a loveseat opposite him. She tucked her feet up beneath her.

"I called Richard. I don't know what I was thinking, because I never call when I will interrupt his sleep. He's very strict about that sort of thing. The next thing I knew, a woman answered. I was shocked, and hung up. I called back. No answer at all that time, just his voicemail coming on. I imagined they were both awake and Richard was asking her why she answered the phone, and she probably said that she forgot that she wasn't supposed to. . . ."

Hearing herself tell the story ruined her composure. He came over to the loveseat, and held her, rocking her gently back and forth, and stroking her hair. She sobbed for a while, feeling the sharp pain of Richard's betrayal.

"I know there could be some logical explanation but, I don't th-think there is one. . . . I thought he loved me." Pulling away from him, she rose to go find a tissue and tidy up a bit. His t-shirt was damp from her tears, and she had wiped her nose on the sleeve of her robe.

She blew her nose and splashed some cold water on her face. Her head throbbed. She came back to the sitting room.

"I am sorry," she sniffed. "I shouldn't have dragged you into all of this."

"No, don't you worry 'bout that."

"Billy, what do you think?"

"That I want to make love to you and rip his damn head off, but I am not sure in what order."

She grinned and then sank back down on the loveseat beside him.

"He doesn't deserve you, Serena. Not that I do, but he really screwed up, didn't he?"

"I don't know," she said, fresh tears falling hot down her aching face.

"What don't you know?"

"Because I am not sure I loved him like I should. Maybe it's my fault."

He got up and started pacing the room. Billy's agitation was endearing. Serena could see that he was as upset as she, and that he viewed this as his problem, too. Amazing. How long had it been since she'd felt someone was on her side?

Billy stopped pacing. "No, I am afraid I have to disagree with you, darlin'. He has no excuse to cheat. He broke the trust between you. That's not your fault. The question you have to ask yourself is if you're gonna turn your back on this, like it didn't happen. I've seen women do that; they think once they're married, or have a baby or somethin' that the guy will act right. But I am hopin' you know that doesn't work."

"I don't know. I mean, I do, but, I just can't believe it. I never imagined. He was the 'safe' guy, you know? My parents practically hand-picked him for me, and it felt like we were all marrying him. He's my brother-in-law's best friend since grade school." She blew her nose again. "Obviously Richard shouldn't be too disappointed. He didn't even wait till we were married to have an affair." She couldn't talk anymore, she was exhausted. She could only cry.

*

The dawn brought a worse headache. She was on the loveseat, in Billy's arms. She looked up at him, and he smiled at her.

"Hey, girl. Some night, huh?"

"Oh, I am so sorry. I can't believe all of this. What time is it?"

"Five thirty-eight."

She sat up slowly. "Will you get me something for a really awful headache?"

Billy went to the phone and called the front desk. She went to the restroom, and when she came back he had fresh coffee, and two asprin in a paper cup compliments of the concierge.

"Do you want me to go? Maybe you want to be on your own, and call him?"

"No, please don't. I mean, the thing I keep coming back to is that he hasn't even called to explain. I can't marry him now. Especially since everything that hurts is because of pride, instead of hurting because he is the love of my life, or whatever," she drained the coffee. "I never knew the difference before, not for sure. So, I am glad that I found out, before we were married. I just don't know what comes next."

"You're talkin' sense at least," Billy said with a smile. "What do you feel up to? Sleep? Food? Or do you want to go out, and try to forget it all for a few hours?"

"I don't want to be bad company for you, and I am not sure what I want to do," Serena said, tucking her tousled hair behind her ears.

"Do you want to fly back early?"

"No, I need time to pull myself together."

Billy was quiet for a minute. "Tell you what I think. It's probably going to be worse if you sit in a hotel room by yourself all day. Why don't you let me take you somewhere, like for a walk someplace nice? And you don't have ta talk or anything, just some fresh air, and we'll see what you feel like from then on. I'll stick around, and remind you to eat and get you to the airport on time. Sound good?"

It sounded very good. Some TLC, without any pressure. She knew Billy would take good care of her, and not complicate her feelings any more than they already were. "Okay."

"All right, then. Could you eat somethin'?"

"Amazingly enough, yes."

"Okay. Then you go dress, and I'll sit here and read the paper they dropped at the door until you're ready. Then we can go to my place, I'll grab a shower, then I'll make you breakfast."

Serena felt renewed by having a task. She showered quickly, put on the only casual clothes that she'd brought along. She clipped her hair up and went sans makeup. Still in the bathroom, she had an impulse to call Richard and acted on it.

"Hello?"

"Whose your friend?"

"Serena, look. It's nothing serious. We can talk about this."

"Talk about what, Richard? What is there to talk about?"

"She doesn't mean anything to me, okay? I know that sounds trite, but it's true. I want to marry you," he pleaded. His voice changed then, to one of authority, as though scolding a child. "Serena, don't do this to us."

"I think you're confused, Richard. *You* did this to us."

There was a frustrated pause. Richard sighed, and Serena knew that he felt frustrated by having to deal with this on a Saturday morning. It was important to have his head clear before he got to the club, or his golf game with her father would be screwed.

"Goodbye, Richard."

"Serena — "

She hung up on him. The laughter caught her by surprise. It was insane to be giggling, but she couldn't stop. She laughed some more, and dabbed a few tears. Relief followed, and with it, a sense of excitement came surging up within her. She had all of the energy in the world, and her headache had totally dissipated. The hurtful episode with Richard seemed surreal.

It was going to be a great day.

# Chapter 11

"Oh, my dear, you do the loveliest arrangements, I dare say!"

"Thank you, Mrs. Smith. Your custom and your compliments are appreciated," Jane replied. "I hope you enjoy Portia's visit, and do tell her I said hello." She closed the door behind Mrs. Smith and locked it. It had been a tiring day at the flower shop, and Mrs. Smith had waved through the window after Jane closed, begging Jane to reopen the store for her. She didn't want to make a habit of that, but Mrs. Smith had always been so kind to her, and she was an old friend of Mr. Collins's in the violin shop next door. For her, Jane would make an exception. She picked up her bank deposit and dashed into the chilly spring air.

The sweet fragrance from the blooming lilacs suddenly stabbed at her heart. Her eyes filled with unexpected tears, and she remembered Lydia as though she'd seen her only yesterday. The idiotic thing was Lydia always seemed to flash by with a contented smile. It would be easier to take if she seemed regretful to leave them all. But, no, Lydia seemed to be content with leaving her loved ones in misery. It was odd to be holding a grudge against the memory of a deceased friend. It put Jane rather out of sorts.

"Jane, are you all right?" Mr. Collins asked. He was locking up the shop next door.

"Oh, yes, Mr. Collins. Just thinking of Lydia. Something about the scent of lilacs can make me melancholoy. That sort of remembering, it comes on one quite suddenly, doesn't it?"

Mr. Collins didn't reply. He was a widower, and Jane reckoned he was thinking of his wife.

"Good evening, Mr. Collins."

His eyes floated back to meet hers, and he touched the brim of his cap.

Jane pulled her cell phone from her bag as she dropped her deposit in the bank slot. She rang Brambleberry Lane.

"Hullo?" sang Clarice.

"Clarice, how are you?"

"Oh, fine, Jane. My legs are good today, and we've been putting everything to rights here. Do come for dinner, I've got a pork pie coming out as soon as you come through the door."

"You're a mind-reader, Clare," Jane said. "I was so glum. Listen, is it all right if I bring a friend? You're sure? Brilliant. And I hope Jackson will be home?"

"Oh yes, he's just come in from the stables. He went riding with the Gaffney children, them what live down the road. See you in a tick."

"Cheers." Jane turned the opposite direction from Brambleberry Lane, and headed back to the high street. She walked up to the navy-trimmed door marked Collins's Violin Shoppe, and knocked loudly.

The heavy door yawned and Mr. Collins shuffled into the doorway. "Why, Jane, is something wrong, love?"

"No, no, I am fine. I just wondered if you'd join me at the Membry's for dinner. Nothing fancy, but our Clarice is a lovely cook."

"The Membrys', eh? Goodness, haven't spoken to Eleanor in some time. Not since, well, you've only just remembered a few minutes ago, didn't you?" His kindly face pulled into a repenting frown.

"Shall we go, then?" Jane said with a smile.

"Yes, dear, let me get my coat. An old man like me takes a chill."

Mr. Collins returned in a well-worn tweed and pulled the door shut. He ceremoniously offered his arm to Jane, and she cupped her palm in the crook of his warm woolen elbow. The fragrance of the budding trees was delicious now, and no longer attached to memories. The sun was setting, shading the sky in pinky tones, and Mr. Collins looked vibrant. He must have been very handsome in his day, and his quick blue eyes were still enchanting. What a dear old soul.

Jane realized how empty with hunger she was, and anticipated the comforting meal.

"We'll go round to the back, through the kitchen as old friends do, Mr. Collins," Jane said as they took the path along the side of the formidable house.

They opened the door and were assuaged with savory smells. "Clarice, I've arrived with my mystery friend. I didn't tell her who I was bringing around, Mr. Collins."

*

Clarice said good-naturedly, "Mr. Collins, we're delighted to have you, dear. How are things at the shop?"

Jackson came running into the room and straight into Jane's embrace.

"Oh, Jacks, you're getting too big for these running leaps. How's Dudley? He didn't throw you off, did he?"

Jackson howled with laughter. "Of course not! Dudley's the best pony in the world. You'd know that if you'd ride with me, Auntie Jane!"

"Darling, you know I am no good at horses. Do you remember Mr. Collins?"

"No. Hello, sir. Do you like ponies?"

"Yes, actually, you and I have something in common, my boy," replied Mr. Collins. "I had a marvelous pony when I was small. A little Welsh mountain, he was, and white as snow. His name was Llanarth."

"What happened to him?" Jackson asked.

"Well, naturally a chap gets too tall for a pony, doesn't he? So, we sold him off."

Clarice gathered everyone into the dining room, just as Eleanor was coming downstairs.

"Well, upon my word! Mr. Collins! What a lovely surprise!"

"Hello, Mrs. Membry. You've been well, I hope?"

"Oh, my, yes. And you're looking fit as a fiddle. Oh! I've made a good joke!"

Everyone laughed and took a seat around the table. Eleanor was about to speak, but her voice was lost when the air was punctuated with shrill sirens.

"Grams, the fire engines!" Jackson yelled. He peeled out of his chair and ran to the window. Red light revolved around the walls of the dining room as the trucks passed by, headed for the high street.

The meal was forgotten on the table, as everyone followed Jackson out the front door and into the front garden.

"Oh, no," Jane whispered. The black billowing smoke was coming from the area where she and Mr. Collins kept shop. "You don't suppose?" she said, turning to Mr. Collins.

Tears shone in his eyes.

# Chapter 12

Billy showed Serena his sparsely furnished condo. "It's really just a place to crash and keep guitars," he said, pulling out a chair at the table for her. "But I can make up for the bad decoratin' with my cookin', don't you worry." He fixed up a tasty frittata, opening a jar of homemade salsa to go on the side, compliments of his mother, and he even remembered to snip some fresh chives and cilantro from the neighbor's overgrown pots at the edge of their patio. After the zesty breakfast, he surprised her with another delight: a motorcycle ride.

"Oh, Billy, this is great. I haven't been on a motorcycle since high school!" She eased onto the seat behind him, fastened the helmet he gave her, and enjoyed the best part, which was having an excuse to hold him tight. They headed out of town and about fifteen minutes later Billy parked the bike at the entrance of some nature trails. The sun's rays were hot, but it was cooler in the woods. At times the trail would narrow, and he would take her hand and lead. Walking was good therapy. She would chat and he would listen. Then she would grow quiet again, trying to remember the last day she'd spent doing something this aimless and fun.

After their walk, he took her for a short ride to a BBQ place that seemed to be popular with the locals. The screen door sceeched softly when you opened it and everyone let it bang behind them. Country music was playing, and there were lots of families eating together.

"How does this work, exactly?" Serena asked. Billy laughed, and pointed out a picnic table in the shade. "You just go park yourself over there, and I'll handle everything." He walked up to the long counter and placed their orders.

Billy returned to her a few minutes later with a whole loaf of supermarket white bread, two baskets of food mounded on red-and-white checked wax paper, and bottles of water.

He placed a basket in front of her. "Smoked trout. Ever had it?"

"No, I don't think I have. At least not like this!"

Serena stuck her fork into the tender fillet. Not fishy. Not too smokey. Just right. She smiled at Billy in appreciation.

"You're just full of culinary surprises, aren't you?" She teased, taking a slice of bread from the bag.

"Well darlin', when you don't smoke, chew, drink, do drugs, or chase low women, you eat."

"This is really great. It really is," Serena's voice broke.

"You all right, honey? Do you want to wrap this stuff up and get outta here?" Billy's face showed his sincere concern.

Serena laughed, embarrassed. "No, no. Actually, I am just really happy. I haven't had a day like this in a long time. You know, just hanging out."

"You know somethin' that always stuck with me, Serena? This really smart doctor I knew told me that we're with certain people because of how those people make us feel. We think we're doin' so much for them, but what actually keeps us with 'em is that we like the way we look to ourselves, through their eyes."

"Hmm. That's pretty profound. I am not sure, exactly, how it applies to me and Richard."

"Well, I am wonderin' who you are through Richard's eyes, or maybe it could be he's never really seen you."

Serena looked blankly at her meal. "I think you've hit on something there. I think Richard saw my family, maybe my looks, my education, and my status at work. And I fit easily into his life. But he doesn't see my dog. Or the new flower garden I made last year. We don't like the same music."

"And those parts of you are who you really are."

"Uh-huh," Serena agreed. "Those are things that are personal, and he only likes the things about me that go on a resume, or that people in our circle know about me. Of course he doesn't reject me, he'll try to sympathize when I have to leave Taffy to go on a trip or something, but it's a stretch for his patience."

She laughed, and Billy's heart gave a jump. He was interested in her dog and her garden. And it was *his* music that she liked best.

"But some of that works both ways," Serena said before taking a long drink of water. "Richard was my ticket into my own family. I know that sounds crazy, but they liked me a lot better when he came to our family get-togethers. Anyway, I really appreciate you being here for me this weekend. I think it made all of the difference in how I processed this. But, I need to say something, okay?"

Billy was worried, but put on his warmest smile. "Sure. I am listening."

"I know that we . . . well, we get along really well, don't we?" She blushed and couldn't look at him for a minute. "My parents were always afraid of me hanging out with musicians, but I never really have. Anyway, when I think of us, I mean if you were ever interested in seeing me, that may not work for me, either. God, that didn't come out the way I wanted it to, Billy!"

"That's okay, I — well, I think I understand."

"You do?"

Well, didn't he? Billy already figured Serena was too smart, too beautiful, too good for him. It wasn't money, really, he probably had plenty of that. Richard was a jerk, but he came from her world.

Billy realized that he'd grown quiet. He was determined not to add to her misery. "Don't feel bad about bein' honest with me. And you're right, I've been thinkin' since I met you that . . . how . . . you're just an awesome woman. But, there's no gettin' around it, that I won't be goin' to college anytime soon, or — "

" — No, that isn't it! Billy, you are a genius, without a piece of paper to say so. Your success says so, doesn't it?"

He was pleased by her compliment, but this was getting confusing. What did she think of him, anyway? Maybe because they had a little chemistry going, he thought too much of things between them.

She said, "My life is in Atlanta. And, to be honest, I guess I can't imagine bringing you home to my parents."

"Most girls can't, darlin'. I am used to that one," Billy's laughter bubbled out of him, causing a few people to look at him and recognize him. They whispered to each other and he regretted drawing attention to them, knowing he was probably going to get a few autograph requests. He gave an even stare to some of the onlookers, indicating that he didn't want to be disturbed during lunch. He usually never pushed off fans, but he usually never ate with Serena Berquist.

Serena continued. "I feel really childish saying that. And even though Richard was *perfect* as far as they were concerned, well, their opinion still matters, although it probably shouldn't."

"Why not? Sweetheart, no matter how old we git, we always want to please our mama and daddy. I don't think it oughta run your life, but I don't believe in tearin' up your family. Fact is, if your parents don't like what you're doin', a lotta times its cuz it ain't right for you."

"So, since my parents were thrilled with Richard, they obviously know what's right for me?" Her voice was tart. She'd suddenly turned on him.

"Uh, I guess I was speakin' more generally. You know, just sayin' that most parents want what's best," he said meekly. "Serena, I know I am not what's best, okay? I can see now that you'd be tradin' way down to start somethin' up with me. I'm sayin' maybe there's a guy that likes your dog *and* measures up for your parents."

"Yes, that would be just right. Very simple requirements. I'll have to go home and find that person this week, and then perhaps I won't even have to cancel my wedding, just change the name on the invitations."

Billy reached out for her hand, but she pulled away with a snap. He could tell that she wasn't used to tenderness, and misread it. Her cold behavior made him pity her all the more, instead of feeling pushed away. He wished that he could have a chance to be good to her.

"Hey, girl, you sure are pretty, even when you're mad."

The smile he was hoping for burst onto her face with unexpected brightness.

Billy knew she didn't want to be mean to him. She was tired and she had been hurt. That smile said it all. "So, you ready to ride? We got some miles to put on to get you back to town."

She rose and followed him to his motorcycle. Minutes later, they were flying down the highway, and he felt her chin come to rest on his shoulder.

Billy said good-bye to Serena, and made her promise to keep in touch. He thought about hugging her, but then thought better of it, and got on his bike. He rode to his mother's house.

She still lived in the old neighborhood where he'd grown up. As a surprise, Yancy and Billy had bought their mother a new home, much bigger, brand new, and closer to them. But she said it wasn't *her house*, and she preferred to stay where she was. They ended up selling the place to a cousin.

Margaret "Mossy" Killian was delighted when she threw open her front door to her youngest boy. She would've loved a big family, but her husband was in bad health early on. So, she'd just been content to love her two headstrong, musical boys and adopt the world in general. It wasn't unusual to find all manner of people having a piece of Mossy's yellow pound cake at her kitchen table at any hour of the day. She kept herself busy with church, volunteering, bridge games and shopping with her girlfriends.

"Honey, I am so glad to see you Shug, give your Mama a hug," Mossy grabbed her tall son around his slim waist and bear-hugged him. "I was just cleanin' because the girls are comin' over tomorrow mornin' for coffee. We're goin' to Trader's Village."

"Is that that flea market thing over in Arlington?" Billy said, slumping into his Daddy's old green chair. Ranger, the family's beagle, came for some attention, and Billy stroked his head.

"Yes. Sandra says she's goin' to do all her Christmas shopping before summertime, and well, we hardly need an excuse to go shoppin'," Mossy said with a chuckle.

"Here, Mamma, take some money," Billy said, leaning forward and pulling some bills from his wallet.

"Honey, I don't need that, you put that away. Now, I am serious, if you leave it there, it's goin' straight to our new ladies project at church. Did I tell you about that?"

"I don't think so. Whatcha' doin'?"

"All them little kids whose parents are gettin' off drugs need a day care till they're old enough to go to school. Why, Honey, with all you been thru with drugs and alcohol was jes terrible, but imagine havin' a little one stuck in the middle when you're tryin' to get your life on track."

"Well, Mama, I'll give you more money than that. How much do y'all need? Does Yance know about this? You know anythin' we can do for kids," Billy said.

"Oh, I'll be callin' him soon enough! Mr. Purdy's workin' on the budget as we speak. It'll give some of our young moms a little payin' job, too. Now, what's goin' on with you? Yancy said yesterday that you had a woman comin' from a museum for one of your guitars."

"Yeah, she flew down from Atlanta. I just dropped her off." Billy was fussing with the crocheted edge of a pillow.

"Oh, I see. She was a nice girl, wasn't she?" Mossy knew her boys inside and out. Billy never felt like his mama pried as much as she just cared so much about everything in their lives. They were close, and Billy needed to come clean.

"Well, Mama, she is more than nice. She's perfect. But she's way out of my league, and she was kind enough to tell me so, so I wouldn't get my hopes up over her. Even though we get along real good."

Mossy Killian waited patiently to see if her son had anything else to say. He was deep in thought. "I think when people want to be honest with you, about anything, that just proves what a really fine person they are."

"Yes, Honey, I think so, too." A silence fell between them. Mossy said, "Oh, my goodness, it's goin' on six-thirty already. Have you eaten? I didn't stop and have any supper."

Billy followed his mother into the kitchen, and kept her company while she ate a bologna sandwich and left over potato salad. He passed on her offer of everything in her fridge, agreeing to a small dish of homemade blackberry cobbler.

"How's this record goin'?" Mossy asked between bites. "You've hardly been around, you been in that studio so much. Did you get that casserole I sent over with Charlie, or did he take it home?" She talked slowly, but somehow always got in three things at once.

"He brought it in, and then complained 'cause we ate it. It's been goin' real good. We'll be wrappin' it up and doin' some finishing work on it startin' this week."

Mossy giggled, pausing with potato salad on her fork, saying, "And that April! Why, she couldn't be more tickled about namin' that album! Land sakes, that child called me on the phone way past her bedtime and told me she'd done something for posterity, or some silly thing. She sounded just like Yancy sayin' it, but I forgit what she said."

Billy shook his head. "Yup. That youngun is a piece of work, ain't she? And I told Yance we ain't seen nothin' yet. She's goin' to get spunkier every year. But she's got a good head on her shoulders, don't she?"

"Yes, praise the Lord for that."

"Well, Mama, I better get goin'. I'll be headin' into the studio early tomorrow mornin."

"Okay, sweetheart. I know you're makin' a good record, and it takes a lot of doin'."

"That it does," Billy said, as Ranger and his mother followed him to the door.

# Chapter 13

Serena had an awful Monday at work. Coming back through the kitchen to let Taffy in, the telephone rang. Serena winced at the shrill, and picked it up only to avoid it screaming at her again.

"Hello."

"Serena. Look, I just want to apologize for this whole misunderstanding." Richard's voice was gentle, but his words enraged her. Again.

She opened the door for Taffy and put her hand on her hip, gazing at the ceiling. She felt like Richard was invading the sanctity of her home by speaking through her telephone.

"Richard. I have a headache. I am going to bed. I can't do this right now. And it wasn't an misunderstanding. *It was an affair.*"

He retaliated. "But I told you it's not really an affair. She's just someone from the office, we were working late, and things got a little out of hand. Of course it will never happen again, Serena, you have my word."

"You're right, Richard, it won't happen to me again, because I am not going to let *you* happen to me again. We're through."

Sweeping through the kitchen, she slammed her phone down on the counter. She was livid by the time she got to the top of the stairs. Her self-pity was acute, and she didn't know how to rid herself of this burning anger. She considered a relaxing bath, and remembered the last time she'd taken one, in her lovely suite at Turtle Creek. Billy had been so good to her.

But he wasn't here now. And he never would be after what she'd said to him. She wasn't even sure why she suddenly had wanted to push him away. She was cold-hearted, like her mother and Caroline, after all. But that didn't mean she deserved Richard. What a beast.

She was standing in the middle of her bedroom. She turned to face Taffy, who was on the bed. Her liquid eyes showed deep concern, and she whimpered when Serena looked at her.

"Oh, poor little Taf!" She went to the bed and scooped up the warm little body. "Mommy's sorry to worry you, puppy. You're a good girl. It's just that Mommy is very unhappy. We need to find someone to love us both, okay?" Taffy licked her hand in response.

Serena suddenly felt compelled to phone her mother. No, she should wait; her head was still hurting.

She sat on the bed stroking Taffy, and the phone rang again.

"Hello," Serena answered. She knew it wouldn't be Richard again. Not this soon. He had too much pride to beg her forgiveness more than once a day. She was safe from him till tomorrow evening.

"Hey there," sang a deep voice. Billy. He sounded so good. She knew she'd liked his voice before, but right now it was healing.

"Oh, hi." She knew she sounded tinny and impersonal.

"I hope I am not catchin' you at a bad time. . . . I just wanted to see how you were gettin' along today. Been thinkin' about you a lot, you know, all this trouble, and I said a little prayer, which should help some."

Serena drank up his kindness, hovering over each word like a hummingbird drawing up precious nectar. She couldn't form a response.

"Um, anything I can do for you? You just name it, okay?" he said.

She drew in a sharp breath and replied. "Yes, okay. I am okay. It's been a rotten day, but, I am doing fine. I have a terrible headache, more than anything."

"You took something, didn't you?"

"Yes, but it hasn't had a chance to kick in yet."

"Well, here's what you do. Turn on your best soft music, nice and low. Getcha a cold washrag and put in on your forehead and take a good, long nap. Then when you wake up, eat something and go right back to bed. By tomorrow, you'll feel on top of the world, I promise."

She laughed softly at his careful, loving advice. It was so like him to believe what he believed, completely, even if it was a headache remedy.

"I'll do that, Billy. And I really appreciate your call, okay?"

"Sure thing. Feel better, Sugar. Goodnight."

She put down the phone, smiling, and followed his instructions to the letter.

*

Billy and the band toiled through another week of long days in the studio, improving and polishing the new album. Billy was exhausted with the work, and though he thought about Serena when the music stopped, he didn't call her again, letting the days roll by.

His feelings were jumbled. He thought she was the finest person in the world, and felt angry with her fiancé. Then his feelings would cool a little when he thought of how quickly she made it clear that there couldn't be a romantic relationship between them, despite their mutual attraction. But what else could she do? She was in the middle of canceling a marriage and she was smart enough to not get involved with anyone else. He was wrong for wanting her come running to him when she had just broken up with Richard. And, like she implied, maybe they just weren't suited.

He couldn't figure out how to benefit her the most — to be a supportive friend, or someone who would respect her privacy and go away. He knew what he wanted. He wanted to be everything good for her — — like a brother she could lean on, a father who could tell her to respect herself, a lover who could prove that love doesn't have to hurt.

Friday afternoon was fun. The guys, worn out from so many hours in the studio, had started horsing around. Everybody was slaphappy. Yancy walked in the studio, and let out a loud whoop.

"Did y'all do a damn fine record, or what?"

"We did a gold—no, platinum—fine record, sir!" Charlie said, with a mock salute.

"Yeah, that may be, Charlie, but you know if they call out the name of that album at the big awards my daughter's goin' to go runnin' up there cause she named the blasted thang!" A round of raucous laughter ensued, and Yancy went over to his brother and held out his hand.

Billy took Yancy's hand and let him pull him to his feet, saying "What's up?"

"I need to talk to you for a second." Yancy said, grinning.

Billy was puzzled, and they stepped out into the hallway. Yancy just stood there, grinning for all he was worth.

"What is your problem, man?" Billy said, laughing. He hadn't seen his brother act this way since he bought him a motorcycle for a Christmas gift three years ago. His "swallowed a canary" expression was rare.

Yancy folded his arms across his chest, savoring the announcement. "You've got a visitor. Just dropped in. Was in the neighborhood."

"Huh?"

"From At-lan-ta."

"You're foolin' Yancy, and that ain't funny, now." A streak of irritation burned through Billy. He was tired, and he didn't know where Yancy was going with this.

"Billy, chill out, okay?" Yancy's expression was serious, and he put his hands on his brother's shoulders. "She's as confused as you are, so cut her some slack."

"What?"

"I am tellin' you that Miss Georgia Peach is here, waiting for you in my office. I am telling you that she isn't quite sure that she did the right thing by comin' here, and I am tellin' you to get yourself straightened out."

"I can't believe it! What did she say?"

"She just walked in with my secretary and says, 'Hi, Yancy'– No, she called me 'Mr. Killian.' Then she said somethin' about likin' the studio. And then she was ramblin', about how she was in Dallas for the weekend, and did Billy happen to be here. And she's waitin' on you, right now."

"I need a drink."

"Deep breath. Let's go."

Billy followed his brother through the hallway, crossed the atrium, smiled at a receptionist as he walked by. A minute later, he was face to face with Serena. Yancy excused himself, a beaming canary, saying he was due at a meeting.

"Billy, I know this is a total surprise. I hope you weren't busy." She extended her hand, and he grasped it, shook it, but didn't let go.

"I can't believe you're here. Sit down. Can I get you anything? Is everything all right?"

"Everything's fine. I just needed to get out of town. I've never really fled like that before. It's very self-indulgent, isn't it?"

"Yeah. I've done it a lot, only we call it touring."

She laughed at the joke. Then they laughed together again, self-consciously.

He couldn't think of anything he wanted to say, except to ask her what she really wanted from him. She spoke next; she'd had time to rehearse.

"Things with Richard are all worked out. I mean, we are totally broken up. Everyone knows, and I let my mother cancel everything. It was her that I had to get away from."

She took a deep breath and paused, but he waited for her to go on. If he wasn't on the same couch with her, he would've felt like a therapist. Yancy's big executive office was a safe-feeling place to dump things. He'd done it before, himself, sitting opposite his brother.

Serena gazed towards the desk and continued. She was talking to herself as much as she was informing Billy about the last week. "Richard traveled a lot, and wanted to golf when he was home. Most of our time together was with other people, with my parents at the club, or at a party. So, we weren't a cozy couple to begin with. It was easy to let him go, after what he did. But my mother, she is humiliated."

"Humiliated?" Billy was lost here. If a woman had screwed around on him, his mother would have felt only compassion for his hurt. He didn't understand Mrs. Berquist.

"Yes, you know, as though I've been stood up at the altar."

"Oh, I see," he said, when he didn't. Billy smiled, embarrassed that he had interrupted.

"Well, she doesn't say that she blames me, but it feels like she does."

"What were you supposed to do different?" Billy was lost again.

"I don't know. Nothing. I mean, she knows it's not my fault, but Richard isn't there to be mad at, so she's taking her frustration out on me. Saying, 'oh, that caterer had the perfect menu for your special day. It's all just a shame.' Or, suggesting that I need counseling. Not Richard, just me."

Billy shook his head. He hadn't met Serena's mother, but he'd seen her type. "She really loves you, and you know that. But she's actin' like you ruined her party plans, instead of feelin' bad that you've lost your whole life with the man you was gonna marry."

"*Exactly.*"

Billy sighed, and was glad he was following this confusing business.

"Did you leave your little dog at home?"

"Yes, with Mrs. Duchak who lives on the corner. She loves to keep Taffy, and she has a dog just like her. They're friends."

Billy smiled. She was so pretty. And she was here, with him, because she didn't want to be anywhere else. Or, at least, she couldn't think of anywhere else to go.

"Are you at Turtle Creek?"

"No. I don't want to go back there. I've got my suitcase in that closet over there. I guess your brother's secretary thought someone would trip over it."

Billy took a minute to size up the situation. "What would you say to seein' if my Mama will put you up while you're here?"

"Oh, that would be sweet, but I don't want to put her to any trouble."

"She wouldn't think a thing of it, but I don't know if she's already got plans or company. I can call her and find out, if you are okay with it?"

"If you really don't think she'll mind, then please call her."

Billy smiled at her and then leaned over and kissed her lightly on the lips. Her mouth was soft and willing, and kissing her was as heavenly as he'd imagined it would be. "Mama's gonna love you as much as I do. I am glad you came. It's a compliment to me that you'd come here when things are goin' bad for you, do you know that?"

"I guess on some level I must, because I didn't have to think twice about coming. I knew it would be okay . . . if I could just get . . . here." He could see that the truth of her own words moved her.

Billy leaned in and kissed her again, slow and tenderly. She put her arms around his neck and held him tightly, drawing strength from him.

The phone on Yancy's desk rang once for another line, and both of them laughed. Billy got up from the sofa in search of her suitcase, punching his mother's number on the speed dial of his cell phone as he crossed the room.

"Mama, what are you doin' this weekend? . . . Uh-huh . . . Oh, really? Well, because that nice girl from Atlanta is back in town, and I was wonderin' if she could stay with you?" Billy turned to smile at Serena, just as Yancy's secretary came to the door of the office. "Okay. Yeah, we'll plan on eatin' with everybody here. What time? Okay. Love you, too." Billy ended the call and said, "It's cool. She's excited."

He turned to Yancy's secretary. "Hey, Sandy, how are you hon?"

"Doing great, Billy. I've got a call for you on line one. Some fellow from England."

"England? He probably wants Yancy, but I'll talk to him for a second. Thank you. Oh, and Sandy, if you don't have plans tonight, Mama's cookin' for everyone, okay?"

"Thanks anyway. Hot date," Sandy said, fanning herself. She smiled at Serena and turned to go.

"We can eat here with everyone, if that's cool with you, and then go on to Mama's house later. Okay? Excuse me a second while I see what this guy wants."

Billy sat in Yancy's chair and picked up the line.

"Billy Killian here. Can I help you?"

A measured voice, with an English accent, greeted Billy across the line. "Good evening, well, I suppose it's still afternoon for you there. I am called Harold Beacon, and I am a solicitor for the Membry family. Does that name mean anything to you?"

"Uh, let me think. Nope, I am sorry, I don't believe I've heard of y'all before. I can't really think of anybody I know in England, except some musician friends of mine. What's this about, Mr. Beacon?"

"Mr. Killian, I have some news that you may find rather shocking. I hope you're at a place where you have some privacy, in case you've any questions?"

"Yeah, I can talk. Go ahead." Billy's face became serious, and Serena leaned back on the sofa and crossed her arms.

"You see, a number of years ago, you had a short-term relationship with a young lady in London. Her name was Lydia Membry."

Billy said nothing. He couldn't recall. There were more than a few girls on every tour.

"Mr. Killian, perhaps it might assist you to know that you were with this young woman the evening you were taken to hospital."

"Mr. Beacon, do you know if she was really pretty and had dark hair?" Billy replied, a distant memory bubbling under the surface.

"Yes, yes, that's right. Quite a beauty, in fact."

"I am sure I remember her, but I never saw, uh, I never saw this girl, Lydia, again after that night. And you're calling because of her? Is everything okay, I mean, how is she?"

"She's deceased, Mr. Killian."

"Oh! Well, um, I am really sorry to hear that Mr. Beacon. I hardly knew her, well, except in the Biblical sense, if you get my meanin', sir, but I sure feel bad about her passin' away." Billy and Serena exchanged looks. Serena looked sympathetic, though she didn't have a clue who died.

"Actually, that brings me to my next point, Mr. Killian. Miss Membry was a decent sort. As far as anyone knows, she never even had another relationship with a man after you. But she did have a child. Yours. And you've just indicated to me that you remember your affair that evening. I should think you would require proof, but of course we can do tests if that seems necessary. I am sure you're quite surprised, sir, and I am sorry to be speaking to you about such intimate things over the telephone, but you understand the circumstances."

"Are you sayin' that I am a daddy?"

Serena's hands flew to her mouth. She got up and walked towards the window, as though looking out would provide answers.

"Yes, Mr. Killian. That is what I am relating to you. And he wishes to come to you, now that his Mummy is gone."

"He?"

"Yes, sir. You have a son. His name is Jackson. I am told by his uncle that he was named for someone you admire, though I never knew who that was. I've wondered if it wasn't your American hero, the one on the note, perhaps, Andrew Jackson — "

"No, Jackson Browne. But you're sayin' he wants to come here? Like to visit me or somethin'?"

"Uh-hum. Well, to be more precise, to trial a living situation with you. Of course, we're moving on the assumption, sir, that you are free from drug use and could act as a responsible parent?"

"Yeah, I guess so. I mean, I want to be. I'm clean. Mr. Beacon, you got me really shaken up here. But, yes, I want him. I am just so shocked, ya know?"

"I understand."

"Why, he must be goin' on, what? Five or six years old already?"

"Yes, sir. He's quite attached to his pony, and we've promised that you'll look into arrangements for having him sent over. You wouldn't mind to do that, will you?"

"A pony? Oh, okay. Yeah, I'll try to find a place to put one. I better be findin' a place to put a kid, too!"

"Very well, then, Mr. Killian. Let's allow this revelation to sink in a bit over the weekend, shall we? Then we can speak again next week about further arrangements. I can call you at this number on Monday, if you'd like?"

"Yes, sir, that would be great. Thanks, Mr. Beacon. I'll talk to you next week."

Billy hung up the phone and looked at Serena. He started laughing, and then stopped. He was a father, and he didn't know what to do with that.

"I guess I have a son."

"You're sure he is yours? Didn't I hear you say that he is six years old or something, yet you never heard about him?"

"I know he's mine. I just know it's true. Maybe she tried to let me know somehow, but, well, if I think about it from her perspective, I didn't deserve to know. I was half-dead at the time, and not exactly the marryin' type, back in those days."

"And he wants to come here? Isn't there someone else over there? I mean, more family?"

"I don't know. I don't care. I am just so, I don't know what I am."

"Well! I thought I had a surprise from Richard, but this takes the cake," Serena cried. "Did you say something about a pony?"

"Yeah. I guess he has one, and wants to bring it with him or something."

"I see. Do you know his name?"

"No. Oh, you mean the boy?" Billy rubbed his hands across his face. "I am sorry, I am an idiot right now. His name is Jackson."

"Jackson. That's unusual."

"Not to me. One of my heroes is Jackson Browne, and somehow she knew that. That's really cool, isn't it? I mean, it was nice of her to remember that. Or maybe she read it somewhere. I dunno."

"Jackson what?"

"Huh?"

"Well, I mean is his last name Killian? Does he have a middle name?"

"I don't know. I am only his father." Billy laughed a big booming laugh, joy coming from his gut. "You like kids, Serena? You gonna stay around for this?"

"Yes. To both questions." She came over to him, leaned over him and kissed him. "And, I even like ponies."

"Oh, good. 'Cause I am gonna need help with that one. I am gonna need help with a lot of things. . . . "

"You've got it, Billy."

"Thanks, baby. Is it too soon to tell you that I love you?"

"Not soon enough. I've been waiting to hear that ever since I left you last weekend."

# Chapter 14

Serena knew that she had to move fast if she was going to be part of Billy's life. As much as he needed help as a single father, he could get too preoccupied with that role and forget her. Already he was talking about going to England to pick up his son, and staying for a few days so that they could get used to one another. She was not invited.

They sat on the patio of a nice restaurant, enjoying the falling temperatures as night began to close around them. A waiter walked by their table, pausing to light candles that were staked in the ground. Soft conversation and music drifted on the air, and Billy was still laughing about some joke someone had made about his sins coming back to haunt him.

Serena was getting irritated. The man had a one-track mind, and right now there was no one allowed on that path but he and his kid. He wasn't thinking at all about how she would fit into this. She was puzzled that such monumental things in one's life could change so quickly, and already she was ready to get serious with Billy. Perhaps that made her a flake? Or maybe one just needed to grasp happiness when it was offered, instead of waiting for the perfect timing.

"You're kind of quiet this evenin'," Billy said. "Everything okay?"

Serena ran her finger along the brim of her glass. "I just don't know what is next for me."

"Meanin' what?" Billy's face was open and relaxed. He wasn't worried in the least about how this whole mess was going to get sorted out.

"Well, my job, for one thing. I can hardly stand being there anymore. I want to be a part of your life, and your son's, but I don't know how. I can't just keep jumping on planes. . . ." She clasped her hands together, wedged her chin on top of them, and stared at him, waiting for him to respond. She realized she'd only flown here twice, but she felt the frustration of the distance between them already. Last week was so empty, and it seemed like life in Dallas was the only reality there was.

"I am not sure what to say, Serena. You know I love you, I have from the moment I laid eyes on you. But I've got a kid on the way from a foreign country, and I am not sure you're over everything and ready to move on, ya know?"

"What are you trying to say? That things aren't over with Richard?"

Billy was stunned at the venom in her voice. "No, I meant that, well, maybe it's too early for me to be proposin' to you. I mean, I need to see about Jackson, he's my responsibility now, I hope, and you've been through a lot. We might need a little time to work things out in our lives, before we can get our lives together."

"So you do expect me to just keep jumping on planes every time you want to see me."

"No, honey, that works both ways."

"You hate to fly, you know that. Unless it's to go to England, apparently."

Billy stared at her with a bland expression. Serena knew she'd pushed things a little too far with that last off-handed remark. But, she couldn't stop now. She had to push for a conclusion with this relationship. Every woman in her position had the right to know how things were. She wasn't going to let herself get strung along. That wasn't fair, because she was willing to consider a future with Billy. He couldn't just "yup and shucks" his way through the next five years. Her days of wasting time were over. Serena drew in a diplomatic breath and changed tack.

"I am sorry, Billy. But you have to look at this from my perspective. I feel like you're going to get involved with your son and forget all about me." Her voice struck a pathetic note, and she starting speaking in a rush. "Look, I know how selfish that sounds, but I can't help it. I want to get closer to you, but I don't know how."

Billy looked at her and smiled. Emotion chocked in her throat, and she didn't mind showing him how vulnerable she was. She surprised herself. She really must love him, more than she realized. She'd been so emotional where he was concerned. And she desperately wanted a stable relationship with him. Starting now.

"Look, baby. I am not sure what the answer is. Let's do this." He reached across the table and pried her hands from under her chin, and held them in his. "Let's take a couple months to figure it out, okay? I want ya to think about what it would mean to leave your parents, your job, everything you know, and move down here. I am goin' to have to concentrate on Jackson some, but then, we should be able to make some decisions. I'll be lookin' at getting a bigger place, and stuff like that. Sound okay?"

Serena pulled one hand away and brushed it under her nose. "Yes, okay."

"Nothin' we're doin' now is forever. I mean, the long-distance thing is temporary. But, I think it's gonna work out just fine, okay?"

Serena closed her eyes and nodded. That's just what she wanted to hear. And she had a scheme in mind to hurry things a long.

# Chapter 15

The acrid smell of ashes pierced Jane's nostrils and stung her eyes. She stood alone, in the middle of the high street, in Hartsbury — a village that she felt she'd somehow never seen before — looking at the building that had once housed a small business office, Mr. Collins's violin shop, her florist business, and Charlotte Lloyd's ladies' dress shop. Jane didn't go to pieces. Somehow her grief over Lydia's death made this tragedy to seem like just another obstacle to face, rather mechanically; another disaster to slog through.

She'd collect her insurance, and begin again.

Mr. Collins wasn't handling the loss as objectively as Jane. He didn't speak beyond a greeting this morning at breakfast. Jane understood. Several of the violins in his shop, including his own personal instruments, were irreplaceable. Like any instrument, they had a set value, but the sweetness of antiquity was lost forever.

Both Mr. Collins and Jane lived in the flats above their shops; likewise, both were left homeless. Eleanor kindly offered them rooms at Brambleberry House for as long as they were needed. In fact, she seemed to have more vigor this morning than Jane had seen in a long while. Eleanor and Clarice had a houseful, and they thrived on nursing the fire's victims. Mr. Collins said that he needed to go to London and see his brother, but he'd return on the evening bus in a few days. He left a phone number with Jane, in case he was needed by the police or other.

Everyone quite forgot the arrival of Jackson's father from America. Eleanor had meant to have a nice chat with her grandson, to let him know that his message, sent through Mr. Beacon, was bringing his father to England. It slipped her mind.

"Pet, go see who is at the door," Eleanor Membry said to her grandson. Jackson slid from his chair at the kitchen table where he'd been coloring a picture of Dudley, his pony, and made his way past Ausfrid lying next to the Aga, and into the passage. The spaniel followed. Jackson pulled open the front door, to find a tall stranger dressed in leather.

"Hey there, you . . . you wouldn't happen to be Jackson, would you?" said the man, bending over to be eye-level. Jackson took a step deeper into the house, away from the smiling dimpled face and cloud of musky cologne.

"Yes," Jackson replied quietly. His hand found the head of his dog.

"Well, isn't that somethin'! I am your daddy. You asked for me to come, didn't you?"

"I suppose."

"Oh, well, uh, is your granny at home?"

"Yes."

The stranger suddenly shoved his hands in his pockets, and looked over his shoulder, down the street. Jackson wondered what he was looking at. He wasn't what Jackson expected. He was quite set on his dad resembling the lead singer of Coldplay, and imagined that he'd be holding a guitar. This bloke was rather odd and spoke funny. Ausfrid stepped forward to sniff his boots. They were the kind that cowboys wear, but all the pop stars on the telly wore trainers, sometimes in bright colors.

The stranger took a deep breath and then refocused his attention on Jackson. The boy could see now that the American was sort of upset or something, and was rubbing his chin with the fingers of one large, multi-ringed hand. The hand was interesting. Jackson hadn't seen a man wear so many rings before, and one of them was like a chunk of gold nugget.

"Jackson, who're you talking to?" Eleanor suddenly appeared behind the boy and rested her hands on his shoulders.

"Oh, my, well, we'd all but forgotten you, Mr. Killian!" said Eleanor Membry, obviously recognizing him in an instant. "I am so sorry. Won't you come in? How was your flight, then? You'll want a cup of tea. Or, well, perhaps you drink something else?"

The stranger started laughing.

"Ma'am, you're just like my momma. She says three thangs at one time. Thank you, Mrs. Membry? De-caf coffee would be nice, if'n you have some. Or water. I am, uh, I am Jackson's father, you know?"

"Yes, yes. Yes, I know." Eleanor looked at the stranger for a a few seconds.

"Please, make yourself comfortable in the lounge, Mr. Killian. I'll get the coffee and be back in a tick. Jackson, would you come and help me?"

Jackson took his grandmother's hand and walked down the passage, meeting Clarice's singing as they came into the kitchen.

*

"Oh, love, I am so sorry I sent you to the door on your own. I should have been there with you, duck, but I entirely forgot he was to come today, what with the fire," Eleanor said to her grandchild. His face was starched and expressionless.

"It's all right, Gram," he mumbled. Clarice had stopped singing and was turned at the waist, hands in dishwater, watching them, her mouth agape.

"What now?" Clarice asked.

"I am getting him some coffee. I think he said decaffeinated. Do we have that?"

"Should do. Try for the yellow packet," answered Clarice, turning back to the sink. Jackson returned to the table and began coloring.

"Jackson, you'll come with Granny when I go back in, won't you, love?" Eleanor said cautiously.

"Yes," the boy replied, focused on his drawing. Clarice and Gram exchanged looks, wishing they knew what Jackson was thinking. He had the tendency to be a tough customer in these matters, quite as indifferent as his Uncle Nigel. The phone rang, and Jackson dashed to pick it up. It was his friend, Toby, wanting him to go to the barn.

"Say yes, Gram, please?" Jackson asked earnestly. His tone suggested that he was afraid, or at least feeling overwhelmed, at meeting his father.

"Well, I suppose for an hour or two, it might be a rather good idea. I've heard there'll be rain, so take your jacket, love." She refrained from saying anything about Jackson's father, waiting in the next room. Jackson had already gone before she decided whether it was a good decision.

"Do you think it's all right, then?" she asked Clarice.

"Well, he weren't very chatty with him, was he now? I don't suppose another hour is going to matter one way or the other, Ellie."

Suddenly the back door opened and Jane shuffled in, looking like a haggard woman who'd been out all night instead of gone for twenty minutes.

"Jane, thank God you're here!" Eleanor exclaimed.

"Why?" Jane said tenuously. "Oh, I am sorry. What is it?"

"No worries, darling. The last twelve hours have been quite a strain. Especially feeling afraid that the whole village might go up or something. But don't let's talk about the fire any more at the moment. Jackson's father's just arrived."

*

"Oh — I, I see," Jane checked her reaction for Eleanor's sake. The child didn't seem to care a toss whether his father was here or not, as she'd just come across him leaving with Toby. Jane suddenly suspicioned that it was Nigel who'd wanted Mr. Killian to come, and perhaps Nigel hadn't been entirely honest with her. She felt that niggling distrust of Nigel, and it made her cross. She couldn't deal with more emotion at present, so kept it under wraps, putting on a brave face to meet the enemy head on. Had it not been for the fire, it would have been mere curiosity that would drive Jane to want to meet Lydia's mysterious lover, but that no longer held any fascination.

"Well, I'll just go and say hello," Jane said, passing quickly towards the front sitting room, knowing the stranger would be installed there.

He was, and was ironing the fringe on the sofa cushion between his fingers. His eyes were locked on a photograph of Lydia and Jackson, taken the year before she died. He looked up suddenly, and Jane was annoyed at the man, just looking at him. He was invading their lives, and for what purpose? Because he felt that being a parent might be rousing good fun?

"Mr. Killian, I am Jane Quinn, how do you do?"

Billy Killian stood to his feet and met Jane's outstretched hand.

"Hello, there, ma'am. Um, are you Jackson's teacher or neighbor or somethin'?"

"I was his mother's best friend." *The one who stood by her when you left her with a child after a one night stand.* "I am quite close to the family."

Billy Killian and Jane Quinn faced each other in silence.

"Well, I've got your coffee and some biscuits, Mr. Killian. Clarice wanted to know if you'd care for a late breakfast? Perhaps they didn't give you anything on your flight?"

"Oh, no, that's okay, ma'am," Billy replied. "Coffee, and them cookies, will be just fine."

Billy slurped his coffee and Jane cleared her throat. They attempted small talk.

*

After three minutes to an eternity, Mrs. Membry returned and took a seat in her favorite chair. "So, Mr. Killian, how long are you planning on staying?"

Billy was stumped. "Well, I wasn't rightly sure. I mean, I could stay a week or so, dependin' on everything." He didn't have the nerve to imply he was taking his son with him. This was going to be harder than he thought.

But he was ready to fight. Jackson had fine features like his momma, but his eyes were Billy's. Billy had wanted to scoop the boy up in his arms, and tell him that he was sorry he'd missed so much of his life so far. He'd make up for it, he wanted to promise. Billy was going to bring his boy home.

"What if he doesn't want to go with you?" Jane said pointedly.

"Well, ma'am, I figure we'll cross that bridge if we come to it, you know? His uncle said that he, that Jackson, asked for me. So, I am here."

"He's only six, Mr. Killian," Jane said sourly. "He's obviously not very interested, as you can see. He's just stepped out with a friend. His life is here, with us. This lark, getting in touch with you, was just a little boy being silly."

"Jane," Eleanor said soothingly. "I am sure Mr. Killian just wants to make sure Jackson is well-looked after. And, naturally, he would want to meet him. Why, after finding out about him, all these years later, you must have been quite surprised?"

"Yes, ma'am, you could surely say that!" Billy smiled at Eleanor's encouragement.

With agitation, Jane sprung from her perch on the piano bench and went to the window. She could just glimpse a slither of black shard from the high street. It was what was left of Mr. Collin's flat. Why was Eleanor being so kind to Billy Killian? What was she playing at?

"Jane, my dear," Eleanor said in measured tones. "Would you mind to excuse us for a while? I wonder if perhaps Clarice might need a hand tidying upstairs?"

Jane was speechless. Dutifully, and a bit stunned, she withdrew, feeling Mr. Killian's eyes on her back as she went. What was going on here? Eleanor, dismissing her, with the cheeky suggestion that she ought to go polish something? Fine, let her deal with the rock star on her own, Jane thought, glaring at the American on her way out of the room.

Clarice was sweeping the kitchen floor. "How do you find him, Jane? Do you think he's a good sort of person?"

Jane picked up the drawing that Jackson had made of Dudley. "It wouldn't matter if he was a saint, Clarice. He's here to take Jackson away. Worse, Eleanor seems to want to help him."

"Now, that can't be, Jane. Eleanor certainly doesn't want Jackson to go, anymore than you or me. Why, that's just nonsense, it is. You can't be thinkin' all together rightly, love, what with the shock of losing your home and your business. . . ."

Jane allowed Clarice give her a firm hug. "I hardly know what to do," Jane said. "It suddenly seems like there hasn't been any time at all. Lydia's gone, and we haven't done anything but run in place. We've worked, eaten, sent Jackson to school, and it all seems a misery, like all I've done is cry and work and survive. But, yet, there's nothing to show for it. No business, no home, and now Jackson may be leaving. Oh, Clarice, I can't bear it!"

Clarice thumped Jane's back reassuringly, as though trying to burp a baby.

"Cuppa tea, love? You'll feel better."

Jane slipped onto a chair at the kitchen table. She tried to think of something constructive, but nothing came, so she decided to concentrate on having tea, calming down, and trusting that things would sort themselves out. The stranger would surely go in a few minutes, and he certainly wouldn't be invited to the kitchen. She was safe for now.

Clarice filled mugs for them and served Jane a piece of cake. "Your favorite," she said, as Jane stabbed a corner of the lemon cake and ate it. She caught her crazed expression in a reflection from a piece of china standing on the bureau, and it made her laugh. It was simply to exhausting to process everything happening, and to be upset with it all. She smiled warmly at Clarice.

"That's it dearie."

"I suppose you're right. And your baking has always made me slightly giddy, Clair!"

Clarice swelled with pride at the compliment, and slowly sipped her steaming tea.

Jane stirred two lumps of sugar into her tea and a plan started forming in her mind. The fire brigade hadn't secured the building, but, as soon as they did, she could see if there was anything to salvage. She'd kept her most important business papers at the bank, but she had a small safe upstairs. And there were some papers in there that she needed. Desperately.

# Chapter 16

Billy walked to the edge of town and up a long lane that led to Hollyhock House Bed and Breakfast. The sun was warm and he took off his leather jacket. He thoughts wandered back to having his second drug-induced heart attack. The darkness had been swallowing him up, and he had called out to God, believing he was dying. Then, everything cleared. He hadn't walked towards a light like other people described, instead he was in a meadow. And the view had been sort of like this one. Glancing across the fields, he remembered the wonderful impressions he had when he graced the edge of heaven. The fence here in this place and time wasn't magnificent, like his divine vision of carved mahogany; but it was rustically charming, and a break in the hedge revealed a large stone house that had stood sentinel over the village for ages.

He crossed the flagstone walk and came to the front door, which was sheltered by a rambling spray of white roses. He rang the bell and waited. Birdsong filled the air, and a gentle breeze blew. Soon, he heard the tread of dainty feet.

The door was opened by a petite woman with auburn hair. "Oh, hullo there," she said in a surprisingly rich voice. "Won't you come in?"

Billy stepped into a foyer, onto emerald green carpet.

"So you've found us here, all the way from Texas, did you?"

"Yes, ma'am. It's a beautiful place you've got here, too."

"Thank you. I am Deborah Fraser, Mr. Killian, and I am pleased that we had a single available for you. You're lucky, you know, as we're often full."

"Yes, ma'am. How old is this house?"

Deborah was pleased with the question. "Over a hundred-and-twenty-five years this farmhouse has stood. It used to be all farms here, with just a tiny hamlet down the road. Why don't you come through to the conservatory, which is my own addition to the property, and I'll give you some tea?"

"That would be real nice," Billy said obligingly.

The conservatory was radiant with light, and a little warmer than anyplace Billy had been since leaving home. He chose a chair that was covered in a faded floral chintz, and let his gaze rest on the stately trees outside.

"Here we are," said Deborah, coming in with a tray. "Have you had lunch?"

"No, ma'am, but I can't say as I am very hungry. This here will be just right, thank you. Can't remember the last time I drank so much tea without some ice."

"Oh, yes, of course. Habit I suppose," she smiled graciously as Billy dropped some sugar cubes into his cup. The china handle was too narrow. Billy pinched it and took a small sip. There was nothin' like iced tea, and he wished he had some.

"The pub at the opposite end of the high street, it's called the Rapunzel, is really the best spot for your meal this evening, if you don't have a dinner engagement," she said. "And there's a television in your room, and plenty of books in the library. You'll let us know if there's anything else, won't you?"

"I am sure I'll get along just fine, ma'am." Billy thought the woman was charming, but she seemed to delay leaving him or showing him to his room.

"And shall I expect you for breakfast in the morning, or perhaps you're meeting friends?"

It was the second time she'd led the conversation around to whom he might know in the village. Billy decided to keep her in the dark.

"I'll be down, ma'am, you just let me know what time."

"Anytime between seven and nine will do," she said, obviously disappointed with his lack of information. "And now if you've finished your tea, I'd be happy to show you your accommodation.

The driver that dropped you in the village not only brought your case, but wouldn't hear of leaving until he stowed your case in your room. You must have given him an excellent tip!"

Billy smiled and wished that were true. Although the driver said nothing, Billy saw him checking him out in the mirror, and knew him to be a blues fan, sure enough.

*

"Good morning, Angel," Billy said with a smile.

"Oh, hi," Serena replied, switching the phone to her other hand, and reclining slightly in her office chair. "I wasn't sure if you'd call today. How's it going?"

"Well, I found a little hotel to stay at, close to their house. It's a real small place, so I am walking everywhere. I am getting ready to go and eat something up on the main street. They call it the high street, but I don't think that's really the name."

"Billy! That's nice, but you know what I mean. You met your son, right?"

"Yeah." Billy had found it easy to speak to his brother about Jackson, just a few minutes ago. But with Serena, he felt sort of defensive. Maybe he should have waited until tomorrow to call, like she seemed to expect him to do.

"And?"

"Well, he was a little shy, I guess. And nobody seems to think he's leavin'. They're kind of acting like I am visiting."

"Oh."

"How are things with you? Is the hospital quiet today?"

Serena sighed. "Yes, I am ordering department supplies, actually. And my mother phoned to tell me that she and Daddy saw Richard at the club last night. He was with friends, some guys that he golfs with, and Mama kept reiterating that he seemed so sad and could hardly look Daddy in the eye. She thinks I ought to feel sorry for him and get back together."

"What do you think?" Billy said, patiently.

"I think if he's that brokenhearted he could be on my door step with flowers, but you don't see him even trying to patch things up. He expects me to come to him."

Billy was getting antsy to get off the phone. Phone calls could be hit or miss with really connecting with someone, and this one was a mile off. He wished that Serena had come with him.

"I am sorry, Billy. Here you are, on the other side of the world, meeting your kid for the first time. I do care, you know. I hope it goes better tomorrow. You are seeing him, aren't you?"

He warmed to her concern. "Yes, his grandmother invited me back in the afternoon, when Jackson gets home from school. We're going to the barn to see his pony, I think."

"Ah, well, that's nice. I miss you. I know we'd be apart anyway, but it does feel like you're farther away than normal."

"Yeah, darlin', me too. It'll be nice to bring my boy home with me next week. Real scary, but, each day will get better. Then we can bring you down to Texas for a visit, okay?"

"Sounds wonderful to me," Serena said wistfully. "I am so fed up with this job I could walk out right now and never feel a twinge of regret."

"Yeah, I know. You've just been so worn out with everything else that it must be extra hard to be there. But we have a lot to look forward to."

"Definitely," Serena agreed. "Bye now."

"Bye." Billy put the phone down and sat for a while on the bed, just thinking. Serena always put his brain in a burn. It seemed a little weird to tell her he loved her again, especially over the phone, so he hadn't. He did love her, but they both knew he was operating in a priority sort of way with his relationships. He loved Serena, but Jackson came first, and that's the way it had to be. He had to think of himself as a father, and get that worked out, before he could have a crazy whirlwind romance with some woman who lived in another state and had been engaged to another man not more than a month ago. It was a lot to keep track of, especially when he had had to empty himself, so to speak, into his music, and the album he just wrapped.

Serena was so sweet, but in a way Billy felt he wasn't reading her right. He couldn't quite wriggle it out, this hesitation he felt. Maybe it's because she said what she did, that first night, about their worlds not quite fittin' together. He tried to imagine them being married, but mostly his thoughts ran to what it would be like to touch her. God, she was beautiful.

"You done a fine job on that woman, Sir," he whispered to the ceiling.

*

Jane spent the afternoon dusting and hoovering upstairs for Clarice, and then making a jam roly-poly for pudding. Although Jane had a lighthearted moment in the kitchen, she was still confused by Eleanor's warm welcome to Jackson's father. Jane avoided her.

As the late afternoon sun was slanting through the windows, she retreated to her guest room in Brambleberry House, Lydia's old room. It was regularly cleaned, but otherwise, as Lydia left it. It wasn't that Eleanor was trying to enshrine her daughter by keeping the room unchanged, but rather that the furnishings were pretty, and there was no sensible reason to change them. The lilacs continued to bloom on the wallpaper, and the bed was a vision of femininity in a slippery, knotted — silk quilt of pale green. The scent of lemon furniture polish lingered.

Jane tried to imagine what Lydia would say about the turn of events the past twenty-four hours. She knew her friend would deeply pity the loss of her home and florist shop, but Jane couldn't determine what Lydia might suggest for a plan of action. In fact, it seemed she was losing Lydia's voice. She certainly hadn't a clue what Lydia would say about Billy showing up, but, then, the circumstance would be much changed if Lydia were alive. Would Lydia find the stranger attractive? Threatening? Or simply a miracle for Jackson?

Worse, Jane was completely baffled by her friends that were alive and mulling around downstairs. Eleanor could usually be described as practical. There was nothing sensible about her siding with the American who wished to take away the child of their hearts.

Jane sat down at Lydia's French provincial desk and opened the lap drawer. She pulled out some cream paper that had a Membry family crest engraved in royal blue on the top. A box of it had arrived one holiday from Nigel, and was still in plentiful supply.

She began a letter.

> *Dear Mum,*
>
> *Hope this letter finds you well. You'll probably try to phone me tomorrow evening, and find the line has gone dead. It's just as well, because I can't talk about it very much just yet.*
>
> *We've had an awful tragedy. Somehow a fire started in the Row and all of the shops were consumed. I am staying with Eleanor, and can't quite get my head 'round the fact that it's all gone. My business, and my home, the old building gobbled up in a matter of minutes.*
>
> *I think that it will take time, but I am counting on insurance helping out quite a bit. Eleanor said that I could stay as long as I'd like, and I shall probably take her up on it. I want to leave off spending any of my savings, because I'll need every bit of it to get going again.*
>
> *Jackson's father has shown up from America. I think he's keen on Jackson returning to the States with him. I certainly don't care for him being about! You were right, in that Jackson does share some of his characteristics. They have the same*

*eyes. At any rate, his timing in being here is abominable, and the sooner he gets off, the better.*

*Hope that you and Hugh are keeping well and that the freeze has finally left off. Spring in the Highlands always seems a tricky business.*

*Don't worry about me. I am quite all right, and still plan to come and see you next month. And I don't even have to worry about closing the shop!*

*All my love, Jane.*

Jane sealed the letter and trotted down the stairs to go and post the letter. On her way out, Clarice called from the kitchen.

"Oh, Jane, I thought you'd gone out, dear, so quiet you were upstairs. Charlotte Lloyd phoned for you."

"Is she here, in Hartsbury?"

"Yes, she said she's just finished with the police, and was going to have a look at the shop."

"I'll see if I can meet her there."

Jane dashed out of the house, and posted her letter on the way down the street. She looked around at the houses. It might as well have been five minutes ago that she came here, instead of fifteen years. She'd lived here in the village with her parents, before their divorce.

She turned the corner, briskly walking towards town. Suddenly it was all too familiar. The charred remains of the shop row were bleak reminders of her once very comfortable life here in the village. It was still unfathomable that it was gone.

Charlotte Lloyd stood in front of what used to be Panache, apparently talking to herself animatedly. As Jane drew closer, she realized that Charlotte was speaking through a cell phone and headset. She refused to acknowledge Jane, even with a glance, until she rang off.

Jane was thinking about how much she missed dressing the shop's window. She'd meant to refresh the scene today. She and Charlotte were going to do pastels, with Jane's tulips, hyacinths, and jonquils sharing spring color with Charlotte's short-sleeved angora jerseys.

Abruptly, Charlotte turned on her heel. She seemed to have aged ten years since Jane saw her last. Her lips pursed together, allowing no breath to escape, and forcing Jane to stare at her in abject silence. She'd never seen Charlotte when everything wasn't under control, and with others dutifully carrying out her bidding. But Charlotte wasn't masterful today, she was just a distraught older woman feeling very much out of her depth.

"Jane, I shan't deceive you. I've some very bad news."

"Let me guess. The shops have burnt down." Jane was as surprised at her surly attitude as Charlotte. It just slipped out, with the strain of the moment. "I am sorry, Charlotte. It's been a rough twenty-four hours."

"I am afraid it's all my fault. I might as well just be out with it. During the renovations, well, I cut some corners, Jane. Had some work done that wasn't up to par, I suppose. The down lighters, you know, over the display window, they were so lovely and bright."

"Yes, I know you adored them, but, what does that matter, Charlotte?"

"The protective surrounds. They'd have gotten too warm, and, that's how it all began."

"That's how the fire started — from your fancy lights."

"Yes, Jane. *My fancy lights.* Every time I try to do something that is above average, bringing a little excitement into retailing, or into my relationships, or anything, it all goes combustible. That's how it was with my last marriage. If I tried to create something special, he just, well, extinguished my hopes."

"Lovely pun, that. Too bad Rolland wasn't still around to extinguish our property."

Charlotte ignored the insult. Jane's mind was in a tumult of thoughts. She studied her landlady, attempting to size up what Charlotte really thought about all of this. If it really penetrated her heart.

Charlotte was somewhat pitiable, with her many marriages behind her, the current state of her red hair, carelessly snapped to her head with a tortoise shell clip. But Jane didn't care. The arrogant woman burned down the row, by quite literally trying to outshine everyone else. How stupid. How unnecessary. How ridiculous.

"There's more."

"Charlotte, I really don't care to hear any more about your personal failings. Really, I just can't."

Jane glanced around. The few villagers that were on the street kept to the other side, opposite the horrific site and the two women in front of it.

Facing the building, Charlotte rattled on, quite determined to confess her sins and be done with it. "I was quite short on cash, but I knew if I could get the ladies coming in, that I'd make the money back, possibly in a fortnight, with the new range from France. So, I did all that I could, to make Panache as enticing as possible. And it was working, Jane. You know that. Your business was picking up, because of what I did." Charlotte had spun around and spit out the last sentence, as though she were daring Jane to deny how skillfully Charlotte had caused them to prosper.

"Business was good, I'll grant you that. But last month's receipts hardly matter now."

"But don't you see, Jane? Why I had to do it? We needed a strong, steady flow of cash. I had to prioritize. I've been on my own, with bills to pay. It's been dreadful, Jane."

Again, Charlotte was manipulating her, first by insisting she'd increased Jane's income, and now by soliciting empathy regarding her past, weaving her story so that Jane would feel sorry for her. Jane was growing tired of Charlotte's theatrics. Jane stared at her blankly, wanting to move towards home, but was somehow unable to uproot her feet. Through a fog she heard Charlotte say, "I never expected to actually *need* the insurance."

"What?"

"Jane, one never believes anything will ever *really* happen. I mean, really, darling. People are caught unaware everyday. I am just like everyone else. I try to take precautions, try to consider everything, but I am just one woman, managing quite a lot on her own."

"I don't understand, Charlotte."

"I used the money for the clothes. The insurance premiums."

"Charlotte, you couldn't have done . . . why, I am sure that's illegal. And, I, well that leaves me without anything. . . ."

"Jane, I've suffered a terrible, terrible loss here, too. You needn't only think of yourself!"

That was the last straw.

Jane found her feet, and pulled up from the engulfing quicksand of Charlotte's self-absorption and cruel news. She walked away, leaving that nasty, criminal woman standing there by the rubbish that was once their livelihood, and their homes. She walked, then broke into a run, ignoring the concern on the blurry faces of people watching her pass. *Damn their eyes! I just want to be away, away, away.*

Upon quitting the village, Jane picked up a run. Her cloak of propriety fell away. As she entered a patch of woods, she let out a scream, did Jane, this woman who never raised her voice.

She kept on running. The woods fell away, the road grew narrower as she got deeper into the country. Feeling the heaviness in her thighs, Jane finally succumbed to her rapid breath, putting her hands on her knees, and bent over, sobbing. Her lungs sucked and burned, sobs blurted out. Her nose ran, and she dragged her woolen sleeve across it. She stood up, heaving breath, and ground her palms into her eyes, as new hot tears traced warm tracks down her wrists.

Pressing hard on her eyeballs, she wished she'd never have to look again. She didn't have the nerve, she must keep her eyes closed. Her head pound and she wanted to run again, but her legs felt so very heavy. Sweat dewed her skin, and she felt slightly sick. She sunk to the ground to rest and regain her composure.

"Darlin', what's wrong?"

Jane smeared her palms from her damp eyes to her hair, and her watery gaze focused on the stranger. It was the rock and roll star, standing on the narrow road in front of her.

"Bugger off, you awful man!"

*

Billy wasn't sure what she said, but it was something like, "the bug, it was tan." Had she been upset by a bug or maybe a spider? Maybe it was crawling around her in the grass.

"Do you want me to kill 'er?" Billy asked, ready to boot the bug back to its maker.

Jane's face felt tight, her eyelids were swollen and she was thirsty. But she could still yell. "How typical of you Americans, and your senseless violence. As though we'd let Jackson go to you, when you're standing there, quite seriously, talking of killing Charlotte?"

Billy said, "Oh, yeah, I remember that story, *Charlotte's Web*. So if I am gettin' you, Charlotte is like, Cockney slang, for spiders, and you're the type that can't abide killin' any creatures, right? Did it actually bite you? 'Cause that could be real serious, ma'am."

Despite being wildly upset, Jane started laughing at the irony. Charlotte had a reputation in town as a Black Widow. Her first two husbands died young. Jane squeezed her arms around her middle with a hearty belly laugh, and an exhausted, "Oh. . ." escaped her lips.

She put her hands on her hips and looked at the surrounding countryside. Perhaps she was going mad. Laughing inappropriately, running, crying. This was sobering, because Jane suddenly wasn't certain of anything. Maybe she was a bit touched. She wrapped her arms tightly about herself and searched her mind for other signs of poor mental health.

At the moment, she didn't have the energy to hate Billy Killian. "I don't come out here very often, anymore. Not since Lydia died. We used to take Jackson on picnics around here."

Jane saw him struggle for an instant, and knew. "So, you would've cared? You would've come, had you known about your son?"

"Yes ma'am, I surely would have."

"Then why do you want to ruin his life now, by taking him away from us?"

"Oh, now look here, miss —"

"No, you 'look here'! We're all that Jackson has ever known. England is his home. How selfish of you to want to take it all away!"

Jane intended to say more, to scream more, and tell him what he ought to know. Clearly, he knew that she was right, because he just stood there, looking at the ground. She'd won a verbal battle with someone besides Lydia. This was quite a day. She felt less the victim, homeless or not.

Why stop there? She continued, yelling.

"You can't know anything about him. He couldn't stay at camp for wanting his granny so much. He's allergic to bananas. That it would quite possibly break his heart to leave . . . *me*." Suddenly her newfound momentum disappeared. Weakness fell heavily over her shoulders. She sunk to the ground. Today seemed a bad dream that refused to end.

Billy kneeled in front of her. "Maybe you're right, ma'am. But I can't just leave my boy and never look back. See, ever since I've known about him, he's been, like, *everything*. If I think about a song, I think about teachin' him to play. If I think about food, then, well, I am glad you told me he can't have bananas."

"This isn't about *you*, and all of the useful things you can learn!" Jane squealed. She thoroughly detested this man. He was dribbling on about Jackson as though he were in a greetings card commercial. Raising a child was his newly adopted vocation. How touching. Jane was sure that the cowboy didn't have a clue. They sat in silence on the grass for a few minutes.

"Do you wanna go to the pub and have dinner with me, Miz Jane?"

"What! No! Certainly you *are* joking, Mr. Killian."

"Well, what are you gonna do, then, ma'am? 'Cause I am gonna walk away now, and I don't really wanna leave you here by the side of the road."

"I shall sit here and do as I damn well please, that's what. I don't curse. But you bloody well make me loose my rag!"

"Okay, ma'am."

"Stop calling me that. I am not over-sixty nor a bloody royal."

"Jane," he said softly.

She snapped her head up to look at him. His hand was outstretched. She sat motionless on the ground.

His arm fell to his side. "Look, honey, I am sorry. I really am. Maybe if you could talk to me, we'd be better at workin' this mess out. I'd like to know what you think. Now, I don't know where you been, but you got a pasture's worth of dirt on your dress, and you can probably use a little somethin' to eat. Come on with me, now." He extended his hand to her once more.

Jane grasped his hand and rose to her feet, but she wasn't calling a truce. "I don't want to talk to you. I am walking back to the village, and I suppose you're walking that way, too."

"That's fine, ma'am. Whatever suits. I just don't know why, if you love the boy, you won't help."

Jane paced ahead. She looked at the trees and breathed deeply of their scent. She allowed the cleansing honesty of the forest around her to help her settle. She answered him in even tones. "Because I don't feel like helping you. And you're wanting to take Jackson away, and I don't want you to, so, what can we have to say to one another?" There, she's said it. That summed it up, and it was easy. She'd at least made a step to reconciling herself with all that had happened. She was behaving logically, and she didn't feel the least bit mental. She'd just been through an awful lot, but she would be right as rain, and start her life over.

Billy spoke, interrupting Jane's internal dialogue. "I thought you loved Jackson."

Jane spun around in fury. "I do!"

He put his hands on his hips and cocked his head to one side. "Then since I am his daddy, you oughta be actin' like a grown up and talk to me. If you have somethin' to say about him, I wanna hear it. If you don't, then I guess I can assume your opinion don't count."

Jane's throat throbbed with pressure. The cyclone in her abdomen was picking up speed. Her voice trembled, but she yelled out anyway, unable to hold back. She'd never had a chance to face down her own father. She couldn't be bothered with this heavy-handed, authoritative approach.

"Who do you think you are? Was that a threat? You suggest what I have to say matters until I refuse to come to the pub with you, then you quite suddenly decide to subtract me from Jackson's life. As if you're God. You don't seem to grasp that I have already fully expressed my opinion! Which is, that nothing matters except that Jackson stays here, and life carries on as usual, with no interference from you. There is no compromise of that scenario that interests me. And if you think you're the only person who has any rights to Jackson, you're quite mistaken."

With that, she walked briskly on wobbly legs, away from the stranger who stared after her.

# Chapter 17

Jane came through the back door of the Membry house at Brambleberry Lane, and was grateful to find the kitchen empty. She'd take some tea and something for her head, and slip upstairs.

Putting fresh water in the kettle, she laid it on the Aga and turned to get the tea and a clean cup. Suddenly, there was Jackson.

"Oh, Jacks, you scared me!"

"Can I have some cocoa?"

"Of course, love."

Seating himself at the table, Jackson propped his head on one hand, just as his mum used to do. What a sweet, bright, and lovely boy. But not at all hers. She turned back to the whistling kettle.

"I am sorry, Auntie," Jackson said with a hush. For what? Did he understand the ramifications of calling his father to England?

She set the cocoa and plate of biscuits in front of him, and sat opposite him, cupping her tea with both hands. She tried to blow over the tea for something to do, but her lips trembled too much. She cradled her chin in laced fingers and let out a sigh. *And I think Billy Killian incapable of handling a child. Look at how I am failing miserably to hold up a conversation.*

Jackson tried again. "It's very sad about your shop. I liked going there, and you lived so close. What will you do, Auntie?"

She slipped from the table for a tissue, from the box decorated with pansies that sat by the telephone. Her head still ached from the last ridiculous outburst, and here she was damming up again.

"I am not certain, sweetheart. I should like to open another shop, but I don't have much money, so it may take some time." Jane blew her nose, and took a long sip of hot tea. The warmth gave her courage. "I do know one thing, though."

"What?"

"I have time more time now to go with you to see Dudley. May I go with you tomorrow?"

Jackson brightened, and his head straightened on his shoulders. "That would be brilliant, Auntie Jane. And maybe soon we can go to the cinema? There's a new one, about a zebra who thinks he's a horse. It looks really funny."

"That sounds lovely, Jacks." Jane swallowed her headache medicine.

Jackson seemed to sense her distress and tried to help. "I've been reading an awfully good book."

"Really? What about?"

"The Native American Indians. They used to ride ponies and kill buffalo, by stabbing them with these long spear things. They painted themselves and the ponies. And they lived in tepees. In fact, Toby and I are putting up a tepee in the garden, if Grams will go along."

"Wouldn't that be fabulous?"

"Mmm. It's time for the Top of the Pops." Jackson went off towards the television.

"Sure, Jacks. I love you."

"Love you, too."

Jane felt strangely as though she were melding into Lydia's life. She'd slept in Lydia's bed, acted as a mum to her child, and had a fight with her only lover. Maybe these people weren't her life or her concern. Maybe they shouldn't even be her friends. Perhaps she ought to just remove herself from the situation. Go to her mum and Hugh in Scotland.

*

Serena threw the yogurt container in the trash and turned back to her computer. Her dissatisfaction was deepening by the hour. If she really intended to be with Billy, then why was she here? She'd always been proud of doing something for herself, being a career woman. But that was getting old. She was a woman first, and she wanted to be with her man. Make a home, take care of his child, and have a child of her own. She was sure that Billy must have a lot of money, and there was no reason for him to need "time alone" with a child that he didn't know. After all, neither parent knows their newborn when he or she is born; they come to know their child together. They're a unit.

Serena picked up the phone and dialed the number for Killian Studios. She was going to need Billy's brother's cooperation for everything to go smoothly.

"Killian Recording Studios. May I help you?" Serena recognized Sandy's voice.

"Hi, Sandy. This is Serena Berquist. I am, uh, Billy's friend from Atlanta. How are you?"

"Oh, hey, Serena. We're busy here, as usual. You know Billy's not here, right?"

"Yes, of course. In fact, he called me from England last night. I was calling to speak with Yancy."

Sandy hesitated for a moment. How irritating. Didn't she recognize that Serena was Yancy's future sister-in-law?

"Just a moment, Serena, and I'll see if Yancy's in."

Almost a full minute later, Billy's brother finally picked up the line.

"Serena? Yancy here. What can I do for you, hon?"

"Hello, Yancy, sorry to bother you like this at the office. I'll get right to the point. I gather you've talked to Billy, and know what a hard time he's having over there?"

"Yeah." Serena felt a stab of nervousness. She was hoping Yancy would be a little chatty with her, but he had his business airs on.

"Well, I am really concerned about Billy," she said, pouring honey into the phone. "He may have bitten off more than he can chew, you know?"

No reply. Serena rushed on.

"I thought it would be nice if I could take some time off work, and come down and help Billy out. And his little boy might be really glad to have a sort of mother figure around, you know?"

Yancy was still silent.

Serena added, "And I know they're bringing that pony over, and I know a lot about horses, so that's another thing that's important to your nephew."

"Why are you talking about this with me, instead of Billy?"

"Oh, Yancy, I just got the idea this morning, and of course it's nighttime in England, isn't it? The truth is, I just don't think Billy needs to have to make one more decision about someone else's welfare. I mean, I want to take care of him, instead of abandoning him to try and take care of a child on his own." Serena laughed. "What does Billy know about kids, anyway? He'd probably think the kid should sleep in a guitar case or something!"

Her joke fell flat. Serena's anxiety rose.

"I think you ought to discuss this with Billy. He isn't due home for another four days, so I am sure that will give you time to contact him. And I am not sure what I was supposed to do about it, anyway?"

She took a deep breath and summoned all the feeling she could. Taking her time, she paused, and then said quietly.

"Yancy, Billy and I have a wonderful relationship going, and this is really embarrassing for me to talk to you about, but, I love your brother. Only he doesn't have the emotional resources for me right now, he's focused on his son. I understand that, and it's one of the reasons that I think Billy is a wonderful man. What would make me so happy, Yancy, is to come down there, and go to Billy's condo and get that place in shape. I am a little concerned, that's all. Billy didn't even think ahead to buy a bed for that child. My maternal instincts are going wild, Yancy. I just want to help make this a smooth transition, and there are so many things that I could do for them both, but I'd need the keys to his place, and, and Mossy's phone number, so we could connect, and that sort of thing."

Serena hoped she wouldn't have to carry out her plans with Mossy in tow, but whatever served her purpose would have to work for now.

Letting out a big sigh, Yancy said, "I understand, darlin'. And Lord knows Billy needs a woman to help make this whole thing come off. I know Mama was going to help, but she's also trying not to interfere, whereas you, well, seein' as how he's lost his mother, and you and Billy are together. . . . Every kid should have a mama, and if you love my brother that much, that you'd come here and do all that work to get him organized, well, I don't want to be the one to stand in the way. Quite frankly, none of us has the time, right at the moment. Even Mama, well, she has her own life. She was always kinda independent, even when we was growin' up."

Serena smiled into the phone, but kept her cool. No need to sound too triumphant. She wanted him to hang up feeling good about this. Sweetly, she said, "I am so relieved that you'll let me help, Yancy. Billy didn't want to throw me into this role, with our relationship being so new, but I love children."

"Yeah, I guess it'll be a good thing."

"Billy is due back on Sunday night, and if I leave Atlanta after work on Friday, that will give me plenty of time to clean, prepare a room for Jackson, and get some food in the house." She sounded like an efficient mommy. This was going to be fun.

Yancy was heartened by her enthusiasm. "Well, okay then. I'll send a car to pick you up at the airport, and the driver will have a package for you with the keys and such, all right?"

"That's so wonderful, Yancy. I am going to take good care of your brother and his boy. It's going to work out beautifully, you'll see. I can hardly wait to surprise him!"

"So, you're not telling him you're coming?"

She hoped she hadn't tripped a security wire, but she went on boldly. "Are you kidding? Billy treats me like a queen, which is wonderful, but he doesn't think I should lower myself to scrubbing the bathtub and cooking a meal suitable for a little boy. If I tell him, he'll try to hire someone to do it, and you know that would be ridiculous."

To Serena's relief, Yancy generously agreed, saying his brother had Serena on a pedestal, but he admired her for bein' so down-to-earth enough to not like it. Yancy made sure his wife had a housekeeper, because he liked spoiling her. Only she didn't act spoiled, which is the way things oughta be. Serena agreed with him, with all the charm that she could muster.

"Okay, darlin' we'll expect you on the seven o'clock from Atlanta on Friday night. We'll get in touch with you on Saturday mornin' to see if you need anything."

"Great. See you soon, Yancy. And thanks."

# Chapter 18

The coach pulled to a stop in the middle of the village. Harry Collins drew a deep breath and ignored the front window, through which he could surely see the remains of his violin shop. His spirits were high, no need to look at the blackened buildings. He brought down a canvas bag from the overhead and walked half the bus length to the door. He was the only passenger and he tipped his hat to the driver, a heavyset woman with smooth latte-colored skin. She nodded in reply as his feet tapped down the grooved rubber stairs. As soon as he was on the street, he walked towards Brambleberry House.

His brother, Ed, and his wife, Elise, had been lovely, and it had made a nice change to be in London. They'd even splurged and gone to an orchestra concert at the Barbican. When the orchestra music swelled to life, he came to life, too. His brother had known how much it would lift him. God bless Ed for that. It soothed his soul like nothing else, to hear the free flowing, passionate strains of Stravinsky's *Rite of Spring*, which grew in intensity with stamping chords to mirror the controlled chaos that Harry Collins felt in his own heart. He released his worry and heartache over losing his shop that night, sitting in the plush seats, listening to the ravishing bassoon solo that so long ago incited it's 1913 debut audience to riot.

The following day, Ed had taken him for a long walk in Hyde Park. They discussed many things, and fed birds. Coming home foot weary and out of words, they were greeted by the welcoming smell of Elise's beef stew. Her secret ingredient was bourbon whiskey cured in oak, and the depth of flavor was a perfect compliment to the sweet carrots, colorful green beans, acidic tomatoes, and zesty turnips that languished in the hearty stock thick with chunks of meat. She served crusty bread, and a heady, sweet Atholl Brose. After the meal, they laughed and drank coffee. Then they moved into the lounge and Ed enjoyed his pipe.

"So you're staying with Mrs. Membry, then," Ed said, between puffs.

"She's a fine lady. And her little grandson, Jackson is there. He's a good boy. Loves his pony."

"Reminds me of someone. Did you tell him?"

"Yes, and he keeps askin' to hear my old stories over and over. I can't imagine they're as exciting as what's on the telly, but I suppose children just need to be at your knee, don't they?"

"Hmm," Ed replied. He knew his brother adored having the little boy about. It had been many years since Harry's own young family had been lost in an accident. His bride was a girl straight from school, and they'd had a daughter. They were married as young teens, against their parent's wishes. Harry was considered a virtuoso violinist at the age of nine, and studied at several prestigious schools. He was abroad, playing at the funeral of a dignitary, when Sheila and the baby were killed. Harry had been devastated.

"So, you'll not have the shop. But you'll be free to get on with what we talked about at the park," Ed assured him. "It'll be a happy ending, after all, you'll see, our Harry."

"I'd drink to that, if I hadn't had a drop too much already!" They laughed and Elise gathered her knitting to her lap. "Still making the blankets for the bairns, are you?" Harry asked, noting the fluff of light blue yarn covering her almost to the ankles.

"Oh, yes. They're better than store-bought. And I put the name on them, too, provided it isn't too long."

The next day, after Elise gave them a full breakfast, the brothers journeyed in a borrowed truck to the countryside south of Romsey, for a day of fishing in the Test. The weather was fine, but the fishing was not. Even so, it made for a good excuse to spend the day out of doors again.

Harry felt as though he'd been gone a decade. He was sore from the walking and the fishing, but had a new perspective on life. His years might confine him to the autumn of life, but in spirit, his heart was full of spring.

Brambleberry House always looked welcoming. The pansies smiled at him as he made his way along side of the house, towards the kitchen. Although he was newly reacquainted with the Membry family, he'd slept under this roof, and Eleanor would be offended if he came to the front door. As Harry rounded the house, he heard voices. Eleanor and Jane were digging in the garden.

Jane saw him first. "Oh, Mr. Collins! We were hoping you'd be back soon. How was London?"

"It was lovely, Jane. My, those black tulips are unusual, aren't they?"

"They were one of Lydia's favorites," said Eleanor. "Not my taste, but I can't seem to dig up anything she'd planted."

"No, of course not, love," Harry replied. Though he'd lost his daughter as a baby, he understood how your children stay in your heart, always.

"Shall I put the kettle on?" said Jane, as a means of thwarting the conversation from Lydia's memory.

"Well, that depends," said Harry with a smile. He added a wink and said to Eleanor, "I was hoping you'd come to dinner in Tunbridge Wells."

Eleanor was clearly gobsmacked by the flirtatious invite.

"Oh, why, Mr. Collins! Harry. I'd be delighted. I'll just pop upstairs and freshen up. It'll only take a tick." Eleanor dashed into the house.

"Mr. Collins, you Casanova!" Jane teased. He felt pleased as punch. "With the dirt she's been into, we've still time for a cuppa. Come on inside, and by the time you've put your case away, I'll have it ready."

"Thank you, Jane."

*

They walked into the house and Jane put the kettle on. She gazed out the window into the garden. Mr. Collins, carrying a torch for Eleanor, how sweet. It was lovely for both of them. The best sort of surprise.

Mr. Collins sat down at the large table.

"You seem perfectly refreshed after seeing your brother. What mischief did you get into?"

"Oh, we had a grand time," Mr. Collins said, taking a bit of his steaming tea. "We went fishing, to a lovely concert, and I've eaten far too much. Our Elise is a fine cook."

"Fishing? Really. Did you catch anything?"

"No. But the countryside is beautiful and Ed and I can chatter on for days. And I've brought you something, dear. But you'll have to wait till later."

"Me?"

"Mmm. You brought me to this house, remember? And you and I, we've been through something, haven't we? Good friends, we are."

Jane came around the table and hugged Mr. Collins by the shoulders.

Eleanor came through. "Now, don't steal him away, Jane!" Her cheeks were pink and Jane noticed she'd dashed on lipstick.

"You kids have fun."

Harry stood and the couple turned to go. Eleanor stopped and said, "Jane, you won't forget Mr. Killian will be round to go to the barn with Jackson after school, will you, love? Bye, now."

Jane was dumbfounded again. She and Jackson were supposed to go see Dudley. Alone. She'd had no idea Billy Killian was invited. Of course, she ought to have suspected it. Perhaps Jackson knew, too, and had wanted her to go along? Or, maybe Eleanor didn't tell him, like she'd "forgotten" to tell Jane.

She used to think of herself as quite an easygoing person. She ought to start moderating her reactions. Mechanically, she walked out of the kitchen and back into the garden. She slumped on a stone seat beneath a Rowan tree covered in creamy blooms.

What was the quote her grandmother said? We're to pray for the ability to accept what we cannot change. *I cannot bring back the shops*, pondered Jane. *I cannot make Mr. Killian leave our lives. But I might be able to convince him to leave Jackson here.*

Oh, Jackson. She couldn't bear him going to America. Like Lydia, he'd become the glue that held them together. They all thrived on his presence in the house. He was their light.

The hope of changing Mr. Killian's mind gave Jane a fresh spark of enthusiasm. No more being nebbish. Time to act as though she had sense. She'd show the stranger that his child belonged in England. He could visit Jackson during holidays, and they'd allow Mr. Killian to take Jackson to the museums and sights in the City. Or, they could go down to the sea, perhaps. Walk through Penzance and eat ice creams.

It would work. She knew it. She went back into the house, to wait on the American's arrival.

Clarice came bumping into the back door a few minutes later, ladened with shopping.

"Oh, hello, dearie."

"Clair, let me help you with those. I was just reading in the sitting room, waiting for Jackson to get home from school." She would be kind to Mr. Killian, but she wasn't going to suggest that she'd been waiting for him, too.

"It is lovely. Yes, Jackson should be along any moment." Jane wondered if Clarice knew that his father was due to arrive, too. Perhaps she and Eleanor were in cahoots.

They chatted amiably as they stowed away the kitchen provisions. Clarice said, "I am planning chicken, bashed neeps, and an orange fool for pudding. And I've got some lovely asparagus. Of course, we'll have an extra guest at the table tonight."

"Oh?" Jane said, casually. "Who do you mean, exactly?"

"Why, Mr. Collins, pet. He's due back any time." Clarice looked at her strangely.

"Actually, he's already home. I guess since I'd already seen him, I wasn't thinking of him as an extra guest." Jane smiled, and Clarice did, too. "He and Eleanor have gone to Tunbridge Wells for lunch, and must have got up to something else as well, to be gone this long," she added with relish.

"You don't say?" Clarice laughed. "Oh my, now there's a treat. I knew something was going on between them."

"Did you?" Jane exclaimed.

"Yes. I caught them sitting out under the tree together, the evening Mr. Collins left for London. She was holding his hand. I must say, I thought at the time that she was only sorry for him, what with him losing his shop. But, now, well, some folks come together with a single glance, and not much time or talk required."

"I suppose you're right, Clarice." Jane thought of Nigel while she peeled swedes. He hadn't come for Easter as usual, so perhaps he'd come soon. As much as she always looked forward to seeing him, she hoped he'd hold off another week. He seemed as eager as the rest of them to turn Jackson over to his father. Perhaps it was Nigel who was setting that standard for everyone else in the Membry household to follow, the devil. What was wrong with everyone?

The bell rang at the front door. Clarice was quiet, as though she hadn't heard anything. So, you did know he was coming, thought Jane. Aloud, Jane said, "I'll go." As she walked to the door, she fixed a smile on her face, willing herself to release ill feelings. He mustn't sense resistance, Mr. Killian only needed to be given opportunity to see that Jackson ought to grow up here in Harts-bury where he belonged.

"Mr. Killian, do come in. I am afraid Jackson hasn't come from school yet, but he should be along soon."

"Hey there, Miss Jane. You're lookin' real pretty today."

Jane blushed deeply at the unexpected compliment. She'd slipped upstairs to change into jeans and a lilac colored polo-neck that Nigel had once said brought out the grey in her eyes. She wanted to look good, but didn't want him to say so. It gave him an unfair advantage. It occurred to Jane that he probably knew that, and perhaps the compliment wasn't genuine. At any rate, he treated her as though the incident on the road never happened, and for that, she was grateful.

"Would you like a cup of tea?"

"No, thank you. I just had some with Miss Deborah."

They sat down, facing each other in a pair of slipper chairs at either side of the fireplace. Jane took a deep breath. She aimed to prove that running mad into the woods wasn't her usual response.

"Have you enjoyed your stay at the Hollyhock?"

"It's fine. I haven't had a whole lot to do, but she lets me play some."

"Play?" Jane said, giggling.

"The guitar. It's what I do."

"Oh, yes, of course. Sorry, I wasn't thinking."

Billy smiled with a kindness that Jane thought was quite sincere. Maybe his compliment had been truly meant, as he seemed the kind of person able to find beauty in all sorts of guises. She wasn't very skilled at being distant and coy. Her words began to tumble.

"You realize, of course, that I don't often yell at people and have a breakdown at the side of the road. I feel very badly about it, really I do."

"Oh, no, ma'am. I mean," they both smiled, remembering her objection to the reference. "I heard about you losin' your store. The barman at the pub was talkin' about it. It's a real bad shame.

It's no wonder at all you're so upset. And you lived there, too, idn't that right?"

"Yes," she replied calmly. No tears this time. What a gift.

"Is there anything I can do to help?" he asked. His brow was furrowed. Jane knew he meant it. She could imagine him trolling through the rubble with her, looking for salvageable treasures.

"No, no, it's all quite beyond help, I am afraid. I'd just had another piece of bad news when I last saw you, and it all became a bit much. After you, that is to say, I'll stay here a week or so. Then I'll probably go and visit my mum. She'll help me sort things out. Her husband, Hugh, is very good at business." Why was she talking on and on? A simple no, thank you, would suffice. Jane fell silent and brushed at some imaginary lint on her jeans. Where was that child?

*

Billy had listened patiently, nodding his head. It was already common knowledge at the pub that Charlotte Lloyd had failed to keep up the insurance payments. He knew Jane had lost everything. Billy knew what it was like to start from scratch. He'd had more money than she had, probably, but he'd needed to reinvent himself to play music again. It had been hard.

Both were quiet, considering their fortunes. Jackson came into the room. Jane noted that he didn't seem at all surprised to see Mr. Killian.

"How was your day, darling?" Jane said, as Jackson came to slouch by her chair. She hoped Mr. Killian noted with what attention and love Jackson was received at the end of the school day.

"Good," replied Jackson. "Mrs. McMillan had her baby and they called it George. We made cards for her." Jackson jumped to his feet, and without a word or glance at Billy, called over his shoulder, "I'll go change, and we can go to the barn." As he directed his remarks at Jane, she thought that Jackson was sometimes the picture of his mother, Lydia, when he felt shy. It was just as well, because surely Mr. Killian would feel excluded from this second encounter with his son. Jane didn't attempt to put him at ease by explaining that he was at times ill at ease with strangers.

Billy Killian sat looking in the direction his son had gone, the smile still on his face. He didn't seem to feel at all slighted by Jackson's indifferent attitude towards him.

He turned towards her and said, "That kid sure is somethin' else, ya know, Miss Jane?"

She nodded, and couldn't help her amusement. She'd never spoken with someone from southwestern America before. He sounded like a John Wayne movie. She kept thinking that Billy would stop speaking that way, that he was just teasing her. She wondered what his life was really like in the United States.

Jackson returned and the trio set off for the barn. Jane noticed that Billy didn't ask Jackson questions, he just let him warm to the situation. Before long, Jackson was talking, entertaining both Jane and Billy with observations of his feisty riding instructor, Mr. Miles. Jackson assumed that Billy had never been properly introduced to a pony before, and explained the finer points of grooming and tacking.

The adults followed Jackson and Dudley out of doors, and watched him ride in the outdoor arena. Two other children were in the ring, too, and they had a good deal of fun playing games on horseback. After Jackson was done, he slipped from the pony and led him back to the barn aisle. Billy and Jane sat on a pair of tack trunks while Jackson thoroughly groomed his pony and gave him not one or two, but three carrots. Dudley was set free to join his mates in the pasture, and Jackson announced that he was starving and may drop dead of hunger. Jane drove them home in her floral delivery van, each of them relaxed in their thoughts. Jane was wondering what sort of afternoon Mr. Collins and Eleanor had, and if they'd eaten lunch too late to sit down with she, Jackson and Clarice.

Laughter could be heard at Brambleberry Lane, as Jackson, his father, and Jane approached the back door.

"Ah, there's my little Prince!" Eleanor cooed as Jackson flew into his grandmother's arms. Jane and Billy joined Eleanor, Harry, and Clarice at the kitchen table. Billy had followed Jane into the house quite naturally, and had already sat down with them when it occurred to Jane that she ought to have shook his hand and said goodbye, sending him away for the evening.

"And how is Mr. Dudley getting on?" asked Harry.

"Very well, Mr. Collins, but he's asking for you to come and visit him."

"Is he now?"

"Yes. He wants to show you how he can go over cavalettis and jumps better than any other pony in the barn."

"Hmm, he sounds a very confident sort of person," Harry said, rubbing his chin. "I suppose he expects some sort of custom in exchange? Sugar cubes, perhaps?"

Jackson brightened considerably. "He'd love some sugar! Clarice never lets me nick from the bowl, so that would be really fab!"

Harry laughed and patted Jackson on the hand.

"Well, now that you've come, we can eat. The table's laid, I've only to put everything out," said Clarice, rising from the table and heading towards the Aga.

Jane was pleased when Billy rose to excuse himself. "I'll say goodbye, then, and let ya'll enjoy your supper. Jackson. . . ."

"Oh, no, Mr. Killian," Eleanor replied, with a hand flying to her cheek. "No, you mustn't go. Naturally, we thought you'd stay."

"You'll stay, won't you?" Jackson said, grabbing his father by the hand. The room came to an immediate stop, and Jane felt her heart quicken. Jackson seemed oblivious to the collective reaction. He was let down to think of Billy leaving.

"Okay, partner," Billy replied, and all moved towards the dining room, each taking something from the kitchen as they went, including Jackson, who carried a plate of rolls. Never mind, Jane told herself. Billy would see what warm family meals he'd be depriving Jackson of.

The food was delicious, and the conversation was lively. Jane cleared the dinner dishes, and Clarice asked who'd have coffee with afters. As Jane entered the kitchen, there was a knock at the back door. It was Toby, asking if Jackson could come out and play. Having secured a rain check for his pudding, Jackson flew out the door, throwing back his head to make roaring noises that were meant to be the battle cry of a Tyrannosaurus Rex. Toby answered with a carnivorous gnashing of teeth and they raced to the back garden to enter the land of the dinosaurs.

As soon as tea and pudding were served, Eleanor clasped her hands together and said, "Harry, tell them, love."

Harry smiled, flipped his tie, and dug at the orange juice saturated sponge with his spoon.

"Well, not that it's a'tall very exciting," he said, taking in the smiling faces around the table. "But I've put together a plan that I am rather pleased about. I hope Jane won't mind me mentioning our misfortune," he glanced at her with compassion. "To explain it properly, I'll go back about a month ago. I was in the pub and my mate, James, says to me, would I like to go in with him as he'd like to expand his fishing business at the castle. At the time I said no, I wasn't wanting to quit the shop, I liked the lessons with the children, and didn't mind my flat above. So he said, fine, he understood. He had only thought I might be ready for a change. So, nothing else was said."

Mr. Collins sipped his coffee, and continued. "I went fishing with my brother and realized how much I'd missed being out of doors. I've always been a bit of a walker, I can go a good distance and not be a bit winded. Mind you, music has been my life, but now that my shop's gone, well, I've decided to take James up on the offer. I rang him from London last week. He said he was glad I'd changed my thinking, and we'd sort it all out when I'd got back. I am going to take my insurance money, and spend about a third of it to double the fishing, and we should have a nice bit of business going. So, that's me."

"Oh, Harry," Jane said.

"There, love, I knew you'd be happy, and no reason to look so serious, what? This'll be lovely."

Clarice abruptly heaved herself up from her chair and left the room. Eleanor stared at her retreating form in surprise.

"I ought to be goin', too," stammered Billy. "Thank you very much, and I'll call ya'll tomorrow, if you don't mind." He backed his chair away, and left through the front door.

"My goodness," Eleanor said. "I dare say that wasn't the reaction Harry and I were expecting."

Jane left her position at the far end of the table, and moved closer to the couple. "Eleanor, please don't be upset." Their puzzled faces studied Jane, waiting for an explanation. "Harry, it won't work. You see, Charlotte Lloyd failed to renew the insurance. We've nothing coming, dear."

Harry looked at Jane with a searching expression, trying to comprehend the news. His lips parted slightly. The hall clock ticked on and on. Eleanor's gaze was fixed on the table, and she folded and refolded the dinner napkin beside her plate. Harry finally stirred, making fists with his hands and pressing them to his chin.

"Jane, you're sure?"

She nodded. "I spoke with Charlotte myself. Billy and Clarice know, because Billy's been to the pub, and Clarice probably heard at the market. I suppose we all thought Charlotte or her solicitor had contacted you by phone in London."

"Unbelievable." Harry said, pushing back his chair. "All my life was in that shop," he said.

"Don't you worry, darling," said Eleanor quietly. "Oh, Jane, you've lost everything, too." She sighed and added, "But you've more years to put it right."

Jane thought it was time to make her exit as well. Eleanor and Harry had formed a strong attachment, and if it was going to weather this storm, then they needed privacy.

"We'll talk more tomorrow," she whispered. She knew Clarice would be happiest left alone to look after things in the kitchen, so she gathered up the last of the plates and cups and saucers on a tray and deposited them on the kitchen table. Neither she or Clarice looked at each other. Jane mumbled, "I am going out for a while."

She could hear Jackson and Toby still running around the garden, sounding more like Native American Indians now. The spring sky still had an hour of light left, and Jane grabbed a jumper off the peg. She slipped out the backdoor, went unacknowledged by the Sioux braves hanging from the tree, and began walking down Brambleberry Lane.

# Chapter 19

Serena had been busy. Every evening after work, she came home and worked on getting her house in order. She had her carpets cleaned on Tuesday evening. Windows done the following morning. She spent hours clearing out closets. Her efforts produced six bags of clothing, several pieces of furniture, lots of books and CDs, knickknacks, and an older television to donate to the less fortunate of Atlanta. When it was time to put her house on the market, she intended to be ready.

As far as she was concerned, her future was in Texas. Billy was a rock-and-roll god. She would be his goddess. She decided that she would take an earlier flight to Texas on Friday. She had plenty of days off that she'd already asked for, since she hadn't taken any of them to plan her wedding to Richard. She'd already passed the idea by Yancy. She was thrilled to hear him say that he didn't mind giving her a key to his brother's place on Friday morning, but that, regrettably Mama would be busy then and most of the weekend with a fund-raiser at church. Aw, too bad.

When it was time to move in permanently, Taffy would fly to Dallas with her. English kids were used to Yorkies, and her dog would add a comforting charm to Billy's condo.

Wednesday morning at work, Serena daydreamed through an early care conference with members from other departments, and was just unlocking her office door when the phone began to ring.

"Physical medicine, how may I help you?"

"Hey there, Georgia peach!"

"Billy! I guess I should say good afternoon, right?"

"Yeah. And good mornin' to you. How ya doin'?"

"Just fine. How are things going with Jackson?"

"Pretty good. Yesterday we went to the pony barn and that was nice, and I stayed on for dinner. I am going to see him again this afternoon, after school."

"That's great, sweetheart. It sounds like it's going well, then. So, you'll be bringing him home on Sunday, huh?"

Billy drew a deep breath. "Well, I don't rightly know. There's a lot goin' on here, and I haven't had a chance to talk to his Granny about it."

Why couldn't he get on with it, Serena wondered, and said, "Billy, that's why you're there, honey, is to bring home your son. Are you saying that you'll be returning alone?" That idea was plenty appealing, and Serena's irritation cooled considerably.

"I thought I might need to stay a little longer. I am just not sure. Maybe through next week."

"Billy, you can't!"

"Why not?"

"Because! I've been working for nearly two years on our blues museum, and you're supposed to attend the grand opening ceremonies with me! Billy, *even Richard* wouldn't have forgotten *that*."

"Oh, baby, I am sorry. It just totally slipped my mind. Yeah, okay, honey, I'll be home before next Thursday, so I can catch a flight over there, and I won't miss any of the preopening and then the weekend. Okay?"

"Fine. But when are you coming home, exactly? This weekend, or early next week, or what?"

"I don't know. Like I said, things have been a little busy here. Are you okay, now? You still sound pretty miffed at me. 'Cause, well, you know I had planned on flying back to Dallas, not coming to you in Atlanta, right? So, it doesn't really matter where I am until we see each other at the museum in Mississippi. Oh, maybe you're worried about me flying, because I don't like it so much?"

"What? No, Billy, I'd just like the courtesy of knowing if you're in the country or not. Oh, I am sorry. I am a little edgy over this whole situation. It's not everyday the person that you're seeing suddenly becomes a parent. It's been a big deal for me, too."

"Yeah, I know. Our timing has been kinda bad, and it's hard being so far from each other. Things'll get better soon, though."

"Yes," Serena said with a smile, thinking, *you have no idea!*

"And that boy, he's awesome. He's the smartest, nicest-mannered, best lookin' kid I've ever met. He's doin' real good in school, so I want to put him somewhere special to keep him challenged, you know?"

"Yes. Of course," Serena was still thinking about her own plans. She decided to drop a little hint. Just for her own amusement. "Actually, I was planning a little surprise for you soon, Billy. That's why I wanted to know when you'll be back from England."

He started to laugh, "Oh, is that right? You're so sweet, girl. Hey, I'll call you tomorrow and let you know, okay?"

"Sounds good."

"I'll let you get back to work now, and we'll talk soon. Bye now."

"Bye."

Serena felt assured. Billy would surely come home soon, with a new son in tow or not, he would be there for her at the museum opening. It was all going to work out. She was struck with a few more ideas of things to pick up for Billy's condo, and made some notes. And it occurred to her that she ought to decorate Jackson's room in some sort of horsy theme.

*

Jane left the police station with the sooty, small metal safe-box, retrieved for her by an old school chum, who was now a higher up in the fire brigade. Paul Ravin had been delighted to send the lads into her condemned flat on a mysterious mission, to find and bring out her box. It was a fine morning, so Jane walked along a path that led to Ashdown Forest. She listened to the birds trill, and saw a bicyclist in the distance as she stepped across the main trail and into the wood. The great trees were soughing with a spring breeze, and she spied a rabbit who froze at her approach, tweaking his nose to and fro to catch her scent. Buttery daffodil were scattered about, and Jane felt a twinge of missing her florist shop. A few minutes later, she came into a clearing, where a picnic table stood. She placed the box on the table, and sat down.

Suddenly, she heard trunching in the underbrush. A moment later, a voice called out behind her. Jane's heart sped in fear as she turned around. It was Billy.

How do he do it? How did he manage to run into her, when they were *nowhere*?

"Sorry if I scared you, there, Miss Jane," he said, grinning. He looked ridiculous. A cowboy on a bicycle.

"What *are* you doing?"

"Well, now, I git pretty bored, ya know? I play for three or four hours, but then that leaves me a long time 'fore Jackson gets home from school. So, I been toolin' around the countryside on this thang I rented from Deborah. Saw you from up yonder, so thought I'd say howdy."

"Oh. I see," Jane said weakly, as he sat down.

"What's that?" Billy said, slinging a finger towards the suspicious-looking box.

"Um, it's the only thing that came through the fire, really."

"Awl, I am sorry, Miss Jane. And it's pretty clear you came out here to look over them on your own, and here I turn up like a bad penny. I'll leave you alone, sweetheart, okay?" Billy was already standing, hands on the table while he kicked one long leg over the bench.

"No, don't go. The most important item in here is something I want you to see."

"Uh-huh. Okay, darlin' as long as I am not puttin' you out. I could kinda use a little break from ridin'," he said with a another big Texas smile.

Jane smiled back easily. Now that she was over the shock of seeing him, it was quite nice to have someone to chat to. Shockingly, Jane felt a sort of kinship with him, since they'd both endured Mr. Collins's dreams dashing upon the rocks the previous night after dinner.

"How's Harry?" asked Billy.

"I don't really know. He and Eleanor were out when I came down this morning, and Clarice was off to see her sister. Despite him being sort of a loner, Mr. Collins seems a very optimistic person, so I am sure he'll think of something. And, anyway, it appears he has Eleanor's support and kindness to help him through. I am sure that is a great encouragement to him. Quite frankly, she's put a roof over our heads, and that's quite a lot, isn't it?"

"Yeah, she's a fine lady. And how about you, Miss Jane?"

"Pardon?"

Billy crossed his arms and leaned towards her. "How are you doin'?"

She flushed at the sweet concern in his voice. She knew that he wasn't being kind to employ any strategy where Jackson was concerned, he was truly interested.

"Honestly, I am not sure. My emotions sort of change hourly, it seems. And this box makes me a little nervous."

"Well, honey, why on earth is that?" Billy said, tilting his head to one side. Jackson did the same sort of head tilt. It was startling. She'd heard people often behaved with regards to genetics, not necessarily their environment, but she'd never seen it demonstrated.

Looking down, she cleared her throat. "I have something in this box that I want to show you, Mr. Killian. It's important that you have all of the facts, you see."

Billy waited quietly while she opened the box, and plunked it down on the table. Without looking at him, she lifted the lid. She sifted through several deeds, policies and letters from her father, until she reached the cream colored paper with the blue crest on the very bottom. Unsure of her voice, she abruptly handed it to Jackson's father.

The handwriting was plump and loopy.

*Dearest Jane,*

*What can I say? You've been my closest friend, and more fabulous to me than I deserve. Even when I think back to our worst rows, you were usually angry because you thought I deserved better or you wanted desperately to help. Today when we came from the church after having Jackson blessed, I started dreaming about what he might grow up to be. I hope he's more like Nigel than me, but maybe not so busy! And I hope he lives here always, where our family has been so happy. We complain, but you know it's a great place. Hartsbury is home.*

*But the reason I am writing this is to put it to paper that, should something dreadful ever happen to me, I hope that you'll look after Jackson as your own. I am really very happy, so it seems silly to be writing something so ghastly, but, I am a parent now and have to think ahead, don't I? I am even going to be quite formal and put this in the post, never mind that I see you nearly every day.*

*Love, love to you, Jane.*

*Lydia*

"Wow, Miss Jane," Billy said. "That's really something. I mean, she thought the world of you, didn't she?"

"But you understand that's not the point!" Jane said. "Don't you see that she wanted Jackson to grow up here? With me, and his family? There is no way I can make her wishes clearer to you than this, Mr. Killian!"

She snatched Lydia's letter from his hands.

Billy sat looking at the treetops, pondering the situation. "Okay, look here," he said, leaning towards her. "I've gotta go home this weekend. There's a museum openin' up, the week following, and I *have* to be there. After that, my calendar's pretty open. I understand why you showed me the letter, and what you're trying to say. But, things have changed a world since his mama wrote that, and I want to take Jackson with me."

Jane bristled.

"Now, wait a minute," Billy said, reaching an open palm towards her, close, but not touching her arm. "You gotta remember somethin' darlin'. I am here because Lydia's brother had his lawyer call me. I am here because I was told that my son wanted me to come. I was invited."

Protesting, Jane argued, "But now you've seen how Jackson is, and how we're doing well, and — "

"And you want me to go away. I know sweetheart, believe me that message is loud and clear. Things in life don't stay the same. I can't undo comin' over here and meetin' my boy. And now that I've met him, there's no way I could just go off and forget him, no matter what an old letter says. He deserves to have a daddy, and I am not even sayin' he has to live with me if he doesn't want to. But I am here cause he asked, and you've gotta give us a chance, hon. Okay?"

Jane couldn't give in, and refused to look at him.

Billy said gently, "Hey, maybe think of it this way. She wrote that letter 'cause she'd plum given up on hoping that I'd be the sort of man who . . . who would come back, and be decent to her and our son. She didn't know I'd be here when she couldn't be, and it was us that made that baby, now wasn't it? You can't play my role if I've come back and stepped into it, Miss Jane. You see that, don't you?"

Jane let out a sigh, looked into Billy's earnest eyes, and felt convinced by his words. She couldn't argue that he was invited. That he did have a right to his own child. That for some reason, Nigel was aggressive in making sure that Billy came here to meet Jackson. She supposed everyone had seen that, except her.

It wasn't entirely his fault, all of this.

Still, she couldn't bear him just whisking Jackson away. "But Lydia's wishes still count, don't they?"

"Yeah. So, why don't you help me then."

She commiserated with him, but she still couldn't see a compromise that would work for Jackson's benefit. "What do you mean, Mr. Killian? Help you do what? If Jackson enjoys the life that Lydia intended for him, he'll stay right here with his family. And you'll be off playing your guitar somewhere. I know you're his father, I respect that. But what kind of life do you intend to create for your son?"

"You wanna go back to this letter, fine, we will. Miss Jane, you know as well as I do that Jackson's mama may have written somethin' pretty different if she and I had any contact with each other. You know she was written' that, not really knowin' that she was gonna pass away not so many years later. Seems to me that the best thing you could do, you know, to be a godmother and all that, is to come with me and Jackson, and see to it that he's all right."

Jane was speechless.

"I mean, I've hardly been alone with him. And, if'n he's havin' a rough time gettin' settled, then you'd be right there to comfort him, and take him home if it ain't workin' out. And I would sure be appreciating it too, ma'am, cause this whole thing scares me to death, but there's nothin' else for it but to jump on in and give it a go." He paused and his hand came to rest on her arm. "Whatta ya say?"

"I scarcely know what to say. It's ludicrous. Absurd. You must be mad. I don't even know you."

"That's the point, idn't it, Miss Jane? Jackson hardly knows me either, but I was told he asked for me to come and that he wants to live with me. I guess we need to be thinkin' what that's like for him. What's he said to you about all this?"

"Nothing, actually."

Billy laughed and Jane flinched.

"You mean, I am sittin' here thinkin' that you're so close to him, and you haven't talked to him about meetin' his daddy? Well, I guess it's time I stop thinkin' you've got it all covered. What about Eleanor? What's up with her?"

"If you mean have I rudely demanded her deepest thoughts on the subject, I am sure I can't help you there, either," Jane snapped.

"Okay, girl, just calm down. Look, I didn't wanna have to say this, ma'am. But, the truth is, I've got a legal right to him."

Jane's heart pounded, hearing the unalterable fact. She knew he was right, and her letter from Lydia wasn't going to challenge Billy's paternity. "Okay, Mr. Killian, if you're determined to uproot that poor child in the matter of several days, and take him away from the only life he's ever known, then, yes, I'll go with him and make sure he's well looked after, on one condition."

"What's that?"

"We'll need to speak with Jackson's uncle, and run the idea past him."

"Why?"

"Certainly you can't just, well, just leave with Jackson and not let Nigel know."

"But, Miss Jane, it was Lydia's brother that got me here. He's the one who talked with Jackson, contacted the lawyer, and made all this happen, honey."

"Yes . . . and how could he do that?" Jane whispered.

"Sweetheart, I don't know why that seems hard for you to understand. I think you must be thinkin' of it all wrong. You maybe have to look at it another way. Maybe he was listenin' to his nephew say what he wanted. Maybe Nigel figured to be a good uncle than he oughta try to give the kid over to his daddy. Nigel probably didn't want Jackson to ever blame him for us not gettin' to meet each other. And Jackson said he wanted to live with me. That must mean that Jackson isn't altogether as happy as you're sayin'. I am sorry that's harsh, hon, but most kids don't ask to leave home."

Jane reluctantly agreed. "Yes, I imagine you're right. It makes sense when you say it." It was strange and emotional for her to hear him speak Nigel's name. Nigel certainly seemed like a figment of her imagination at this point; sort of as though he were off somewhere with Lydia, watching them all play out this drama from afar.

Billy took her out of her reverie about Nigel by taking her hands in his. "You've been through a lot here lately. Trust me when I say the best thing is for you and Jackson to come with me. It doesn't have to be forever, but help me through the next couple of months, all right? I promise I'll be as good to y'all as I know how."

"Oh, all right. All right. What do we do next?"

"Well, I'll get on the phone and make the plane reservations. We need to leave in the next two days, so we have some time to settle in, and then I can make that museum opening next weekend. There's already been a letter sent from my attorney to Jackson's school. But both of us need to touch base with everybody, you know? Talk things over, as we get a chance to. Especially with Jackson. I've kind of just let him get used to me, but now it's down to the wire. You pack your things and Jackson's. And in the mean time, we'll talk to Jackson's granny and Mr. Collins, whenever it seems right. Deal?"

"What? Um, yes, it's a deal. I don't have anything to pack, because I am wearing some old things I'd left at Eleanor's house at one time or another, so I'll look about for some cases for Jackson."

"We'll go shopping when we get there, and get you some new things. Stop worryin' Miss Jane."

"Can we actually, just . . . do this? It all seems rather sudden."

"Honey, everybody knows that's why I came to England."

# Chapter 20

Jackson placed his books in the house, and then went to wait in the garden for Aunt Jane. He thought she'd be here when he came from school, but she wasn't. Gram and Mr. Collins were in the sitting room, having what sounded like a serious talk. The garden seemed the best place. The air in the house seemed stale with worry. Everyone was upset, but trying not to show each other. It was all rather dreary. Ausfrid nosed his pant leg, then jumped up on the bench beside his master.

Aunty Jane finally returned. He could hear her footsteps pattering up the stone walk, then a deep breath as she came towards the gate. Maybe Aunt Jane couldn't breath very well in the house, either. He felt sorry for her, because she'd lost her shop and her flat. He didn't have any money, but he wrote an e-mail to Uncle Nigel to tell him to give her some. He always seemed to have a lot. He even paid for Dudley's boarding at the stable.

Aunt Jane almost made it to the back door of the house before she noticed he and Ausfrid in the garden. She seemed lost in her thoughts.

"Jackson. Hello."

Aunt Jane was nervous, but Jackson didn't feel scared. He knew that grown-ups had a hard time getting on with things, so he just decided to let her know where he stood.

"I want to go."

"Where, darling?"

"America, of course. You're worried about that, aren't you? Worried about me? But you don't have to be."

"It's very far away, Jackson. You might not be able to imagine how different everything can be."

"But I must go, Aunt Jane. I promised Mummy."

He should have told his secret, but it seemed very private at the time. He needed a secret then. It kept Mummy close, for a while.

She wasn't as close anymore, but he understood what she had told him better. He hugged Ausfrid. Dudley and Ausfrid wouldn't understand. That was the bad part. He wasn't sure if they'd come with him on the airplane or have to be left behind. Maybe Ausfrid could sit in the seat next to him.

"Jackson, what do you mean, that you promised Mummy?"

"When we last spoke. She said to be good. She said that my father would come for me, and that he was going to take care of me. Uncle Nigel would see to it. And that she was happy for us. She wanted to see him again, but she said that was quite impossible because she didn't have time."

"When? When was this?"

"When she was in hospital."

"But Jackson! Darling, you didn't go to see Mummy in hospital. Your grandmother thought it was best, remember?"

"Yes, I know. I rang her."

Jackson knew that Aunt Jane would be surprised at this. But why should she be? Did they think he was such a baby that he couldn't find a number and ring someone? And it wasn't like Mummy was at work. She was lying there, resting, so she wouldn't be annoyed that he'd rang her, like she would have done had she been busy nursing someone.

"You just rang her up, on your own? But how?"

Aunt Jane was just being thick now. Why bother answering her. She looked completely baffled, so he finally said, "Like you do. I called her mobile. And Mummy answered."

"Before she died?"

"Naturally." Had Aunt Jane gone crackers? She'd been acting more than a little strange.

Ausfrid yawned and a whine escaped. Jackson knew how he felt. This conversation was getting rather boring. And he was getting rather hungry, too.

"How did she know your father would be coming, Jackson?"

Aunt Jane's brows were furrowed. Jackson knew she was asking to make sure that she wasn't caught out of all of the grown-up conversations. Maybe she thought that Billy was lying about never having talked to Mummy. Or that there was something Uncle Nigel wasn't telling. Why couldn't they just ask each other?

"I don't know." Jackson sighed. His stomach rumbled. Clarice had been at her sister's house, so she hadn't been here to bake something for tea. But there was a box of biscuits from the grocers. He thought he might put some Nutella on top of one.

"Jackson," Aunt Jane's voice grew serious. He looked at her. Her eyes were mostly chocolate-colored. Like Nutella. But they were rather red. She had been crying, and that made Jackson feel sad and just a little frightened, too.

"It had been a very long time since Mummy had seen your father. So, maybe you are the best judge. You've met Mr. Killian. Do you like him? I mean, are you keen to go live with him? Because you like him, of course, not because of what Mummy said?"

"Yes. He's brilliant."

"What makes you say that?"

Aunt Jane was missing the obvious. It would have to be explained to her. Her eyes were shiny, and Jackson didn't feel very hungry now.

"Because he's sort of a cowboy, and he plays the guitar really, really good. Like he gives concerts to people and makes records. I think he must be an all right person, even though he has a funny way of saying things. And Gram is so old. I love her, you know I do. But I want at least one parent. Everyone does."

This must have been the right thing to say, because suddenly Aunt Jane hugged him very tightly. He felt Ausfrid's nose with his fingers, and Auntie Jane's hair tickled his mouth. Both things, the wet and ticklish, made him laugh. He was glad that he could say what needed saying, and make Auntie Jane happy, too.

"I have another question for you, Jackson." She released him, and looked at him intently again. His stomach did a little flop, because he wasn't sure what was coming next.

"Jackson, you don't have to answer me today, all right, darling? But I wonder what you might think of me coming with you to America? To sort of be your nanny for a while?"

Jackson was gobsmacked. He didn't have to think about it!

"Yes, please! You need someone, too, Aunt Jane. I mean, not a father, but someone. We'll go together! It'll be fab!"

Aunt Jane clapped her hands and Ausfrid barked. "Then we're off!"

She straightened and spun around like a young girl instead of someone grown-up, and Jackson bounded after her into the house. Now he was hungry again, and felt like having tea. With Aunt Jane.

# Chapter 21

"Only five more hours to go," Jane remarked sullenly, as she reclined her head against the puffy vinyl seat. She'd only flown on short trips to Scotland and back, and never up front with the businessmen who studiously worked on laptops and nursed whiskey and sodas.

"Yeah, I try not to think about it," answered Billy. "I used to think I couldn't fly at all without being stoned. I am doin' better, but I still don't like it all that much. Good day to fly, though. The nasty weather can double the time, if ya know what I mean."

"Mmm." Jane looked again at Jackson, who had his nose in a book. She felt the need to keep looking at him, and remind herself that she wasn't at all mad. It was logical that she should be going to live for a while in America, with her dead friend's son and a man she barely knew. As you do.

She had a sense of panic about the whole affair shortly before they left. She'd prepared herself for an emotional goodbye between Jackson and his grandmother. There was none. Remarkably, with Mr. Collins at her side, Eleanor had said farewell to Jackson as though he were going to day camp. Clarice was equally in control, and they got off and into the car for the airport. It had all been rather easy.

Until Jackson opened the paper bag that Clarice had tucked into his backpack. He opened it and pulled out some candy. Peppermints, chocolate drops, and bubblegum.

"Oh, lovely, some treats," Jane said. By then, Jackson was blubbing, turning the candy over and over again in his fingers as though they were worry beads. Jane and Billy exchanged tense glances over Jackson's head.

"Darling! Whatever is the matter?"

Jackson sniffed, trying to compose himself. Jane knew he hated himself for being a crybaby. He wiped his nose with the back of his hand, and then dried it on his jeans. Jane thought that she ought to have a tissue, but didn't. What kind of inept child minder was she?

He finally spoke softly, "They're from the shop. Doris and Eddie's. I'll never see them again. Mum used to take me there, after picnics."

"Oh, my love, that is rather a sad thought, isn't it?" Jane hugged him and it was like hugging a hard-bodied teddy bear, with unseeing eyes, whose head rolled back away from you when pressed close. She couldn't think of anything else to say and he was very far away in his thoughts, with his mum. Whom she'd never replace.

That's when her panic grew, escalating to a choking feeling. Vicious painful pulsing in her neck, and nausea welling up from her guts. Jane thought that she might lose consciousness and slam head first into the plastic table on the chair in front of her. She tried to take a deep breath. Her chest felt weighted and her panic escalated. *Oh, my God! I am going to die!* One hand flew desperately to her throat. *I want off this aeroplane . . . now!*

Billy suddenly covered his hand over hers, shocking her a bit, and thus rescuing her from her mental tailspin. Her breath began to deepen as she looked down at his hand, so warm, heavy and strong. She couldn't look at him, but all went calm and the terror passed. Jackson looked out the window with his head in the clouds, and Jane laid her head back and closed her eyes. Billy held on.

She didn't know if he knew, but she was grateful for his touch. She would get up and go to the loo, but not now. The next few minutes were spent in sweet relaxation, and telling herself all would be right as rain.

*

Serena was pleased with herself. She's spoken to Billy yesterday, and he confirmed that he'd be on the plane for home the following day. She expected his limo to draw up any moment.

His bachelor's pad had been transformed into a home, under her loving guidance and a lot of work. She'd began with the little boy's room. She bought twin bunk beds for him, so that he could have a little friend over. Serena imagined that he'd have a hard time choosing which he wanted to sleep on, but, little boys being predictable, of course he would settle on the higher bunk. The room already had beige carpet, the same that ran throughout the condo, which worked wonderfully well with the cowboy border she'd wrapped around the room. Below the border, she painted the wall a masculine blue. She added a sturdy oak chest of drawers, a desk that was ready for books and a computer, and she even purchased a television and small stereo with its own corner shelving unit. The boy's room had a small adjoining bathroom, and she continued the look in there, purchasing blue, red, and brown towels that were embroidered with the same western theme. The towel rack was fashioned out of rope, which matched the rope rug lying on the floor in front of the bunk beds, and that brought it all together. Thoughtfully, Serena left fresh soap and shampoo in the bathtub. Of course, Billy wouldn't think of packing those for Jackson, and the poor child wouldn't have any toiletries to speak of. She added a blow dryer beneath the sink, extra toilet paper rolls, and, mostly to amuse herself, a rubber ducky.

Yesterday, she decided that Jackson's room was well-decorated, but needed some personal touches. She copied a picture of Billy from the internet, and put it in a frame. It looked really good, as though he'd had the picture taken just for Jackson. Then, she hung a few horse posters on the wall, and added a few classic books. Billy's son was sure to be thrilled. Serena could imagine Billy's lavish praise, he'd remark that Serena hadn't forgotten a thing. He'd see what a good mother and homemaker she was going to be.

The rest of the condo needed some work, too. She hired a maid service to do some deep cleaning. They washed windows, shampooed the carpet, steamcleaned the furniture, dusted the mop-boards, wiped out the kitchen cabinets, and even powerwashed the patio. Billy's condo wasn't too dirty, but the regular maid service he had in every two weeks didn't do the extras. And everything had to be perfect.

Serena had taken particular delight in spiffing up Billy's bedroom. The large master suite contained a monstrous king-sized bed with a black duvet cover, a side table, and an empty armoire in a dark mahogany. Serena had been surprised at the antique piece, and asked his niece April about it. Apparently it was inherited from a relative, and also apparent was the fact that Billy didn't seem to know what to do with it.

Billy's huge walk-in closet was the most fun. Serena enjoyed snooping. There were lots of expensive suits, several pairs of jeans, and dozens of elaborate shirts. Comically, he kept his socks in a small basket on the floor of the closet, next to a basket of clean white cotton t-shirts and underwear, all unmatched and unfolded. Serena guessed that the large, empty basket was for the dirty items, and that he or the maid just carried this basket to the washing machine when necessary. Actually, it was a pretty handy system for a bachelor, and Serena speculated if she would change it when she moved in. On the shelves above, Billy had three neatly folded sweaters, and stacks of notebooks. Jackpot! She stood on tippytoes to get the notebooks down, and picked a few to read later.

A quick survey of the master suite bath proved that it was bare except for a few toiletries and a collection of six white towels. It would take about five minutes to strip away any evidence of anyone living there, and Serena did just that. The towels were tired, and the duvet was unexciting. Without hesitation, she put them in the garbage. All linens would be replaced.

Several days later, the master suite was now resplendent, and could've easily been mistaken for a room featured in a decorator's magazine. Masculine for Billy, but all to her taste. Hired painters warmed the cold walls of the bath and bedroom with a modern, neutral shade called "Driftwood." Serena chose creamy-colored linens for the bed, accented with raw silk pillows in sage green and a chocolate diamond design. The tapestry window treatments were a cream-and-chocolate scroll pattern, and gold rimmed frames held sepia-tinted photographs of old musicians, jamming on their instruments together. She knew Billy would love those, and she'd used her contacts at the blues museum to get copies of these vintage gems to frame. The mahogany armoire was moved from its stodgy position of lining up with the doorway, and was now slanted in a corner, a focal point that balanced the bed. Serena added a gilded mirror, a palm tree in a sage green ceramic pot, and filled in a spacious, empty corner with a comfortable chair in cocoa-colored leather and a small side table for magazines and beverages. She carried the decorative theme into the bath, which was now invitingly adorned with natural wax candles, a fuchsia orchid, a landscape painting and fluffy sage rugs placed on the wood floor.

The master suite smacked of deep comfort, casual elegance, and tastefulness. Serena knew she could be happy here until Billy bought her a spacious new house; they would need a few weeks to shop. Her goal was to talk to him about their new estate next weekend. Surely they'd have a few minutes alone at dinner after the dedication of the blues museum, and by then he'd be ready to ask her to stay forever. Until then, she'd play it cool, be available for invites to family events, offer to sleep on the roll-away sofa bed (for which she'd brought proper bedding, laundered it, and stashed it into the hall closet), but of course she counted on Billy to be a gentleman and give the master bedroom to her. Or share it. Serena smiled at the thought, but she knew that Billy was a little too religious for that since he'd become sober, and there was his son to think of. In time, and she could be as patient as a cat playing with its prey.

Serena knew that Billy loved soul food, so she had a big pot of soup beans on the stove, and fresh cornbread waiting on the counter. No doubt he was tired of eating that awful pub food, and longed for something from home. The best part was, he'd be surprised that she could cook. Actually, she seldom did, but she had a fool-proof recipe from her mother's chef, and she'd begged Mossy to bake some cornbread.

"Oh, honey, it's best fresh. I could have y'all for dinner on Saturday," Mossy had said. But Serena wasn't about to share Billy with his mama in the first 24 hours of his arrival. They hadn't spoken about Billy's son. Serena figured that her future mother-in-law wasn't sure how much Serena knew. That was okay, because Serena didn't want to get into a conversation about the boy; it was easier to keep her surprises for Billy a secret that way. The only glitch could be if Yancy had been keeping Mossy up to date, but, if so, Mossy didn't let on that she saw anything out of the ordinary with Serena waiting for Billy at his condo. Eventually, Mossy had done what Serena asked, and Serena made a very quick trip in Billy's car to pick up the cornbread. She bought some bread, peanut butter and jelly at the store on the way home, just in case the English kid wouldn't eat beans. PBJ must be universal.

Serena's heart nearly skipped a beat when she heard a car pull up outside. Not wanting to appear too eager, she flipped on the television and pretended that she was deeply immersed in a gardening show. Then there was the roll of the lock of the front door, and she heard Billy's voice talking about how his place wasn't very fancy, but how they'd get a long just fine. Ha! He was in for a big surprise! His droll little rabbit hole now had the sophisticated air of a show house, and was filled with the smell of southern cooking. Her palms were sweating as she turned on the sofa towards the door.

And in walked a woman.

# Chapter 22

Stunned, Serena spat out, "Who are you?"

The woman said nothing, stepped aside as a boy with dark hair came in. The woman held the boy firmly by the shoulders, as though to keep him from venturing further towards the dragon in her pit of huge sofas. Billy came in last, still jabbering about the humble state of his home and dragging his luggage, upon which balanced two small bags.

Serena quickly willed herself into a state of smiling composure.

Billy pulled the suitcases in through the door, turned, and shut it. Then sighed and said, "Well, it's good to be home, ya'all." He turned to see Serena in the family room.

He was silent, and starring at Serena. The British people starred at him, noting his shocked reaction. Serena stared back at the trio by the door.

Serena put a big, tolerant grin on her face, as though she'd shoved a coat hanger sideways in her mouth. He'd better start being thrilled that I am here, Serena thought, or there's going to be hell to pay.

"Uh," Billy uttered. Had he actually forgotten her name? His reaction seemed to indicate that she had no right to be here. Serena was willing to chalk this up to jet lag, if he'd cooperate — now — with the damage control speech that she was about to make.

"Billy, sweetheart, you *are* surprised, aren't you?" The English people now turned to look at her. She'd better make this good. "I'll bet you're surprised that I was able to get off work, after all. But, of course, I couldn't wait to meet your son!"

She clasped her hands together and looked adoringly at the child. Only at the child. Whoever the woman standing beside him was, Serena made it clear that she wasn't worthy of being acknowledged. They were in Texas now. The United States may not be big enough for the both of them, and Mary Poppins would have to fly back home.

The child might prove to be easy to love. He was beautiful. Serena was enchanted by his lovely dark hair and striking blue eyes. Billy was cute enough, but this child was off the charts gorgeous. His mother must have been a real looker.

At least Billy wasn't saying anything negative about her, so these people would just imagine he was pleasantly surprised.

"Can you smell that home cooking, baby?" she cooed, walking towards Billy. "Don't y'all stand there in the doorway, come on in!" She graciously welcomed them in, as though she had long been mistress of the house. They did as they were told, and Billy finally found his tongue.

"This is Jane, and, of course, Jackson."

Serena stood quietly, forcing him to finish. He did.

"Ya'll, this is my friend, Serena."

"Soooo nice to meet you, and welcome to the States!" She walked over to Jackson and leaned over to be on his level. "You are so handsome, just like your daddy. I've been so excited to meet you."

"Thank you."

Serena melted hearing Jackson speak. "Oh my, you're so adorable! You sound just like a proper little Harry Potter. You and I are going to get along just great! I like horses, too, did Billy tell you?"

"No."

"Well, I do, so we'll have to ride sometime soon, okay?"

Reluctantly, Serena looked at *her*. It could hardly be helped, at this point. Again, she waited for Billy to break the ice. He could begin by explaining what the hell this woman was doing here. He didn't.

"How do you do," the woman said quietly. "I am here as Jackson's . . . nanny . . . for a while, till he gets settled in." Serena relished how quickly this person, Jane, looked to the floor after making her little announcement. She knew who was in control, and that was good. Serena ignored her and turned to Billy, kissing him on the mouth. He stood like a statue. Covering up her annoyance, she said, "You must be exhausted and so hungry. Come over and have a bite to eat."

Billy looked flustered, as the trio remained standing by the door. "Actually, our flight came in a little early, and we ate on the way home. But, thanks anyway. We are tired though, but if you want me to drive you to your hotel, I will."

That was too much.

"Excuse me?"

"Well, if I give Jane my room, then Jackson and I can share the sofa bed, but I am not quite sure where to put you this evenin', darlin'. I am sorry."

Keep cool, Serena cautioned herself. She crossed her arms and parried back. "But, I've got a surprise for you! I've redone Jackson's room! There's space enough for both of . . . *them*, there are bunk beds. I'll take the master suite, and, Billy, you can have the sofa bed. One big happy family!"

"You did what?" Billy started laughing. Finally, a little joyful reward for all of her hard labors. She was warming him up now, winning him away from his traveling companions.

"I couldn't have you bringing your little boy here, and he not have his own room!" Serena affectionately tweaked Jackson's chin as she said this. Time to play the family card, and keep Billy's happy feelings simmering. "And of course Yancy was excited to help, so he gave me your key, and your little niece told me where to find some nice horse pictures, and your Mama even made cornbread to go with the meal that I slaved over!"

It worked.

"Don't that beat all! Let's go see what you done, then," Billy said, reaching out to hug Serena to his chest.

Serena proudly led the way to Jackson's room. She had all of the lights burning, in anticipation of the grand unveiling. "Tadah!" She said, waving her arms.

"Oh, baby, you have been busy." Billy turned to Jane and Jackson. "There's was nothin' here but some extra guitar cases when I left for England."

Desiring all of his comments to be to her, Serena redirected Billy. "Billy, look here, honey, I even bought Jack a desk, so that he can do his homework, and a T.V. Oh, sorry, you call that a telly don't you? Anyway, I tried to think of everything, and the bathroom matches this room. Go on and take a look."

Billy obediently headed for the bath to have a look around. Jackson, getting excited that the room was to be his, padded after his father. He was smiling. Billy came out of the bath and walked to Serena, who was perched provocatively on the desk.

"This looks really great, Serena, thanks so much!" He gave her a kiss on the cheek. A little impersonal, but it was a kiss. She caught him by the arm and said, "Wait till you see our room. I mean — your room!" She laughed seductively and Billy looked embarrassed. She didn't care if they'd never shared a bed. She wanted to drive home her point to all present: she was Billy's lady.

But he suddenly turned her comment upside down, becoming Mr. Good Example for the kid. "Well, you know it wouldn't be our room unless we're married, and I don't think Jackson and I are ready for that just yet, are we partner?"

The kid smiled, locking Serena out. Never mind that now, she told herself; she'd scored a lot of points this evening, and ultimately, she'd win. It was obvious that Billy was surprised, but, luckily, he wasn't overly territorial, or into decorating, to care overly much about what she had done to improve the place, so, as she suspected, he wasn't angry. Once again, she bolstered herself with a lifetime of debutante training. Her mother and Caroline would have been proud. She smiled warmly, slipping her hand into Billy's. He was looking deep, deep into her eyes, and she knew for a second that he'd forgotten the others who stood in the room behind them. Perfect, she thought.

"Come see the master suite!" Serena whispered with new enthusiasm. She wasn't going to call it *his* room, but she'd be sleeping there tonight, taking her rightful place, so no need to be upset by temporary arrangements.

The trio followed Serena into her piece de resistance. Billy whistled, and Serena tingled. He did that when he was too impressed to say anything. She'd learned that when she asked him to describe a blues guitarist legend he'd seen in concert. She glowed at the ultimate compliment.

"I had no idea this place could look so good. It's really, really nice." Billy and Jackson made their way to admire the bath.

Jane answered, as though Billy had been asking for her input. "I must say, it is fabulous! You've done a lovely job." Serena didn't mind Nanny speaking if it was to give a glowing compliment.

And you look so out of place in a gorgeous room, Serena thought. The woman standing before her was average in everyway. Boring brown hair, twirled into a plastic clip at the nape of her neck. A dowdy rain coat, jeans beneath, with flat black shoes. Jane's face was bare of make-up. Her features were pleasing enough, but she lacked any interest. Her brown eyes were as large and vacant as a doe's, and were studying the pictures on the wall as though she were at a museum. She was obviously impressed with Serena's decorating ability. Serena guessed by her dull clothes and pale face that the woman had no taste, but at least she was bright enough to admire Serena's.

Perhaps Billy had always been a sucker for strays. Serena decided that the nanny was a stray. And nothing else. Truly here for the child's temporary benefit. She wouldn't bother being jealous over the mousy English girl, but she would immediately launch a campaign to get her sent home.

Coming from the bathroom, Billy was still showering her with praise. "It looks amazing, girl. I didn't know you were so talented at this stuff!"

Jackson yawned and politely covered his mouth. He had manners, of course. Serena liked this kid better all of the time. Her mother and sister would think him divine. So cute. And that yummy accent!

"My partner's tuckered out, aren't you son?"

Serena wondered what Jackson called Billy. They seemed very at ease with one another. They must have done some serious bonding in England. Billy left the room; Serena's grand unveiling was over. Everyone followed him out. He was moving towards the luggage still propped by the front door.

"Us men will bunk together, and you girls can have the larger beds, all right?" Billy looked at Serena. If he was hoping she'd give up the master suite to the hired help, he was quite mistaken.

"My things are all in the master suite, since I've been here, working so hard for the last week. But I have some fresh sheets and a new comforter for the sofa bed, so you'll be very comfy, Jane."

Jane said thank you and Billy picked up her case and put it close to the sofa. "Serena will make that up for you, love, if you want to use that little bathroom off the kitchen, there, okay?"

She smiled at him.

Serena inwardly seethed. *Love?* So, Billy was even talking like them, now? There was some comfort in the fact that Serena had heard that English people call *everyone* that; it couldn't be anything special. Obviously, with his kind words to Jane, Serena had just received an order from the man of the house to make up the guest bed. No problem. At least she'd be tucked comfortably in Billy's king-sized bed. Serena retrieved the sheets from the hall closet and began her task of making up Love's bed, while she rooted for necessities in her suitcase.

A woman's work being never done, Serena turned off the soup beans on the stove and divided them so they'd cool faster. She'd just finished putting them in the fridge when Jane came from the powder room.

Serena smiled wickedly. The Englishwoman was wearing a shapeless, ugly fleece gown, peeking out from beneath an equally Victorian robe.

# Chapter 23

Jane woke to birds singing. She'd been sleeping deeply, and didn't recognize the cathedral ceiling with a large brass fan hovering high above.

Then it came to her. She was in America.

Seized by homesickness, she wished she'd kept her plans to visit her mum and Hugh in Scotland. She turned onto her side, snuggling deep in the covers, praying for at least five more minutes of privacy before the others came wandering into the sitting room where she lay. She thought about the woman sleeping in the master suite, who had evidently surprised Billy beyond words.

Serena obviously despised her from the first moment, and Jane knew today would not likely bring about a change in her attitude. The American woman was attractive. Tall, blonde, incredibly thin, with a beauty queen's face and brilliant white teeth. But she seemed the worst sort of person. She'd regarded Jane with disdain, seemed counterfeit in her affections for Billy, and the most ghastly bit was that she seemed to consider Jackson as a doll of some kind. Jane wanted to go home, and take Jackson with her. She felt that everything probably would have worked out all right, but with this woman's interference it seemed nothing short of a disaster.

"Are you awake, Jane?" Serena called out. Evidentally, the blonde had been in the kitchen the entire time.

Reluctantly, she sat up. Serena was already dressed, leaning by a cabinet where she stood over a spread newspaper, drawing circles around items that were of interest to her. Today she was turned out in a silky scarlet dress that had orange dots. She cast the paper and her pen aside. As she turned to spoon coffee into the machine, Jane noted that Serena's suntanned shoulders were bare, and a floppy, flirty bow fastened the dress at her neck. Her sleek hair was parted on the side, one side tucked behind a neat little ear. Jane thought of the khaki skirt she would wear later, which would produce the effect of looking rather like a sack of potatoes next to Serena's rendition of Marilyn Monroe.

"I wonder what time it is in England. I guess that doesn't matter now, does it?" Serena sang out. Was she trying to rub it in, supposing that Jane was probably feeling out of her depth? Serena took strawberries from a massive black fridge, ran them under water, slicing them. "I am making us waffles for breakfast, but don't feel like you have to help this time, okay?" With this came a searing look and a cool smile. What did that mean? Was she indicating that Jane was to serve as sous chef from now on?

Whatever Serena's game, she seemed to sense Jane's lack of enthusiasm for being here, and she was determined to make Jane feel it. However low Serena's opinion, Jane certainly wasn't going in for another bird bath from the lavatory, like last night. Still feeling soiled from yesterday's travel, she wanted a steamy, proper soak.

"Do you mind if I use the bath in your room?" Jane asked politely.

"That's fine. Only don't be too long, because then everything will get cold. It doesn't take you very long, does it?"

Jane ignored the question, and got her kit from her case. Her wrinkled clothes looked positively dismal. "Have you an iron somewhere?"

Serena was reaching in the cupboard for a mixing bowl. "*Have I* . . . a what?" Serena replied in an agitated, southern twang.

"A clothes iron?"

"Yeah. It's in the laundry room, of course. That door left of the powder room you've been using."

Jane started towards the laundry room, realizing that she might have to postpone a proper bath until after Serena's meal. She made a quick visit to the small toilet, then went to the laundry area. She unfolded the board, set up the iron and waited for it to warm. There was a small window in the room, but it faced the brick exterior of the condominium next door. Jane crossed her arms over her robe, and stood thinking about the overbearing woman who was making breakfast for Billy and his son. No doubt, she'd rather Jane weren't here, and probably wished that Billy's home were large enough to send Jane to the maid's quarters. Serena seemed a lot like a rather nasty girlfriend of Lydia's who was inappropriately called Grace. Grace had been wealthy, her father owning a company that made high-end mattresses fashioned with royal crests. Money had a way of making some people more unattractive than the strain of poverty.

The iron was puffing steam, and Jane set about the task of releasing wrinkles from her inexpensive cotton top and skirt. Not an easy task.

Charlotte had had so many pretty things at her shop next door. She'd often tried to tempt Jane with a twenty-five percent discount, but Jane couldn't see the point in spending a small fortune for one smart outfit that would make the rest of her wardrobe look worse by comparison. It seemed wiser to invest in her business, and she'd planned on taking on some help. Someone to make deliveries would be lovely, and increase her business. Jane felt a little charge of creative energy at remembering her business plans, but then her chest ached as it dawned on her, again, that her shop was gone. This was silly, she thought, pulling the two-pin plug from the wall, when there was nothing to be done about it.

Jane reluctantly ventured towards the large room that was half sitting room, half dining room, feeling a bit embarrassed that she hadn't thought to make her bed immediately. Its rumpled sheets looked sad contrasted with the beautiful setting Serena had created at the opposite end of the room, where she'd put beautiful linens and fresh flowers on the table.

Serena, Billy and Jackson were already seated at the table as Jane emerged. "Oh, there she is . . . finally!" Serena chirped. No chance for a bath, or dressing at this point. Pulling the tie of her robe tighter, Jane tried to walk with dignity towards the table. At least she'd taken a minute to clean her teeth and splash her face, although she was sure of having a horrible case of bed head.

The blonde sat at the top of the table, with "one of her boys" on either side. Jane took a chair by Jackson. Serena passed a dish with waffles and strawberries to Billy. Billy responded with, "Ladies first," passing the dish to Jane. The twitch of Serena's lip was almost imperceptible.

Jane took a waffle and some berries and passed the dish across to Jackson, who followed his father's example and gave it to their hostess. Billy took his portion next, and Jackson was given the dish. He paused and picked out a waffle.

"Don't you like strawberries, Jackson?"

"No."

"Well, you do like waffles, don't you?" Serena asked with a mellifluous voice.

"Not exactly, no. I mean, it's a bit like having pudding for breakfast, isn't it?"

"Pudding?" Serena said disbelievingly. "Pudding is, well, like soft ice cream or something. This is nice and fruity, don't you think?"

"Yes, I suppose so," Jackson answered.

Serena suddenly changed her tone. "You are so adorable, do you know that? And silly, too, calling my waffles pudding."

Jane wasn't sure who was more confused at the language differences. She had to defend Jackson. "He means that it's rather like a dessert, what with the fruit mashed and sweetened with red syrup."

Serena didn't appreciate the linguistics lesson. She glared pointedly at Jane, and then completely turned the subject.

Jane sighed, and wanted to spit out the overly sweet ruby stickiness that ruined perfectly lovely strawberries. How rude could one woman be? And at this hour of the morning. Jackson miserably stabbed a fork at his cold waffle and managed to swallow down half of it. Jane wished Billy had said something to defend them, but he didn't. He just sat there with a grin on his face, as though they were a sort of happy, albeit strangely blended, family.

The meal drew to a close, and Jane said, "Serena, thank you for breakfast. I'll do the washing up. Jackson, have you made up your bed?"

The boy nodded yes. Jane thought he seemed a different person. He was usually running around mad in the mornings, enough energy for four. He must be angry. Or perhaps he was as homesick as she.

"Jackson, I'd like to take you over to my mama's house. She's your other granny, ya know?"

Another nod from Jackson.

Jane felt protective instincts welling up inside. They'd only just gotten here. She knew she wasn't particularly invited, but she didn't care. She didn't mean to abandon him to the Killian clan.

She slipped an arm about Jackson's shoulders and said quietly, "I'll go with you, if you'd like."

His response was quick and surprising. "No, Auntie Jane. Thanks, but I'll be fine." He looked up at her and she realized that he was willing to go with his father anywhere.

"Well, I am definitely coming with you, young man," Serena said, standing up from the table. Giving weight to her proclamation, she added, "I need to return this cornbread, and let you all explain to Miz Mossy why you wouldn't eat any of it last night."

*

Jane realized she was quite relieved to have a few minutes on her own.

The blonde leaned deeply on Billy's arm and Jackson trailed behind, as Jane watched them leave from behind the curtains. Right. She was the hired help, after all, and if Jackson didn't need her, she'd just as soon stay away from Scarlett O'Hara. Jane giggled, thinking of how she and Lydia would've made jokes about Serena. As soon as they vanished in Billy's seldom used Lexus sedan, Jane dashed towards the phone.

She placed a call to Brambleberry Lane, and felt a surge of relief when Eleanor picked up the phone.

"It's so wonderful to hear your voice, Eleanor!"

"Jane, you've only been gone hours. Is everything all right?"

"I don't know. It's all so different. I thought I'd be helping Jackson cope, but he seems suddenly as though he's been with his father the whole of his life. And Billy has a miserable girlfriend that intends to keep him on a rather short lead, and thinks of me as a servant or something. I don't think Jackson likes her any better than I, but as long as Billy is in the picture, he gets on quite well. Father and son are even sharing a room, they've got a pair of those bunk beds. I feel quite out of sorts, Eleanor!"

"Oh, dear," Eleanor replied sympathetically.

"The three of them have gone out, so I am on my own and meant to do a little housekeeping before they return."

"Housekeeping? But you've only just arrived. Why have they left you behind, Jane?"

"Well, I am the nanny, so I suppose that's what I am to be doing if I am not required with Jacks. As long as Jackson is all right, I don't mind, really. I am just surprised how he seems to have taken to Billy, much more than I imagined."

"Jane, that poor little lamb can't be that brave, can he? To go off with them, without you there? Perhaps we just think of him as a baby, and he is growing up, isn't he? Ah, well, I just hope it works out well, all around."

"I am sorry that we left so suddenly. Anyway, enough about us. How is Mr. Collins getting on?"

Eleanor laughed. "I have a bit of news."

Jane settled herself comfortably on the sofa and waited.

"Jane, Mr. Collins and I have decided to marry."

"Oh, Eleanor! That's wonderful! Darling, I know you'll make each other so happy."

"Thank you. Life never stops, even when you're our age. I must say, I feel younger. To think of me, having another beau after all these years. And he was just in the village all of the time. It's you, what did it, Jane. You brought Harry to me, that evening, dear. I am sorry, I am babbling. But there's more. We're putting a bit of money together and Harry is going to invest with James. He says he's too young to retire, and he's sure we'll make a tidy profit. It's all so exciting, Jane!"

"How wonderful!" Jane replied. It seemed as much had happened at home as the tumultuous hours of acclamation that she'd already been through here.

"We're selling the house. Harry'll want to be closer to work, you see. And this place is too big for us, we think. So, that's sort of like saying goodbye to an old friend, too, I suppose. The properties we've been looking over are quite charming!"

*Selling the house?* Jane was speechless. Too many changes to grasp at once. Brambleberry Lane, going to the estate agents? Was Eleanor rushing things a bit?

"That's the silver lining, but there's a bit of dark cloud, I must say."

"What's that, then?" Jane said, fearing some disaster. She realized that she was still a little shellshocked from losing her own home and the shop. She didn't want anyone else to change residences, or finish digging up her roots in the village, like Eleanor's decision to marry and move would effectively do.

"Clarice has decided to go and live with her sister. Don't mind me, Jane," Eleanor said, suddenly teary and sniffling. "It's just that you've all left so quickly, I haven't adjusted, yet. Clarice has been here for so many years, and with you and Jackson gone, I am only glad that I have Harry, you understand. Of course, it's rather an odd trade, I suppose, for I doubt Clarice would leave if Harry wasn't coming in, but it seems I can't have both. And of course I'll no longer have a large manor house, needing help to keep up." She stopped to blow her nose, too short a distance from the phone.

Jane's tummy twisted inside. She realized that her life in Hartsbury had closed. The shop was gone, her home was gone, but that was just the beginning. Life as she knew it at Brambleberry House had changed too, even more than when they lost Lydia. Eleanor and Harry would be happy, that was balm to Jane's heart. But Jackson would probably stay with his father in America. Nigel had not come home at Easter, and when he next visited his mother, there would be none of Clarice's cooking, and perhaps not even a guest room for him at Eleanor and Harry's new home. Jane had no reason to return to Hartsbury, really. The people she knew there seemed distant; everyone in the village seemed severed from her through heartbreak. Brambleberry House had been a formidable shelter for all of them over the years. Now it would be just another address on an estate agent's list. People coming in, poking about. Making remarks about the old-fashioned wallpaper on Lydia's bedroom wall. Jane felt panic icing in again. And this time, Billy wouldn't be here to save her. She took a deep breath and tried to remember multiplication tables to divert her feelings of anxiety. Eleanor talked on about the little dinner she and Harry would have for guests after tying the knot, and Jane tried to listen.

When Jane said goodbye to Eleanor, she felt she said goodbye to belonging anywhere.

# Chapter 24

Billy stared at the little hand flung over the side of the top bunk. Jackson's hand seemed so small, but Billy knew from watching his niece, April, grow up that kids were little for a very short time. Thank God he was getting to know his son at all, but tonight he had a strange craving to know what the missing years had been like. What was Jackson's first word? How had Lydia celebrated his birthdays? Billy had been sober for all of Jackson's life time, yet he'd still missed it. He couldn't blame Jackson's mama, she only knew what he had been like before. He was a real mess, and didn't deserve to be involved with his son.

Today had been just amazin', Billy thought, smiling to himself. Mama, Yancy, and Lisa and April had all been just as smitten by Jackson as he was. When they first arrived at Mama's house, Billy could tell that his mama was really strugglin' to not scare the boy by lovin' on him too much. Billy and Yancy and his family were kinda the opposite though, and got a little too quiet. Serena broke the ice, and started telling Jackson what she knew about each of them, starting with Mama.

"Your Grandma Mossy is one of the finest cooks I know," Serena said. "You'll probably beg to come over here and eat. Oh, and there's Ranger, of course. He likes to be pet behind the ears. You two will be great friends."

Jackson had made friends with the old dog right away. Billy smiled again, remembering that later, when they'd sat down to eat, Ranger was at Jackson's chair beneath the dinner table, his chin pushed against one of Jackson's knees. His boy sure did love dogs. They'd have to think about gettin' one.

"And this handsome gentleman here is your Uncle Yancy," Serena had told Jackson. "He's your daddy's only brother. He can play the guitar, too. And he's super smart. Uncle Yancy has his own recording studio, and lots of famous people make their records there." At this, Billy's brother, stuffed his hands deep in his suit pants pockets and sort of pumped his head. He was a little emotional, and Billy was real thankful that his brother was touched to meet Jackson, and Billy liked what Serena said. "Uncle Yancy also likes collecting vintage cars, and he'll take you for a ride in a convertible. Have you ever been in one of those?"

Jackson shook his head no. "We've too much rain to bother much with them, I suppose."

Everyone laughed. Jackson immediately looked down and started petting Ranger, moving his head just as his uncle had done. Idn't that something! Billy thought. He's like my brother, too!

Next, Serena turned to Yancy's wife. "And this is your pretty Aunt Lisa. She owns a ladies' clothing store in Dallas. Aunt Lisa loves to read books by her pool when she has a day off. Of course, she doesn't have much time to relax, because she has to keep Uncle Yancy in line!"

More laughter all around.

"Finally, your cousin April. She's good at lots of sports. I don't know too much more about April, yet, except that she and your daddy are very good friends!" Billy hugged April by the shoulders and she giggled.

They had a good meal of Mama's fried fish, runner beans, fried potatoes, fresh tomatoes, and a skillet of cornbread, hot from the oven. Mossy said, "Jackson, have you ever eatin' food like this, son?"

Jackson replied, "Sort of. It's a bit like fish and chips, really."

His sincere answer tickled everybody, and Billy couldn't help but reach over and tussle his son's hair. Jackson smiled, even though he probably didn't know why everyone thought he was funny. Serena helped him understand by squealing, "Isn't he adorable?" and "Muh!", smackin' a big kiss on his forehead. Conversation clipped along at a nice pace, and Jackson seemed relaxed and enjoyin' himself. Billy kept close watch on him.

After the meal, everyone sat around talkin' and makin' room for dessert. Jackson leaned in close to Billy and said, "I shouldn't like to wander about. . . ." Billy was half listening to Yancy, and replied, "Huh?"

"I need to go," Jackson whispered.

"Why son? I thought you was havin' fun? Everybody's happy you're here. Do you miss Jane or somethin'?"

"No. Not that sort, like leaving. I mean to the 'ed."

Billy stared blankly at his son, wishing Jane were there. "To the what?"

Jackson widened his eyes slightly, showing impatience. "You know. The head."

Billy still stared, speechless. What was the kid trying to say?

Jackson tried again. "The loo. The water closet. Where people rest!"

Billy was caught from the belly up in a big fit of laughter. Jackson was beyond smiling, though, turtle-backed, still, and hoping Billy would get over himself and show him the way. Jackson was horrified of going into the kitchen, instead of the right direction, and somehow in this house they both looked the same. Serena, who had been listening without interruption, saved the day, again, by discreetly leaning over to Jackson and saying. "See the hallway leading towards the street? Go that way. First door on your left."

Serena had smoothed everything, and Billy was grateful. He closed his eyes, and dreamed of her.

*

At seven the next morning, Jane had tried to be quiet while making Jackson his breakfast. Billy was lured from his bed as well by the smell of bacon and eggs frying. Jane and Jackson heard him shower and then he appeared, shaven and dressed. "Smells awful good," he said, grinning.

Jackson and Jane were seated at the table and eating quietly. "We were in need of a proper fry-up this morning," Jane replied, and smiled back.

"Jane makes the best breakfast, next to Clarice, but Clarice isn't here, so Auntie Jane's is best," Jackson said with authority, shoving the last bite of thin, streaky American bacon into his mouth.

"Such praise," Jane retorted. Before Jane could offer breakfast to Billy, the master suite bedroom opened, and Serena's scent reached over their breakfast and into the room. Jane thought she wore too much. She was just too much of everything, but to each her own, Jane decided.

"Good morning, y'all. I am dying for some coffee." Jane stared in disbelief at Serena's attire. It was quite normal. This morning she wore a simple white T-shirt and jeans. Billy didn't seem to notice.

She poured herself coffee and joined them at the table.

"Well, Jack, you and I are in for quite a day!"

Jackson stopped eating, and began fiddling nervously with his food. He didn't respond to her. Jane knew he was retreating inside.

Jane spoke for him. "What have you got in mind, Serena?"

"I am taking Jack horseback riding, of course."

Jane didn't care what Jackson thought about that. She didn't want to surrender him to Serena, and it sounded at the moment as though no one else was invited.

"Just the two of you?" Jane countered.

"Yes. Why not?"

Jane drew in a deep breath and pondered what to say. She felt powerless. Of course, she was indeed powerless, she thought dryly. *You're just the nanny.*

Billy stepped in. "Oh, honey, you can't take my boy away from me the second day he's here! Jane and I will go, too. We don't have to ride, but we can go, and then all grab lunch together. Sound good, Partner?"

Jackson immediately brightened. Jane knew that Jackson trusted his father completely; there was no distance between them, only challenges to be faced together. For her own part, although it seemed no one else considered it, Jane craved some fresh air. She hadn't left this flat since she arrived the day before yesterday.

The quartet piled into Billy's car and Billy followed the directions that Serena had written down when she phoned the stables. The sun burned hot already though it was only ten o'clock. Jane was glad that she'd bought a few summer-weight clothes at the charity shop before leaving home. Her old wardrobe would have been stifling here in Texas.

Miles of white fences stretched into the flat horizon. Eventually they came to a large sign indicating the stables entrance. Billy turned right into the long sweep, lined with trees either side of the lane. Serena and Jackson were simmering with excitement. Jane doubted that Serena's excitement had as much to do with riding as it did knowing that her expertly laid plans for the day were unfolding.

"Now, Jackie, let me tell you what I've been up to, okay? This is a big confession that will really blow your mind!" Serena said, adding juicy flourishes with her manicured hands. Jane's nerves grated at the boy's new nickname, and she felt totally disinterested in Serena's forthcoming "confession." Serena just couldn't resist whipping everything up into a frenzied production. Lydia would have said she was so OTT (over the top). Jane smirked secretly at the thought.

"I've signed you up for a *whole series* of riding lessons! You'll come here once a week, just to keep up your skills, until we can get you a horse of your own. You'll have to talk your daddy into buying a farm around here. There are a couple for sale."

Nice move, Serena, Jane thought. She's been shopping for the family spread.

"*And*," Serena added dramatically, "You won't be riding a little pony here. You're a big boy, and we'll find you a cowboy horse. What do you think of that?"

Jackson was gobsmacked. And delighted. "A horse?" The excitement thrummed through his high-pitched exclamation. He was impressed. In the rear-view mirror Jane could see the crinkles of a smile pushing around Billy's eyes. Poor Dudley, so quickly forgotten. She felt ridiculously offended on Dudley's behalf.

Billy parked the car under the meager shade of a tree, and Serena and Jackson fled the vehicle as though it were full of bees. Jackson took the hand Serena stuck out to him, and Jane could hear the blonde saying something about going to the stable office to let the instructor know they'd arrived. Billy and Jane followed at a slower pace, and watched as they spoke with a man in a cowboy hat. He was pointing and Serena was smiling and charming and Jackson was staring at the man's hat, scarred boots, and the chewing tobacco he fished from his pocket. Jackson's first real cowboy. Jane knew Jackson should want to tell Toby, should he remember Toby's existence.

Serena turned and smiled at Billy, gesturing that she and Jackson were to go to the big indoor arena a short walk down the lane. Billy and Jane followed a long behind, and then settled themselves on indoor bleachers by the riding area. They could see Serena and Jackson in a barn aisle off to the side, patting a small, compactly built chestnut horse. A petite woman with gray hair was speaking to them, appearing to have Jackson's rapt attention.

"He's thrilled!" Jane remarked to Billy. She'd been so miserable since they arrived that she couldn't help enjoying watching Jackson's delight. "My, but that horse is quite large, though, don't you think? I mean, he obviously is small for a horse, but compared to Jackson's pony, he's quite the upgrade."

Billy said. "I reckon. They all look big to me. Well, I suppose Dudley didn't, but he isn't grown yet."

Jane laughed out loud. The strain of the last two days melted into hilarity.

"What?" Billy said, laughing with her.

"Dudley *is* fully grown!" Jane was wiping tears from her eyes.

"Huh? Don't ponies grow up to be horses, or somethin?"

"No!" Jane shrieked with laughter. She was drunk on silliness. Her stomach hurt, and she rocked on the bleachers. "When . . . when I met you, I thought you were a cowboy! Was I ever mistaken!"

Another fit of laughter seized her. Billy smiled good-naturedly, but couldn't figure out why it was all so funny.

"I am sorry," Jane said, gaining control. "You poor man. I've shown you the whole range, haven't I? Anger to the point of madness, running across the countryside, and now I am in fits. Oh. . . ." Another giggle, and she was finally done.

"It's good to see you happy, Miss Jane. It's been hard on you comin' here, I know. And Serena's kind of uh take-charge type. She surprised me, but good. I had no idea she'd be at my place when we got there. I mean, it was real nice."

Jane didn't say a word. She just didn't care at the moment. She wanted to just sit, and enjoy the breeze floating in through the big barn door. She would've given anything to have this conversation with Billy yesterday, but, today, she just didn't want to be bound by the huge transition they were all going through.

"Anyway, there's somewhere I want to take you, tomorrow."

Jane suddenly cared again. "Me?"

"Yeah. I know Jackson won't like it as much as this, but I know you're gonna love it."

"Well. I shall look forward to it. Thank you," Jane said.

*

The next morning brought an abundance of dazzling sunshine, and stifling heat. There was no breeze to speak of in Dallas. The four were packed into the car for Billy's "outing for Miss Jane," but

Serena took the backseat with Jackson. Clever, Jane thought. She need only become mates with Jackson, and then she has both he and Billy on a lead.

Jane was irritated with Serena's animated conversation, not to mention her movie star glamour. Today's outfit was a shapely yellow cotton sateen dress. Serena wore high-heeled wedge sandals that were trimmed with silk white roses in the center, and her hair was piled smoothly upon her head. When Jane spoke to Jackson about horseback riding last evening, his speech was peppered with, "Serena this, and Serena that." Jane was bloody sick of the woman, and they'd been in America only three days.

Billy pulled the car into the entrance of The Dallas Arboretum and Botanical Gardens, and was rewarded a smile from Jane.

"There are sixty-six acres of gardens here, Jack," Serena said. "It's very pretty. And I've made reservations for us to have tea. Just like England, right?"

*So, it wasn't Billy's idea. Serena wants to show Jackson that she can drink a cup of tea. And why would you imagine Billy had planned an outing for you, Jane?*

"No horses?" Jackson said with a whine.

Jane turned and shot him a look. He pretended not to notice her discipline, and turned to look sweetly at Serena.

"Sounds fab," he said, beaming an angelic smile at his blonde angel. Serena impulsively smacked his forehead with a kiss.

Jane began another round of positive self-talk. Jackson may choose to behave in a spoiled fashion for a moment or two, but if he turns it on Serena, she probably won't have it, either, Jane considered. Concentrate on enjoying the moment.

The garden was lovely. The last of the azaleas were in bloom, rising pink and resplendent against the blue Texan sky. They toured the DeGoyler mansion, a squat, white stone Spanish style house, where their tea lunch was served on a terra cotta veranda. Serena entertained them with jokes and witty observations about the oilman's mansion. Jane relaxed and enjoyed her company. Billy affectionately kissed her hand, then tassled his son's hair. Jackson was comfortable with his touch. Billy took his Australian-outback-styled hat from his head and plopped it onto Jackson's. "I need one, don't you think, Auntie?"

"Quite right," Jane answered easily. The simple prop made him look like Billy's son in a way that was difficult for her to witness. She supposed it was another reminder that Jackson would only be hers to share for a very short time.

After lunch, they walked on through the last area of the garden. Surprisingly, there was a refreshing, shady fern garden, fizzing with water sprayers. Jane sighed deeply, listening to Jackson and Billy chatting about why football is called soccer and why the Dallas Cowboys shouldn't be playing football, when, as Jackson astutely pointed out, they mostly carried the ball. "It ought to be armball, really," he observed.

Suddenly, Serena was beside her and linked her arm through Jane's.

"You're enjoying this, huh?" Serena said. Jane didn't mind admitting it. The gardens were beautiful, and lifted Jane's mood tremendously.

"I was just thinking how lucky I was, working with flowers everyday. I had a florist shop," Jane said.

"Billy told me. And about your losing it."

"Yes, I miss it. I liked keeping a shop, and everyone popping in all day long. Loved dressing the windows, and handling all those fresh blooms. The fresh smells. It's silly, isn't it? But it made me happy."

"That's why Billy wanted me to check this place out, because he knew you loved flowers."

So, he did have something to do with it.

"It's been lovely. And I appreciate you minding the details. Lunch on the patio was so pleasant. Sorry, I can't complement the weak tea, but the food was delicious," Jane said, and the women laughed together. That was a first, Jane realized.

"Speaking of window dressing," Serena said, drawing Jane to a stop and facing her. "We're going shopping tomorrow. Just us."

"But — "

"No arguments!" Serena said, smiling and shaking a finger towards Jane. "You're in desperate need of clothes, and I love doing make-overs. The boys are going with Mossy to meet some relatives in San Antonio, and they need some man-to-man time. So, we'll do what girls do, and go shopping. Okay?"

"All right, Serena. So long as you know, I haven't much money, so — "

"That's not a problem, honey. Billy has loads, and we're going to help him spend it. He gave me his credit card!" Serena laughed wickedly, sending her earrings into a rocking motion. She was beautiful, and Jane felt sorry for Billy, as he probably couldn't deny her anything.

# Chapter 25

"It seems the sun would just burn itself out," Jane commented to Serena. "It's so constant, here."

Serena laughed. "Yes, well, you get used to it. Where I live, in Georgia, we have lots of sun, too. I can't imagine living anywhere dreary, like England. Didn't you get sick of all that rain?"

"I suppose it is as you said, it comes up to what you're used to," Jane replied.

Soft rain, very early on a Sunday morning. She could hear the pattering of an English shower on her roof, in the flat above the store, as she snuggled deeper beneath the covers. Jane remembered such mornings fondly.

Jackson walked over to her flat. She made scones, and served them with lashings of butter and strawberry jam. They'd sat down and ate, and talked. Then they played cards for hours, read stories, and Jane walked home with him to Brambleberry.

Thinking again of Brambleberry Lane, she felt an ache. It was still hard to imagine that Eleanor had listed it with an estate agent, and it was no longer the shelter for the Membry family. Or herself. Jane wondered if Eleanor would even go and meet the new owners, but she knew she would not. Eleanor was so taken with her new life, so excited about beginning a new chapter with Harry Collins in their new cottage, and Harry's new position at the fishery.

No matter what sort of estate Billy's money could buy here, nothing would be as special to Jane as any home, however humble, in England. But, enough of that. She must accept her lot. She was here, and no where else to go at present. There was no such thing as home.

*

The shopping mall was *huge*.

Serena was fussing with her handbag, applying fresh lipstick. She was psyched and ready for her quest: Operation Make-Over Jane.

Jane tagged along behind Serena, as she talked endlessly about the rules of fashion. "It's not necessarily that you need a designer wardrobe, Jane. But the materials should be good quality. And most importantly you have to know what suits your figure, you know? You've got a nice body, hon, but you wear those big floppy clothes."

"But they're comfortable, and practical for working in the soil," Jane objected. She loathed the idea of being transformed into Barbie. "I know it's quite warm here, but I shan't want to look, too — "

"Too much like me," Serena retorted. "Just trust me, Jane, okay? I mean, at this point we don't even know what size you wear."

"I do."

"I mean in this country, Jane." Serena had wheeled around the first department store with ease, casually picking up separates from racks with what seemed like ruthless abandon. "Okay, that ought to be a good start, let's go to the dressing room." Serena herded Jane into the changing area, and took a chair right *inside* the changing room.

"Aren't you meant to wait outside?" Jane said, bundling the clothes modestly under her chin.

"Oh, I am sorry. I usually shop with my sister, and we don't care if the other sees. We can talk better. Tell you what, Jane, when you get an outfit on, just step out and let me see, even if you're not totally sold on it, okay?"

"All right."

Serena moved outside. Jane hoisted the hangers onto a peg on the wall, and began peeling off her clothes. She slipped into a loud printed dress and immediately felt foolish. Standing there, looking at her reflection, Jane didn't recognize whom she was meant to be.

"Jane? You must have something on by now? Come on out."

"No."

"Well, why not? I just want to see."

"It's totally unsuitable, Serena. I'll move on to the next."

Jane took off the ugly tropical print, and looped it hurriedly onto a hanger. Such a waste of time. She really only needed a few more pairs of cropped trousers or something.

Jane stepped into a dress and ran up the zip. She flipped her hair from beneath the thin straps and pressed the skirt across her thighs. She looked into the mirror, and felt a twinge of gratification. *This one would do nicely.*

Shyly, she opened the dressing room door, but didn't step out. Serena stood from the Queen Anne chair positioned by the 3-way mirror.

"Oh, Jane! You look so good! That purple just looks wonderful with your dark brown hair and dark eyes. I couldn't wear that color very well, it's too inky, but I had a feeling it would sing on you!"

Buoyed by Serena's praise, Jane stepped out and took a turn in the showcase mirror. She saw a graceful woman, in a simply cut cotton dress. She thought how well the necklace that Nigel gave her would look with it, and that seemed almost more important than the frock itself. She wore it always, so it was one of the few beautiful things in her life that the fire hadn't consumed.

Serena began instructing. "You see, that gentle A-line works on your curves. You have a classic hourglass figure, Jane. How do you feel?"

"I can't believe it. I feel a million dollars!" Jane whispered.

Serena smiled like a beauty pageant contestant. "Terrific! Now get back in there and try a few more!"

Jane and Serena walked away from Marshall Fields loaded with three dresses, four casual summer outfits, four pairs of shoes, and several handbags. Not all of them were for Jane. Serena spent

Billy's money like water, and it seemed signing credit slips renewed Serena's strength to shop on. Serena's mission was all inclusive: she'd even made Jane get measured for a bra and supervised her while they searched for the perfect pair of knickers. Jane wanted to crawl into a hole, but she couldn't argue with the evidence of heavy wear, and the holes that made spider webs of her old foundations. Jane wasn't even allowed to put the old ninnies back on, and watched as Serena dumped them into the dressing room bin.

After loading their purchases into the boot of the car, Jane discovered with some despair that Serena wasn't finished with her. She drove them to a salon, and before Jane grasped the situation, she was wet-headed, gowned and presented before a hair dresser.

"How long since you've cut your hair, darlin'?"

"Oh, I don't know. Maybe a year."

The hair dresser and Serena exchanged a dramatic eye roll. Serena stepped back and folded her arms.

"Antoine, you can see she has thick hair, so I thought some layering, to take the weight off?"

"Oh, honey, I agree," Antoine said with a flick of his wrist. "I think we ought to take off quite a bit of length."

*Hello, I am still here!* "Excuse me," Jane interrupted. "I like my hair long."

Antoine and Serena looked back at her in the mirror. They didn't expect insubordination. "Well, for today, maybe just here?" Antoine held a comb to the top of Jane's shoulder.

"No shorter, please." Jane said.

Serena didn't leave for a moment, but parked herself at the beautician's chair next to Antoine and chatted about this season's trends. Antoine finished Jane's haircut, and began drying her hair.

"What do you think, sweetheart?"

"Oh, it's quite nice!" Jane said. Her hair fell in gentle curves around her full cheekbones, and her large eyes were revealed with a long wispy bang. To his credit, Antoine had left Jane's hair slightly below her shoulders, the longest layer lay against the swell of her breast.

"Isn't she adorable?" Antoine squealed to Serena. He'd become playful now that his work was being appreciated. "Brows?" he said, arching his.

"Definitely," Serena replied.

"Off you go to the wax room," said Antoine, dramatically swishing the cape away and releasing the chair to the floor. Jane stepped off the chair and meekly followed Serena.

Into another chair, and looking at her new sandals to avoid the bright light that shone on her face, Jane felt a technician wipe beneath her eyebrow with a strong smelling, cool cotton pad. Then the woman eased hot wax onto the unwanted hairs. In a matter of five minutes, Jane's heavy brows were sculpted into a new shape. Lydia had always done her brows for her, but since Lydia passed away, Jane had let them grow in.

Jane and Serena munched on pita sandwiches and were given sweet, iced tea, on their way to the next beautifying stage. Jane was given a pampering facial, and then sent to yet another room for a make-up lesson. Serena, with boundless energy, sat on the sidelines, giving directions to each person, as though she were Jane's personal beauty guru.

Once more, they piled bags of plunder into the boot of the car, this time consisting of cosmetics, hair products, and expensive skin treatments that Serena insisted Jane must use.

"Ready for more?" Serena said.

"More?" *What more could she do to me?* Jane thought.

"Yeah. It's only five o'clock. Billy won't be home until late tonight, if at all." Serena started the car and began driving from the salon lot. Jane recognized the area, and knew they were a few minutes from the condo, but Jane wasn't sure exactly where Serena was heading. That became a lesser issue than what was being done with Jackson.

"What do you mean 'if at all?'" Jane questioned. "He didn't say anything to me about Jackson overnighting elsewhere."

"So?" Serena said.

"So? Oh yes. I'd quite forgotten. I am just the nanny. No need to consult me, I suppose," Jane hissed.

Serena was silent.

"Where are you taking me? Or am I just meant to go along with whatever you people decide for me, like Jackson?"

"Oh, Jane, stop being such a drama queen," Serena said tiredly. "I'll take you to Billy's place if you want. Just calm down."

Jane felt quite put in her place by Serena's remark. She starred out the window. The last thing she wanted to do was give Serena more evidence that she was overreacting. Had she always been so emotional? Jane berated herself for not being able to go along with things. Then again, why was Serena doing all of this for her? Jane hadn't noticed Serena mentioning any friends. Perhaps she didn't have any. Perhaps, in her own way, Serena was trying to forge a relationship. Jane tried to let that sink in, and foster compassion, but it didn't work. She just wanted out of this bloody car.

Minutes later, Serena pulled the car into Billy's garage. Without a word, the two women gathered their purchases and headed into the house. Serena took her bags into the master suite. Jane had no where else to put hers, so tried to make a tidy pile by the sofa that folded out to make her bed each night. The slippery bags just kept sliding off one another. The messy appearance of her life — tumbling bags belonging to a chic new person that she didn't recognize, and the old cases full of frumpy clothes, started to depress her.

Serena stayed for a while in the large bedroom, and Jane was glad for the privacy. She was holding her face in her hands when Serena was suddenly standing in front of her.

"Do you like pizza? You have that in England, don't you?" Serena's voice was breezy.

"Of course," Jane said. "And yes, I like pizza."

"What do you say that we order one, and watch a movie or something?"

"Sure." Jane answered indifferently. But, actually, it sounded like rather a nice evening.

"And you can stop stewing, Nanny Jane. I phoned Billy, and they expect to be back tonight around ten."

"Brilliant." Jane was glad for a temporary respite. But she couldn't wait until tomorrow morning, when Serena and Billy would leave for their weekend trip, to dedicate some museum. She needed a few days' peace.

# Chapter 26

"And then what did you do?" asked Jane, as she folded the last of Jackson's clothes. They'd had a marvelous day, all to themselves. Serena and Billy had left very early in the morning for the airport.

Jane and Jackson visited the park down the street. Then they took a bus and Jackson applied for a library card and checked out some books. Then they walked to a local farmer's market, and bought fresh fruit, warm with sun and glorious smelling, which they'd had with sandwiches for their lunch.

"I played outside with my cousins. They have a big sandbox thing in their garden, and you have to be careful of ants because they breath fire or something, I am not sure. We're going back to see Uncle Calvin, because it will be someone's birthday next month, in San Antonio. And we'll go out on Lake Medina, then, on a boat."

"Did you see much of San Antonio? What about that place you told me about, where they fought a battle?"

"The Alamo. Not this time. Daddy says we're to go next time."

*Daddy?* "When did you start calling him that?"

"Serena said I ought to, before we left. So, I did. After the first time, it was quite easy. He is my father, you know."

"Well, of course, darling. I was only curious. What would you like to do, now?"

"Josh and Jeremy, those boys from two doors down, will be here, straight away. They come from school at 2:30. I don't know, until then." He got up to take his library books to his room, as Jane thought a quick nap might be in order, to revive her from the sun.

*

The waiter finished pouring non-alchoholic champagne for the happy couple.

"I love you, baby," said Billy, hunched over the table to be even closer to his fiancée. "I don't know what I woulda done if you hadn't said yes."

"I don't know what I would have done if you didn't get around to finally asking me," Serena replied and leaned in for a kiss.

"Finally? C'mon, now, I haven't known you more than a couple of months!"

"Four."

"Okay, honey. Four months. Not too long to wait, specially since you live in a different state."

"Not for long."

"No, not for long. So, you're Miss Planner. When do you wanna get hitched?"

"Get 'hitched'? Very romantic, Billy. Actually, I don't want any fuss. I had all of that going with Richard, and the whole idea of a wedding seems abysmal."

"Well, whatever makes you happy, honey, you know that'll work for me. It's my touring schedule to work around, is all."

"Let's just get the paperwork and go before a judge."

"Oh, now, Serena, are you sure? That's not really your style, is it?"

"What is that supposed to mean?"

"Well, now, don't get upset, darlin'. I just mean, you're so classy, and you like to do things right. Do things big. I don't want you regretting' anythang later on."

Serena put down her champagne flute. Billy understood he was on dangerous ground. "Darlin, I am sorry. . . ."

"Billy, I don't want a big wedding. You know my parents won't ever approve of you. They don't even like events like this weekend. No matter how many people get together to celebrate the musical legacy of my grandfather, and build museums like this in honor of his music, it will never make sense to them. We don't make sense in a lot of ways, but I *know* we'll be happy. Here's what I want:

I want to get married quickly. I want you to buy me a big house that I can make our home. And I want me and you and Jackie to be a family. "

Billy beamed, hanging on her every word, and pumping his foot like a dog wagging his tail.

"Let me tell you something else," Serena continued. "I was so sure that's what I wanted that I've already got my stuff in storage, ready to move down here. I've even been looking into a good school for Jackie. I adore him, Billy. I'll take good care of him when you're on the road, and we'll always be waiting for you when you get home."

Billy was quiet, unable to trust the emotion in his voice. He just nodded his head. He'd been at the very bottom in his lifetime, and now he was on the mountaintop. He never thought he could be so full of joy.

They smiled at each other for a long time. Then Billy said, "I know a guy with a real nice jewelry store. We'll go as soon as we get back to Dallas."

Serena excused herself to go to the ladies' room to freshen up. After washing her hands, she reached into her bag and applied a thin coat of gloss to her lips. She grabbed her comb to refresh her hair.

Her relationship with Billy had turned out to be everything that she wanted. She had come to see that she was a little more like her mother and sister than she had thought, but he didn't mind if she quit her job and became a lady who lunches. It was best for Jackson and Billy that she be tending a home base for them both. More importantly, she loved Billy because he was an amazing person, so kind, and a brilliant musician. Whatever her own faults might be, he was pure gold and she felt humbled that he really did love her. Her heart was touched at what a good father he was to Jackson; Billy was a natural. They were going to be happy, happy, happy.

"What?" Billy asked her.

"Nothing, I am just happy, that's all. I am glad that we're flying back this evening. I can't wait to tell Jackie the news. He's been waiting for a family, I mean having both a mom and a dad, for a long time, Billy."

"Yeah, I think he has." Billy's mouth shoved into a hard line.

"I didn't say that to make you feel guilty, sweetheart," said Serena, pushing her hair out of her eyes. A sudden wind ruffled the canopy as they left the restaurant and stepped into their limo.

Billy handed his fiancée into the car, scooted in, and closed the door behind himself.

"I know that's not what you meant, and I didn't really take it that way," Billy whispered. "I don't think we can be responsible for things that we don't even know 'bout in life. It's hard 'nuff just to do your best with what you do know."

"Mmm, that's true."

They snuggled close in the backseat for the ten minute drive to the airport. The plane was waiting at the gate when they arrived. Belted in the small aircraft, the couple discussed the blues museum dedication, and the excellent turn-out. "You are such a charmer during interviews, Billy," Serena teased. "A little flirtatious with that lady from *Rolling Stone*, I noticed. I am going to have to keep an eye on you."

"You've got nothing' to worry 'bout, baby. I was just bein' friendly."

The small jet grew dark. A bolt of thunder cracked in the distance, and the plane began to feel like a bucking bronco. Serena could see that Billy was getting a little nervous. He had never liked flying sober. She recalled him telling her that he had a panic attack, returning from England. Apparently, Jane was a comfort to him, even held his hand when he reached out, like a child. And he admitted this kind of situation had him wanting a drink.

"It was as worse as anytime since I left rehab," he'd told Serena. "But I knew I couldn't, because I can't trust myself. I knew Jane would've called me on it." Serena was glad Jane had been there, and she was thankful that Billy wasn't making this flight alone. She fished for a something to say to divert his attention.

"I spotted a house close to the horse barn that I want you to take a look at," Serena said. "It's an old estate, once owned by a Yankee who'd made a bundle in trains with Mr. Vanderbilt."

"Uh-huh. You been shopping' darlin'?" Billy said with a chuckle. "I'll buy you whatever you want, long as I got the money. Jackson would like bein' close to them horses, wouldn't he?"

"Yes, but of course he could keep his own, at this place. There are 53 acres."

"Whoa!" Billy whistled. "That's a lot of property."

"Well, we'll want our privacy, won't we?" Serena winked at him.

"Is there a garden?"

"A garden? I thought you'd be more interested in building a recording studio out there!"

Billy wiped the perspiration from his upper lip, and forced a smile. "I was thinkin' about Jane. She'll probably wanna see what she could grow here."

*Excuse me? Jane, gardening at my house?* Serena's thoughts were in a jumble that had nothing to do with bumping across clouds. *Won't the wretched woman be going home soon?*

"Billy, I don't know — "

The captain interrupted Serena, his voice seemed as though he were on the other end of a telephone, distant and tinny in the small space. "Folks, I am sorry about these rough conditions. . . ."

He no sooner got the words out of his mouth, and the plane seemed to fall like an elevator dropping to the ground. Serena clapped her hand over her mouth, in an effort not to lose her dinner.

The captain choked out a short curse, his mind obviously on guiding the airplane through the angry wind. "We'll be landing in about ten minutes." With a loud click, he disconnected.

Serena looked at Billy. He was ashen. She put her hand on his cheek, and he appeared not to feel it. He stared away from her, out the window. Her heart squeezed with pity for him, and she made herself swallow the words she wanted to spit at him about the English nanny.

What a joke, she'd felt like she was babysitting the dour woman, and Jane was more irritating than any spoiled child. In fact, that's what she was. Sure, Jane had had some hard knocks lately; Billy had told Serena about Jane losing everything. But she wasn't *doing anything* about it. Jane just wanted to be part of their lives, instead of getting her own.

If they made it off this damn plane alive, Serena was going to see to it that some things changed, and soon.

# Chapter 27

Monday morning found the foursome at the breakfast table together. Serena allowed Jane to make the meal, figuring that Jane ought to be doing something to earn her keep.

"So, today, we're goin' shopping for one of the biggest diamonds in Texas, and then tomorrow, I am goin' to Austin to start rehearsals." Billy said, cramming his mouth full of eggs. Jane was a good enough cook, but he'd added spicy salsa to his eggs.

"Rehearsal? Are you going to make another recording, then?" Jane asked.

Serena thought, *So, now Billy has to clear his work arrangements with you, Nanny?* She shot a cold glance in Jane's direction.

"Naw, Miss Jane. We're rehearsin' for our new tour, and that's just a good place to meet right now. We've got eighteen dates lined up, and we fly out next week. Mmm, you make strong coffee, Miss Jane, but I sure do like it!" Billy laughed, and drained his cup.

"I don't understand," Jane said.

*She admits she's clueless. That's a start.* "About what, Jane?" Serena answered.

"Well, if I am not mistaken, Austin is a bit far for you to come back here, tomorrow evening. And then you'll be leaving on tour. What about Jackson? He hasn't seen you since Thursday last, before you went to the museum dedication."

Jackson became very interested in the sausages on his plate. *Oh, this ought to be good.* Serena cleared her throat and sat back to watch the entertainment. Billy was staring blankly at the foreigner. This would teach him how easily they could do without her. It was time Jane learned the reality of the music business, and Billy was going to give her a crash course.

"Jane," Billy began slowly.

*Just tell her how it is, Billy!* Serena could hardly sit still.

"I believe, Miss Jane, that you're right. Jackson should come with Serena and me today."

*What?*

"You don't mind, do ya, baby?" Billy turned to her with serious eyes. It was time to be on her best behavior. She could see that Billy felt he'd made an error as a father; he would be defensive if she didn't support him.

"Of course! I always love having Jackie with us!" She grinned warmly at Jackson, and was rewarded with a smile. Actually, even though it wasn't as romantic buying wedding bands with a child, she loved spending time with the darling little boy. And leaving Jane behind at home made it even better. "The three of us can drop by the house I want to buy, because I'd like for Jackie to see it, too," Serena added for good measure.

"Miss Jane, it's got lots of room for a garden. Why you could have your own flowers out there — "

"Billy," Serena cut him off. "I think running a florist shop is a little different than turning 53 acres of sunbaked pasture into a flowerbed." Serena smiled her most charming at Jane. She couldn't read the woman's thoughts; Jane had a good poker face.

"What happens when you go on tour, I wonder?" Jane said, still worrying at Billy's obligations like a dog with a bone. She looked squarely at Billy, like a callous British headmistress. Uh-oh, honey, thought Serena. You just don't know when to stop.

"Whatta ya mean?" Billy said, still jovial about giving Nanny Jane her own garden space.

"About Jackson? You're his father." Jane said flatly.

"He'll miss me, won't ya partner?" Billy ran his palm down Jackson's eyes and nose and the boy tossed his head, giggling. "But that's what we talked about, 'fore we came, right, Miss Jane? That you'd be Jackson's nanny and help him get settled and stuff. I am a musician, shug, so naturally I am gonna be out on the road. You knew that, surely."

Jane looked at the table. "Yes, of course. You'll travel, I know. It just seems a bit premature."

"Whatta mean, Miss Jane?"

"Well, we've only just gotten here, really. I suppose I didn't expect you to go on tour until Jackson began school in the fall."

"Oh, I see where you're comin' from," Billy said.

Serena was struggling to keep her peace. To everyone's surprise, it was Jackson that spoke.

"You shouldn't try to make him feel badly. It's what he's meant to do," Jackson said, obviously to Jane, but still looking at the table.

"Darling, I don't wish to make your father feel badly, I was just concerned — "

"No one cares, but you. You're making a mess of everything, Aunt Jane," Jackson said.

"Jackson! I — "

"You're not my mum. And you're not even my aunt, even though I call you that. You're not even to be my step-mum. That'll be Serena. Why are you trying to make everyone do what you want them to do? You don't want to do anything that we like. You don't ride. You don't know anything about Daddy's music, either." Jackson jumped to his feet, raising his voice to a shout. "I don't need a nanny, because I am not a baby. I've never had one before, and — "

Billy put a hand on Jackson's shoulder and said, "That's enough, son. Everybody here cares what you think, but right now you need to quiet down, okay, Partner? Go on, go play."

Serena was impressed with Billy's loving, but authoritative handling of his son. And, unexpectedly, she felt sorry for Jane. It was clear that the woman thought only of the child, and she'd had a big part in raising him when they lived in England. But that still didn't change the fact that, like Jackson said, Serena was going to be his step-mom. She suddenly felt a maternal instinct to go to

Jackson, and reassure him. Although he was angry, he was still a little boy and going through a lot of adjustment. She put a hand on Billy's for a moment but avoided looking at Jane. Who wanted to look at Jane? One didn't know what to say, so it was easier just to look the other way, thankful that you weren't in her shoes. But, at least, reasoned Serena, Jane's shoes were more attractive now than the grubby ones she came here in.

*

A while later, Billy came to speak to Jane. "Are you doin' okay? I know I haven't known my boy very long, but that don't mean I am not sorry for what he said to you earlier."

Jane had been lost in her thoughts, with a library book in her hands as a foil in case someone had interrupted her. What would Lydia have thought of this woman? Serena was materialistic, selfish, and manipulated everyone to get her own way. Yet, Jane must also admit, that Serena was passionate, with an indomitable spirit, and her world would revolve around the boy they all loved so much. But it hurt to let him go, and maybe it wasn't right. What if Billy and Serena's whirlwind affair was over by the time Jackson was ready to go to school? What if —

"Miss Jane, can you talk to me, honey? Pretend like we're back at that picnic table, ya know? You trusted me then, and told me what you thought. That's how we got here, 'member?"

In a desperate whisper, Jane asked, "Do you really love her?"

He answered quietly, but fervently. "Oh, yeah, I am head over heels, have been since the first moment I laid eyes on her. That's why I asked her to marry me. I am not the sort that goes around proposin', Miss Jane. Believe you me. Why are you askin' me about that?"

"I am sorry. I just want to make sure. I, I didn't really know. The night we arrived, we weren't expecting things to end up quite like this, were we?"

"Yeah, things kinda got pushed along a little too fast. But that's okay by me." Billy smiled and got up to get Jane a tissue from the table by the sofa. He returned with the whole box, knowing that Jane could need a few, once she got going.

"Miss Jane, to be real honest with you, I don't mind that 'bout Serena. I need a woman like that to keep me where I need to be. She don't put up with any messin' around, that's for sure. But she also knows how to keep her place, if I need to put my boot down. And I am doin' that for you, Miss Jane. I promised you, 'fore I brought you here, that you'd have a home. And some money of your own. It ain't your fault that Serena is part of the picture, and I wouldn't like to go back on my word."

"But I am sure that when you said that, you were thinking of you and I. Serena didn't factor in, she was a new girlfriend to you, living elsewhere. But now that she's to be your wife, I don't see that she'll want me around."

"Jackson needs you around."

"I am not so sure about that. I cannot believe he spoke to me that way. It hurts to be so . . . quickly replaced."

"Aw, you know kids, Miss Jane. They say things they don't mean. Especially when they start growin' up. I know it seems kinda soon like, me goin' on tour, but that was all planned a long time ago, you see? Lots of people involved with all of that, and lots of money, too. Serena'll have her own things to take care of, what with quittin' her job, movin' down here, and tryin' to set up a house. She'll need you to look after Jackson as much as I do. She just likes to rule the roost, but we don't care none 'bout that, do we Miss Jane?"

Billy took her hand. "You're gonna be just fine here, hon. Don't be forgettin' that you still ain't more'n three weeks from losin' your house and business and all. Best to just take each day as it comes, ya know? There's time."

Jane sniffed. She loved his attention, his strength, and she drew from it. Americans must be better at handling unpleasant emotions or something. She straightened her shoulders, and felt able to cope. Serena entered the room, but Billy didn't pull his hand away from Jane's. He simply looked up and said, "I think we got 'er all straightened out, sweetie. How's my boy?"

"He's fine. Can I get you anything, Jane?"

"No, thank you." Serena seemed truly compassionate. Jane felt that they could be friends, so long as Jane didn't challenge her plans in any way. And, after all, she had been wrong to assert herself there, hadn't she? They were going to be Jackson's legal guardians.

"So, what are you planning on doing, Jane?" Serena asked, as she took a seat by Billy. "I only mean for today, of course." Serena amended her question with a caring smile. Jane could see from the dip of Serena's shoulder that she had put her hand on Billy's thigh beneath the table.

"I wouldn't mind to just stay here the afternoon, if you don't mind. It seemed that Jackson wanted to be with you alone."

Billy's mobile phone rang out. "Sorry, I didn't realize that ringer was turned up so loud! . . . Hello?"

*

Jane was glad to leave the emotionally charged scene and spend a few minutes in the powder room. A splash of cold water further added to her feeling of a fresh start. If Billy wanted a nanny, he would get a good one. And that would amount to keeping her end of the bargain, and Jackson would just have to adjust to her staying for a while. She would begin doing nanny things, like reading again with Jackson, and making sure his mind wasn't going to mush. She would happily send him off with Billy, his fiancée, or the other members of the Killian family, as required. Granted, she loved her charge a lot more than any other hired child minder ever would, but she was determined not to be obstructive. And she'd have to keep a dry eye, now that she wore a touch of makeup.

Jane thought that her new resolve sounded brilliant. It also made her wretched to think of how her life had come to this: no home, no dreams, no plans for her future. How would she gain a life of her own again, when Jackson no longer needed her?

She dried her hands on the thirsty, decorative towel that Serena had placed in the powder room. Perhaps she ought to discuss planning meals, and the logistics of moving house, with Serena? To some degree, Jackson was right. He certainly didn't need a full-time nanny. He'd be going to school in a few months.

She fluffed her hair, admired her new haircut, and tidied her expensive make-up. Pretty good stuff, that. Jane took a deep breath and joined Serena and Billy in the dining area. Billy was just finishing his phone call.

"Looks like y'all are having company while I am in Austin."

"Oh, really," said Serena. "Who?"

"Jackson's uncle."

Jane couldn't believe her ears. "Nigel?... *He's coming here?*"

# Chapter 28

Even as confident as she was, Nigel's impending arrival threw Serena into a tailspin.

She didn't have any details to operate from, and no way to get them. Billy hadn't thought to ask any questions about what airline Nigel was arriving on, and what time. Jane rather enjoyed witnessing Serena's frustration.

"We know he'll be coming from London, right? There can't be that many flights from there, so we'll just call the airport," Serena said.

Jane flipped her tidy plans back at her. "Actually, Nigel could be coming from anywhere. Munich, Paris, Barbados, Geneva. Even from another point here, in the United States."

"Seriously? What does this guy do?"

"Not quite sure."

"Jane, you can't know somebody for that many years and not know what they do!"

"I know that at one point he was managing the affairs of a Middle Eastern royal family. He may have gotten on, perhaps signed on with one of their companies or other. It's not something he's been able to discuss much over the years. But you needn't worry about making arrangements for him. Nigel defines capability." Jane felt a warm sense of pride settle over her.

Serena was puzzled. Jane supposed that she didn't like men that she couldn't easily size up. "Billy's lawyer said that Jackson's uncle would pay us a visit. It's like in a contract somewhere or something. Gosh, I hope this isn't some legal adoption thing. I won't know what to do, and Billy would just say, call so-and-so. And where will he stay? Does he expect a room here, do you think?"

This was so amusing that Jane laughed aloud. "He'll stay where he likes, and he isn't one to share a bunk bed with Jackson, that I can tell you."

"Okay. I am glad you're enjoying a good laugh at my expense, Jane. I am just trying to make everything nice for everyone. As usual, you don't appreciate it." With this Serena turned on her heel and left the room. Jane heard the bedroom door slam.

It's like we're lovers having a row, Jane thought. This is getting stranger by the day. Jane rather liked it when Serena threw a fit; it meant that she and Jackson would enjoy a respite from her presence, usually for at least an hour. Jane heard the television click on in the master suite. A good sign that Serena would be out of the way for a while. She often could be heard talking on the phone at the same time, the din from the television covering her conversation. Jackson was building something out of clay on the desk in his room, talking animatedly to his creation. He'd passed the dinosaur phase, and he hadn't seen as many cowboys as he would've liked in Dallas. It seemed his preference was now for conquering outer space, and needing a good spaceship made of Play-Doh was probably the order of the day.

Jane continued making her bed and tidying the room where she slept on the roll-away sofa. She, too, was nervous about Nigel coming, and it was odd that he didn't seem bothered by the fact that Billy wouldn't be home. One thing was certain, it was highly entertaining to see Serena's discomfort.

The British were coming, and Serena Berquist wasn't in control.

Jackson acted indifferently towards his uncle's impending arrival. Perhaps he had a new sense of loyalty to his father, so didn't want to show excitement, even though Billy wasn't home. And Jackson had long been used to saying goodbye to Nigel so shortly after saying hello that maybe the child just felt vexed at another adult coming and going. Her best guess was that Nigel would check on his nephew, and then be off, perhaps even within twenty-four hours. Unless it was something to do with legal matters, in which case he may stay another day for a meeting. Jane smirked, pleased that her own distress was less than that of her hostess. The Americans dealt with she and Jackson's lives as they wished, but it was fun to think that now Nigel had the ability to control the circumstances for a change.

*

Jane passed a football back and forth with Jackson in the commons area, across the street from Billy's residence. She was abruptly replaced by two boys with whom Jackson was friends, and they delighted in passing the ball between themselves and then surprising Jane with her turn, sending the ball too quickly by her to keep up. They all were having a good laugh, but then Jane began to feel dizzy watching the zigzagging ball. The air was hot and heavy, as usual, and she decided to let the boys carry on without her. She returned to the condo, just as Serena emerged from her bedroom with a piece of paper.

"Jane, listen to this, and tell me what you think," she quipped. "Now he's bound to be hungry, so I've prepared a list of appetizers to have on hand."

"For Nigel?"

"Of course." Serena had finished pouting, but she was obviously still tense.

"He doesn't care for anything too spicy, so you might want to leave off the one with the peppers," Jane supplied.

"Right," Serena said, crossing the starter off her list.

Just then laughing could be heard outside, and the front door opened. Nigel walked in, carrying his squirming nephew.

"I found this lad outside, shaming Becks," he said to no one in particular, tickling Jackson and causing him to howl with delight.

Jane hadn't imagined how seeing him would overwhelm her so. The blood rushed to her cheeks as she thought, oh my Lord, he's gorgeous. She stood rooted to the carpet. Nigel dropped Jackson onto the sofa, causing more hysterical giggling, then turned and faced the two speechless women.

He ignored Serena. "Jane, you look amazing," he said, stepping forward to give her a kiss. She reached out to steady herself, putting a hand on his broad, suited shoulder, meaning to utter her thanks, but found no voice. "It's been ages. I missed not coming home for Easter." His eyes locked with hers, his face was so close, and he held her hands. Jane prayed not to pass out.

Serena spoke. "Hi, I am Serena, and, uh, welcome." Jane hadn't seen her so completely off balance before. She felt her stomach curl into a knot as Serena laughed self-consciously, sexily, and ran her hand through her long blonde hair. *She's just the sort of girl I've always imagined him with,* thought Jane tersely. *What if they get together? It'll be all my fault.*

"How do you do," Nigel said coolly.

"What did you bring?" Jackson said.

Serena played the offended parent. "Jackson, that's such a bratty question! Your uncle has just walked in the door, for goodness' sake."

Nigel and Jackson both ignored Serena's admonition, as Nigel reached a hand into his suit coat. "Just so happens I picked this out for you." He handed Jackson a small computerized game, and the boy squealed with delight. "Spot on, just what I've wanted! Thank-you!" He turned and sped towards the door, calling out, "I am going to show Josh and Jeremy."

"Kids, huh?" Serena said with the weary tone of a taxed parent. She didn't imagine how silly she looked apologizing for Jackson's quite normal behavior.

"Well . . . *Nigel* . . . You must be starving!" Serena cooed, pursing her lips as though she'd said something naughty. Jane thought she may very well be sick, although she knew Billy probably wouldn't think a thing of Serena's outlandish flirting, had he been there to see it. How could he tolerate her carrying on that way, Jane didn't know. She remembered how ridiculous Serena acted towards their good-looking waiter at the tea lunch they'd gone to at the botanical garden.

Nigel wasn't completely immune from her silliness, and smiled in return. But he continued to stand close to Jane, almost as though to protect her from Serena's girl-meets-boy ritual. Simply having Nigel near flooded Jane with a sense of security, of rightness, of *home*.

Jane decided to proverbially throw a wet towel on Serena, and remind her that she and Nigel weren't alone. She turned to him with a personal question, one she knew that Serena couldn't follow, and one that had been on her mind. "Has your mother found a buyer?"

"She has, actually," Nigel said.

"Oh," Jane replied. She knew Serena would think her answer an awfully flimsy, poorly orchestrated response, but Jane didn't care what she thought now. Serena couldn't understand what a loss Brambleberry House was, to any of them. Worse, she wouldn't care, unless understanding it would endear her to Nigel for the time being.

Serena wouldn't tolerate being ignored, even if only for a few seconds.

"Please, come and sit down. Like I said, welcome to our little home. I am in the process of buying something larger, but we've been cozy here."

You're not the one sleeping on the sofa, Jane thought miserably.

Serena settled herself beside Nigel, and what with both of their long legs taking up the space between the huge sofa and the chrome table, it seemed easier to for Jane to sit opposite them on a small chair. It was quite low, and it sat next to a guitar on a stand. It must be where Billy liked to play music, sometimes, although while Jane had been there he had gone over to Yancy's recording studio to play with the members of his band. Jane felt like a adolescent, forced to sit with the grownups. The only way to be comfortable was to sort of collapse, legs crossed, elbows over her thighs.

Serena chattered on about her ambitions for securing an estate and Nigel was attentive. That must of been easy for him, Jane thought. But while he gazed at Serena, Nigel gracefully stood. Jane couldn't hardly breathe, for drinking in the sight of him all over again. He stepped over to Jane, offering her his hand, even as he answered Serena's question. Jane instinctively took it, and he guided her to his previous seat. Serena faltered a bit, watching as Nigel slightly drew his hand down and deposited Jane on the sofa, but she soldiered on in her explanation of the local realty market. Nigel then seated himself by Jane and slipped his arm across the back of the overstuffed furniture, causing Serena's eyes to sweep back and forth at the two people who had suddenly been arranged as a couple in front of her.

Feeling cared for and dignified on the sofa, Jane melted at his gentlemanly gesture, and felt tingles spreading through her body at having him so close. Though he was seated behind her, she was close enough to catch a trace of his divine cologne. Oddly, she was shocked by how *British* he seemed. She longed for home, and listened intently to his deep, sexy voice, savoring the familiar pronunciation.

"But I guess we don't pay nearly as much for property as you do in the UK, right? Did I hear you say that Jackson's grandma just sold her house?"

"Yes, that's right," Nigel said. His imperious manner warned Serena that being so common as to ask about the price of the sale was not on. Serena hesitated, and Jane knew that she was working out what to say next. Jane guessed that Serena wouldn't ordinarily be so flustered, but, then again, she'd never met Nigel. She was clearly out of her depth.

Another toss of her golden hair brought a smile to Nigel's lips, and Serena giggled softly. *Oh, please.* Jane knew it was time to speak up again. Slightly turning her chin to her shoulder, she said, "Do tell us what exciting place you've come from."

"I arrived in Houston, yesterday. I finished business there, and then rang Jackson's father."

This solicited another girlish giggle from Serena. "Rang! Such a quaint way of saying that you've called someone. I love your accent, Nig-ule." She kicked off her high heel sandals, and tucked her feet up under her, as though he were going to tell her a story.

Nigel tipped his chin slightly at the compliment.

"Mr. Ralston?" Jane inquired.

Nigel replied instead to Serena. "Our Jane remembers everything. Yes, Mr. Ralston. And before you ask, Jane, his wife has passed away."

"Oh, dear," Serena said, her face held just so, implying deep compassion. "Poor thing. Was it cancer or something?"

Nigel shot a glance at Jane, and then casually looked at Serena. "No, she rather liked the bottle."

"Oh, I see," Serena answered pertly, in a voice to reassure her listener that Serena would never engage in such a vile behavior. Jane found that she was becoming well acquainted with Serena's many moods and various expressions. It didn't seem to dawn on Serena that she was perhaps a little closer to unseemly behavior than she cared to recount; she was marrying an ex-junkie. Jane felt herself quite ungenerous, thinking of Billy in that way. She reflected on how far Billy had come in conquering his addictions. She worried for a moment, hoping that Jackson would never tend to be like his father in that area, genetics being what they are. But then she glanced at the man seated slightly behind her, and dismissed the thought.

"Jane, shouldn't you offer our guest tea or something?" Serena scolded.

Jane was caught off-guard. Was she actually hoping to banish me to the kitchen, Jane wondered. She could almost imagine Serena saying something in her absence, such as, "You can't find good help these days." Indeed, Serena had been in two minds for days about just how Jane was meant to serve her. It was rather confusing for everyone. But in front of Nigel, it was bloody annoying.

"Nigel only takes tea in the morning, Serena. But perhaps you'd like something else?"

"Uh, no, Jane. Thank you."

Unabashed, Serena spouted off the next thing that came into her head. "What do you do?" With her arms crossed, she gave herself a little squeeze. Jane knew that Serena didn't care what Nigel said, only that he was handsome, he was here, and anything he said entertained Serena, given his accent.

Nigel answered, "I work for a conglomerate, comprised of sixty-seven different companies."

"That's not what Jane said," Serena replied. "She said that you were employed by some king or something. That sounds far more intriguing, you know."

Many thanks, Serena. Jane stared at her lap.

Nigel replied, "One of our main shareholders is an Arabian prince, and I used to personally manage a number of his companies. We've added more companies since then, and they are very diversified, so I've had to be a little thinner on the ground in the last year."

"Mmm, I see," Serena replied.

Jane knew that she did not. Serena was an intelligent woman, but she enjoyed interacting with men as the proverbial dumb blonde, trying to charm them into saying silly things to stroke her ego. Her purpose was not to understand, but to ensnare. Jane wondered if Nigel liked women this way, and how often he had cashed in on this type of flirtation.

The whole situation was becoming irritating, and she suddenly felt quite cross. Now Serena was talking about who knows what, and Nigel was listening attentively. The thrilling environment created by sitting close to Nigel on the sofa had taken on a strange sort of smothering feeling, as Serena seemed to lend the room a sickening energy with which Jane could no longer cope.

"Excuse me, I am going to check on Jackson," Jane said as she slipped from the sofa, and managed to navigate Nigel and avoid his gaze. She went straight to the front door and walked out. Jackson was playing ball with Josh and Jeremy, and Uncle Nigel's computer game abandoned until this evening.

Jane stood for a few minutes watching the late afternoon sun. Feeling guilty that she was behaving so badly, but needing to retreat, she crossed the street and turned left of the grassy area where the boys were playing, and went to sit on a bench beneath a tree. There was a small planting of flowers on either side of the bench, with a butter yellow azalea clinging to a large stone. The heat was tolerable here, beneath the canopy of leaves, and Jane felt herself relax. Strangely, it was rather like the stone seat in the garden at Brambleberry House.

What an odd thing life was, she mused. Here she sat under a tree, in America, with Nigel a short distance away. She'd wondered this afternoon if he would seem quite different, in this setting. Jane had only interacted with him back in England, when he was surrounded by family or people who knew something of him. But he was remarkably the same. Globally suave, probably; able to come off well in any culture or climate. She had been surprised to see him in a lighter weight suit, of a lighter color than his wool suits that were made up for him in London.

Then her nose felt prickly and to her horror she suddenly gasped out a sob. She'd never been so emotional in all of her life as recently. Perhaps she needed medication.

On some level, Jane supposed that she'd wanted to remember Nigel as part of home. Not holding a stupid conversation in a condo with Jackson's future stepmother. Jane was used to being the ignored female when grouped with captivating, beautiful women like Serena. But she'd never been pushed aside in front of Nigel, a man she deeply respected, and, it was true, had carried a torch for, since she was about seventeen. The Membry family, and Jane, of course, had heard some off-handed details of several of his girlfriends, each more glamorous sounding than the previous, but Nigel had never once brought any of them home to Hartsbury.

She acknowledged that she wanted to be alone with Nigel. Not that she could work out why; they'd only ever been close through their shared intimate knowledge of his family. He wasn't interested in her. But he was *home*. Though he probably thought her silly and plain, at least he knew her for herself, not as someone's nanny. She needed someone in her corner, even if he wouldn't approve of the mess she was making, taking money for looking after Jackson — how absurd! — and having nearly daily rows with Serena.

Seeing how attractive Nigel obviously was to Serena, and how she wanted to impress him with what a fine mother she would make to his nephew, it seemed unlikely that Jane and Nigel would have two minutes put together. Then he'd be gone, as he always had done. Only this time she wasn't sure if she could bear it.

But what else was she to do? Perhaps she ought to ask Billy to loan her the airfare to Scotland, and go for a while to her mum?

For the moment, she was stuck here, loathing the possibility of just how well Serena and Nigel might be getting along. Surely that was none of her business; she wasn't a chaperone, for goodness' sake. And better Serena reveal herself and disappoint Billy now, instead of after becoming his wife.

Knowing that she must be mature and return, Jane re-entered the Killian residence. Adjusting momentarily from the glaring light outside to the cooler, slightly darker interior of the condo, Jane heard Serena laughing. *From the bedroom.*

*Oh, God, now what do I do?* Jane panicked and called out Serena's name. Stupid. Luckily, there was no response from the bedroom, and she could hear Serena's voice chattering away. She chose to stay in the house, to cover for Nigel and Serena should the boys decide to come in for a cool drink or something.

Time to make tea.

Drawing the water began to slow down her heart. Waiting for the boil sped it up again. Finally, the click. Dropping a bag into the mug, she suddenly heard the bedroom door open. *Steady while you pour, Jane!* — Ouch. Damn.

The kettle went down with a plop just as Serena came into view on the other side of the counter. She looked amazingly cool.

What to say?

"Nigel left just a minute ago. And Billy says to tell you that you'll get checks in the mail from him. It's just easier to put you on the studio payroll."

Nigel gone? Billy . . . on the phone. Serena always spoke to him on the phone in private. In the bedroom. Jane let out a sigh of relief.

"What?"

"Oh, nothing, just looking forward to sitting down with a relaxing cuppa."

"Why don't you want to drink your tea the American way, Jane? Nice and cold. You look as though you melted out there."

"Yes, it's hot." All the same, Jane felt like a leg of lamb, being half-frozen in the cold blast of the central air conditioning.

Jane felt quite smug, and in a totally different mood than a few minutes ago. She was composed now. Well, with the exception of a slight burn from the kettle.

Serena went to the fridge and poured herself a tall glass of iced tea. "Nigel said he'll be back around seven. He wants to take Jackie to dinner. Isn't that sweet? Just the two of them?"

"Yes, very nice."

"You could've warned me that he's the best looking man in England, Jane! I was stunned."

"You seemed to get over your shock fairly well." "What's that supposed to mean?" Serena planted both hands beside her iced tea, and Jane wondered if her heels dug into the lino, too, preparing for battle. Jane's calm mood lifted into the steam coming from her tea.

"Oh, come on, Serena! You were pulling him something rotten."

"Let me repeat, since you're talking all English village colloquial now, or something. What's that supposed to mean?"

"I shan't fight with you. If you want to flirt, it's your business."

Jane picked up her tea, intent upon going to her room, but realized that she didn't have one. So, to the sofa, then, and try to find a magazine on the way there. Why am I being made to feel badly, she thought.

Thinking of Nigel gave her courage. It seemed insulting now, to her old friend, to imagine that Nigel and Serena would get carried away with themselves as soon as she'd left the room. Jane had been a fool to imagine such a thing. What was wrong with her, these days? Surely Nigel's description of Serena wouldn't be anything but "rather forward."

"Are you trying to say that I was inappropriate? Because Nigel didn't think so. Men and women usually enjoy a little chemistry, Jane. That's what gives life spice. It hardly means that I am loose, or unfaithful or something. I swear, lady, you act like such a prude."

Serena's comment hurt Jane's pride, and now her emotions slammed back into a negative direction. She felt hopelessly naive. Of course Nigel had thought Serena very beautiful. Billy had mentioned to her that Serena had been engaged once. To a businessman, he'd said. Serena's ex was probably a lot like Nigel. And surely she was the kind of trophy Nigel would love to possess, wouldn't he?

Wait a minute, Jane argued with her lower self. Nigel wasn't taking Serena and Jane out to dinner, only Jackson. That counted for something, didn't it?

"What's wrong, Jane?" Serena baited her. "Don't you have a starchy little British come back this time? And why are you blushing? Oh," she threw her head back and laughed haughtily as she seated herself on a bar stool. She put down her iced tea and began to study her manicure. "I think I understand. You've probably been in love with Nigel for years, huh?"

Her laugh cut Jane to the core. But there were no foreboding tears rising behind Jane's eyes this time.

"Listen, Serena, I told you that your behavior is none of my concern. Likewise, my relationship with Nigel is none of yours. I'll thank you to kindly bugger off. *That's* English for — "

The door opened and three thirsty little boys came dashing in.

# Chapter 29

Jane glanced once more at the clock. She couldn't concentrate on the paperback in her hands. Nigel and Jackson were staying out a little later than planned. After Nigel collected Jackson for dinner, Serena had immediately left. She gave Jane no explanation of where she was going, but Jane was given her cell phone number, in case of emergency.

She was thankful for the peace and privacy, but had no doubt that, somehow, when Nigel and Jackson arrived home, Serena would be in their wake. Then Jane would have to sit with them and no doubt Serena would be in good form. She could kill a few minutes by tucking Jackson up in bed, but after that, there would be no where to go, seeing that her sleeping quarters were in the main sitting room. She'd tidied the condo; cleaned the bathrooms, including Serena's. Done the hoovering. The kitchen floor sparkled and everything was immaculate. Jane enjoyed the comfort of the domestic tasks, but now there was nothing left to do. She'd tried watching telly, but it proved more mind-numbing than the book. Phoning Eleanor was out of the question due to the hour. Plus, she was probably in the middle of changing phone service. Jane wished she was the type to initiate a call, but Eleanor, much like Lydia had been, always waited for others to take the lead.

However long she waited, it seemed quite sudden when Jackson and his uncle returned. Jane stood up. Then sat down. Then picked up her book, in the space of seconds before the door opened.

"Hello. Did you have a lovely time?" Jackson ran immediately to Jane and sat beside her on the sofa, snuggling close. He hadn't been this affectionate towards her since arriving in America, and Jane felt a clutch of love in her heart. Jackson was tossing around a mint, probably proffered from the restaurant. Nigel stretched out on the sofa with them. Jane remembered his chivalrous motion of removing her from the little chair earlier, and felt so grateful to him for the kindness.

"We had a good dinner, but not one of the Mexican food places. We went to this restaurant with food from Thailand, and it had lots of elephants about, and it was really very good, wasn't it, Uncle? Then we went to play mini-golf."

"My, that does sound like a good time. And you're ready for bed, are you?"

"No."

"I think yes, mate. At least go change and clean your teeth. Then you can say goodbye to Uncle Nigel."

"All right." Jackson dramatically hauled himself from the sofa, and then picked up a running pace towards his room.

Nigel spoke for the first time. "And how was your evening?"

"Well, I tidied things up for a bit."

"And?"

"And that was about all."

"Jane, you're a poor liar. I can imagine that the Southern belle was quite enjoying winding you up after I escaped."

He hadn't enjoyed Serena's advances then, Jane wondered. Or, was he speaking only about how the two women failed to be chummy?

"We had a row, it's true. We're just very different people I suppose."

"She must not be in at the moment, or you wouldn't be holding court with me on your own."

"True. She went out after you, I don't know where."

"I assume those are your cases, there?"

"Yes. Why?"

"If you've left anything in the bath, you'll need to collect it. As soon as Serena returns home, I am taking you to the hotel with me."

"I don't understand, Nigel."

"This isn't acceptable, darling. You're sleeping on a sofa. Jackson said that mostly you spend your time tidying and doing laundry, and I can see that you haven't any privacy."

"Well, yes, that's true. But. . . ." Jane stammered.

Jackson returned, running again, in his pajamas. This time he went for his uncle and climbed on his knee.

"Uncle, did you have a favorite book?"

"Yes. Asterix."

"But I've seen Asterix!"

"Amazing. What have you been reading?"

"Aunt Jane and I are still going through the Potters. But we haven't watched the latest film, yet. It's supposed to be brilliant, but I want to read the books, first. It's taking an age. Auntie, can I have cocoa?"

Jane was about to answer, when Serena came through the door. She had showered and changed before she left, so was in a dramatically eye-catching outfit. Her many packages betrayed how she'd spent her time.

Nigel stood as she came in. "Retail therapy?"

Serena laughed as though it was a private joke. Jackson said that he hadn't cleaned his teeth. Please, Auntie. Jane rose from the sofa and made her way into the kitchen to make his cocoa.

While she was in the kitchen, Nigel and Serena exchanged words that Jane couldn't hear, and didn't want to. Although Nigel appeared not to approve of Serena's behavior towards Jane as a guest, Jane hadn't sorted out exactly what his response was towards her, as far as "men and women's chemistry" was concerned.

How patronizing Serena had been. It was true Jane had had only two short-term boyfriends in her lifetime, but there was no need to speak to her as though she were an imbecile about human relationships. And she preferred to think of herself as ladylike, not as a prude, thank you very much.

Jane gave Jackson his cocoa in his favorite thermos, and he headed to his room. Jane assured him that she and his uncle would be in to say goodnight.

Jane walked cautiously towards Nigel and Serena. Serena turned to her with a forced smile and said. "Well, we'll see you tomorrow afternoon for lunch, then." She started to walk towards her room carrying her shopping bags, adding, "Sweet dreams," over her shoulder. Obviously Serena was aware that Jane was leaving with Nigel for the hotel, to refer to lunch.

Jane and Nigel bade goodnight to Jackson, and Jane had a bit of worry at leaving Jackson for the first time with Serena. "Yes, Auntie, I'll be fine," he said. "Of course I'll clean my teeth when I am done with my cocoa." He did seem rather ready for them to leave *his* room, his room in *Texas*, in the *United States of America*, where his *father* lives, Jane thought to herself. What would Lydia think of this? Nigel brought her back to the moment with a lift beneath her elbow. Accepting their kisses, Jackson immediately turned back to the computer.

Without another word, Nigel picked up her case, her shopping bags, and showed Jane through the door. A limo was approaching the condo.

# Chapter 30

It was a balmy night. Nigel sat closely to her in the long, sleek vehicle that drove them away from Billy's residence. Embarrassed, she smiled at her lap and turned to look out the window. Within a few minutes, they pulled up in front of the exotic, multi-balconied ZaZa hotel. The driver helped Jane out of the car, and she was greeted by a large, lit splashy fountain. Soft music played in the distance, floating from an open bar, and she hesitated, listening.

"Shall we?"

Jane smiled a joyful consent. Nigel dealt with the porter, sending her cases upstairs, and offered his arm to his companion. They were given a table at the edge of a lush garden, poolside. The water reflected like modular cubes of ice outlined in blue beneath the strung party lights.

"You're far more beautiful than I remembered," Nigel said.

Jane was gobsmacked. She stared at him disbelievingly. Don't wake me up, thought Jane, as her pulse raced. Nigel smiled at her stunned reaction, and Jane laughed luxuriously, her voice carried away on the gentle breeze and the band's music.

"Serena gave me a make-over. She could best Trinny and Susannah, you know. I clearly know *What Not to Wear*, but I admit a little regret at giving up my khaki trousers. Although it can't be denied I look a bit smarter after all of her Herculean efforts."

"Darling, that's a little polish, that's all. But it does suit you." Nigel signaled for a waiter, and ordered Cosmos for them. Jane admitted to being hungry, and added a small plate of mandarin short ribs.

The drinks came almost immediately, and Jane thought the citrusy concoction was an absolute delight. And she drank in Nigel's handsome face, looking over a wedge of pineapple that was pinched on the side of her ruby glass.

"Jane, I have an ulterior motive for bringing you here." Nigel looked uncharacteristically ill at ease. He grinned sheepishly, ringing his finger 'round the rim of his cocktail glass.

The fantasy atmosphere seemed to tip to one side, and took Jane sloshing with it. She felt slightly dizzy. Her thoughts went a bit mad. *Oh, no. He's in love with Serena. He's going to leave me here, and head back to Billy's place. He feels badly, but needs to confess.*

"I have quite a confession to make."

*I'll say*, thought Jane. Determined to kindly hear him out, she took another long drag on her drink, and then boldly set it aside. The waiter came with her food. She couldn't eat it now, with the cold tonic coating her stomach, and the dangerous fizziness floating about them in this magical place. She realized she must have looked to be ignoring him, taking in the exotic poolside surroundings and with a startled expression, she gazed up. He took her hand. For once in her life, she didn't want to touch him. How would his holding her hand make his announcement of bad news, whatever it was, any less difficult?

"I am sorry. My timing is poor. You look rather distraught." Nigel apologized.

"No. . . well, yes. But it's my fault." Deep breath. "I've just been processing so many changes, so many emotions, that I feel a bit odd. And what with the heat here, and sleeping on that sofa, it's all left me a little exhausted," Jane felt better, admitting the challenges she'd faced since coming to America. She calmed down, and smiled at him. "But, please, I am all right, Nigel, so please continue."

Another smile. He was a god. Did he know? His eyes were so blue. Sparkling.

"Jane, I've been doing a lot of thinking. You see, I've been preparing to leave my job."

She refused to entertain thoughts of possible illness or other calamity. She firmly told herself that she was done having inner hysterics, that they'd become quite an awful habit, She drew a deep breath and prepared to hear him out.

"It's always been the arrangement, actually. When you're hired on, you're told that you'll be at the beck and call of the prince for five years, or less time if you don't suit. And you're told coming on that you'll be paid handsomely, but that you'll give up nearly the whole of your life for those years. Family, everything, comes second to the job. Oh, I am doing this badly, Jane. It sounds as though it's all about me. But it isn't. I couldn't be more concerned for your happiness."

"My happiness? Nigel, I am sorry, I don't understand."

"No, I don't suppose." Nigel rubbed his forehead in agitation, and gave a clipped laugh. "I got an excellent response from Jackson, and was full of confidence about this earlier."

"Nigel. Come to the point, please."

"I've booked you on the return flight. We leave tomorrow evening. For home, Jane."

Jane heard herself gasp softly.

"Of course, if you refuse, I shall respect your decision."

"Why?"

"Why, what?"

"Nigel, why am I flying to England with you tomorrow?"

"Because I love you, Jane."

"Be serious."

Nigel became earnest, leaning in towards her. Close. So close. "I am quite serious, my love. I've dated, literally around the world. And . . . you're so very special."

"Me? But you've scarcely spoken to me, all these years. Unless you wanted something."

"I am rather shy, I suppose."

"Nigel, you cannot tell me you're shy. You've been more than authoritative with me. About Jackson."

"That was sort of like business, though, wasn't it? I had an objective. *Personal* feelings are quite different. I've never been good at expressing them. Quite hopeless, really." She laughed again. "I am sorry, I feel this drink is messing with my head. I shall wake up, somewhere, with Serena peering down at me and ridiculing me." She pulled one hand away and supported her spinning head. "I really ought not to drink, Nigel. I can't handle alcohol, but it was so pretty, wasn't it?"

Through spread fingers, Jane saw that his head was cast down. Was it possible that she might have accidentally hurt his feelings? Could this be real? How could she get on a plane tomorrow? She was Jackson's nanny. It wasn't over, yet. She had something important to do, perhaps. Or perhaps not. Maybe she wasn't ever needed, by anybody, to come to America, after all.

"Nigel, I am sorry, darling. I am just shocked. Thrilled, mind you. But surprised. Tell me more!"

It was Nigel's turn to chuckle. He squeezed her hands. "Jane, I know it's outrageous. I am sorry I've been silent all these years, doing my work, but I couldn't start with you and then get on a flight and leave, next day."

He stopped and studied her face. Jane was amazed to see the love in his eyes. For her.

"This is the grand scheme, Jane, all right? I should like to go into politics. I don't need the money, so people'll know they can trust me, won't they? There are some things in the county that are too disturbing not to do anything about. That by-pass road proposal, that would round the village, for a start. No real representation. And the mismanagement of historical properties. I want to do something useful."

"That's lovely," Jane whispered. "The village? You said the village."

"Yes, of course, Hartsbury. Home."

Icy fingers tickled Jane's middle. "There isn't any . . . home. You, you actually feel, still rooted there? I — "

"Jane, listen. You've only lost the shop, darling, and your flat; the village is still standing, love! And everyone misses you."

"They miss . . . me?"

"Yes. I was there last week, checking in on the upstairs bath. And they all asked after you, everyone misses you awfully — "

"The upstairs bath?"

"Yes, darling, you know it needed work," Nigel said. "You've not put it together, have you?" He smiled. Like a pirate.

Jane stared back. It couldn't be. "You couldn't be talking about the wonky toilet at . . .at Brambleberry House?"

"Yes, darling. You're looking at the new owner. I had to keep it under wraps, didn't I? Mum was trying to work out what I should inherit years from now, which is madness, I don't want — or need — anything from her. But I confess I've always had a bit of love for the old heap, and well, you've always been the heart of that house, Jane, quite as much as my family. Mum knows, now, that I am the mystery buyer. A good laugh, that. So, you'll like living in the old house, won't you? I should think it might even be a comfort to Jackson, to be able to come back. Of course, you'll want to put your own touches on the place. Tear down the old wallpapers for a start. The garden's already looking seedy."

All of Lydia's roses. The lilac wallpaper. She'd keep them always. "Oh, Nigel."

"Darling, I am sorry to spring it all on you. That's it in a nutshell, really, my being a country politician and us living in the same old house we've come and gone from for ages."

Jane continued to stare. It was all so wonderful. An answered prayer. . . .

"But, again, that's all me. I would give anything to make you happy, Jane. You could do whatever you like. Start another shop, go to school, organize the church jumble sale or just have a lovely time being a kept woman. Whatever you wish, darling."

"But what about Jackson?"

"I've been in touch with Billy. In fact, I spoke to him again, today. And I had a bit of a chat with Serena about Jackson, yesterday. I'll come to the point, Jane. She has her moments, but she is intelligent, and genuinely is interested in the care of my nephew. Somehow she has a way with Jackson. He's content with them both. I am sorry, darling, but it's true, and she's about to become his stepmother. He wants to stay."

"Yes, of course, you're right."

"Serena has properly laid plans about where Jackson should go to school, and I was rather impressed with her initiative. Billy's family is close by, and wishes to be involved in Jackson's life, as well. Jacks thinks they're a decent lot. So, I should think Jackson should get on all right, despite Billy's lifestyle as an entertainer. We've discussed him coming to visit, and have set a holiday schedule. We've even had a chinwag about Dudley, but now that Jackson's been on a horse, a pony is out. Harry is rather happy with Jackson's spaniel, and Jacks made a gift of Ausfrid to his new grandfather. And Serena seems to have a Yorkie somewhere to be the family's new dog. Darling, you look so lost, but I assure you this is all for the best. It's sort of as though we'll have shared custody, so you needn't worry that you're saying goodbye to him forever, Jane."

"But how can we just leave him?"

"Because we must let go. Darling, think about it this way: we'll have children of our own."

The depth of Nigel's words struck her heart. Her heart's desires met his words.

"You're happy, then?"

"Ecstatic. And silly, that's all. Nigel, say it, please. . . ."

"I love you, Jane. I want--desperately — for you to marry me. End the loneliness for both of us. Become a family. Jackson has always thought of you as his aunt, and now you surely will be!"

"But, why? I still don't understand, Nigel. You've got to be on the U.K.'s most desirable bachelor list or something. . . . Why me?"

"Jane! Have you so lowly an opinion of yourself? I respect your humility and sweetness, but it's only me. Lydia's brother. We've known each other for ages, I've been secretly in love with you for years, you must know that. I've acted a complete fool when you've come to the house, scarcely could say a word. So often I've thought about how there's a special energy when you come 'round. It was you I always hated leaving most; didn't you ever notice that I usually got away to the airport when you were away from the house?"

He stroked her cheek. And he wasn't done, yet. "You're so brilliant, Jane. You took that woman's failing florist's business and made a go of it, all on your own. You ingratiate yourself to everyone you meet, Jane. Why, you even got a rock star to bring you to America. I can't think of anyone I'd be so honored to share my life with, to raise a family with, than you." His passionate voice became a lover's whisper. "There. That really wasn't so frightening once I got going."

He held Jane's face in his hands, watching her comprehending smile, and the love dancing in her eyes. Nigel leaned over and kissed her tenderly, careless that his silk tie lashed through the saucy spare ribs on Jane's plate.